THE PLAYER AND THE PAWN

THE PLAYER

AND THE

PAWN

A NOVEL

WILSON CARTER

Published by Deep End Dynasty

Cover and interior design by Christian Storm

ISBN (ebook): 978-1-967746-03-3
ISBN (paperback): 978-1-967746-01-9
ISBN (hardcover): 978-1-967746-00-2
ISBN (audiobook): 978-1-967746-04-0

Printed in the United States of America
September 2025

For the Seekers and the Seeds

PROLOGUE

Although Caleb Calvarri had entered the NSA headquarters thousands of times, he had never before entered undetected. No security guard testimony. No video footage. No fingerprints. No alarms. No suspects. No arrests.

Miles away, his gloved fingers flew over the keyboard, each keystroke burrowing deeper into what Deputy Director Hamilton Everton had once boasted was an "impenetrable firewall." Tedious. Repetitive. Necessary. Each stroke brought him closer—to salvation or ruin. He pressed on, driven by love of country and fear of what might come.

Inside the digital network, he escalated his privileges, exploiting outdated software patches and dumping credentials as he moved laterally through the system, inching closer to the core servers. With a practiced hand, he deployed his creation—Memory Mole—embedding it deep into the kernel, ensuring it would remain undetected, even during the most rigorous security sweeps.

He paused, jaw tense as the gravity of his actions pressed in. This wasn't just a breach. It felt historic.

"C'mon, Memory Mole, you were made for exactly a time like this."

A distant whir jolted him, a spike of adrenaline shooting through his veins. He forced calm. *You've got time.* He rose slowly, wincing as bruises flared with pain. At the door, he peered past dimly lit shelves of old newspapers and magazines. All clear.

Back at the computer, he scanned the room. The air was thick, oppressive, as if the walls themselves conspired against him. The faint scent of industrial cleaner clung to his senses. His eyes flicked back to the monitor, willing the program to work faster.

The vacuum stopped. Silence. Then the hum of the ventilation system. A cold, stale breeze chilled the sweat on his skin.

"I will support and defend the Constitution of the United States against all enemies, foreign and domestic," he whispered. "So help me God."

He was the best—an elite hacker whose reputation preceded him. At Stanford, he'd cracked a code that had stumped two decades of students. At Berkeley, he hijacked the cybersecurity professor's system mid-lecture, triggering an early class dismissal due to "system glitches." At the NSA, he exposed vulnerabilities that left everyone scrambling. He was good. Some thought he was too good. His reputation was as dangerous as it was prestigious.

The on-screen display blinked:

129,140,163 Files available.

84.05% Complete.

He wiped the sweat from his freshly shaved head, feeling exposed without his usual blond hair. His six-day beard was of little comfort.

The vacuum resumed, louder and closer. The cleaning crew was drawing near.

93.65% Complete. He looked around the room. The desk—his only option. Without hesitation, he dropped to the floor and crawled underneath, pulling the chair in front of him in a futile attempt to disappear into the shadows. Just moments later, the door clicked open.

His pulse pounded as he crouched beneath the desk, breath shallow, controlled by sheer will. Footsteps moved across the carpet—measured, deliberate. Terror flared like dry kindling. Every muscle tensed, coiled. The shoes stopped just inches away.

He held his breath. Above him, the custodian breathed softly, each exhale almost syncing with his own hammering heart. Muscles burned.

Stay still. Don't think. Don't move.

A voice echoed from the hallway—muffled, indistinct, but close enough to send a jolt of panic through him. Feet shuffled. The door slammed. Startled, he jerked upward, slamming his head against the underside of the desk. Pain exploded through his skull. He winced, biting back a curse.

Then came the ominous click of a key in the lock, followed by the vacuum's return.

He exhaled slowly. He couldn't lose control now. Steadying his hands, he slid back to the computer. The sweat on his temples met the icy dread coiling in his stomach. The oppressive sensation of being watched had seeped in from the walls.

100.00% Complete.

A fleeting smile crossed his face.

Focus. Focus. You're not finished yet.

The urge to flee gnawed at him, but he stayed. One name, one face, one lead—someone he had once met. Someone he had to find. He inhaled, fingers dancing across the keyboard.

Seconds dragged. His heartbeat thundered with each forbidden file he unearthed. This man—he had to be the answer. He craved the truth. Yearned for it.

But as he would soon learn, truth could shackle you just as tightly as any lie.

CHAPTER ONE

Three weeks ago, it had all felt simpler. Before everything twisted.

The blue ball rocketed off the front wall, then the side—fast, sharp, precise. Caleb moved on instinct. No hesitation. His body coiled and released as he lunged, racket slicing upward in a clean arc. The sound of the strike echoed through the court, swallowed instantly by the white walls.

Focus always came easier here.

The ball skidded back along the sidewall, but Hamilton Everton was already there. A backhand, brutal and low, barely missed his ankle before dying in the backcourt.

"Fifteen-thirteen," Everton called, panting. "You've still got some work to do, kid."

They stepped off the court, sweat streaking their arms, adrenaline still burning. Caleb grabbed his water bottle and took a long pull, the cold sliding down his throat like relief. His pulse hadn't slowed. He didn't need it to.

"Six years today," Everton said, a note of nostalgia threading through the words. "The first time we met."

The memory landed hard, clear and vivid.

"Your invitation felt more like an ambush," he said, grinning. "The Player and the Pawn. Escargot. Crème brûlée. An evening of firsts."

Everton chuckled. "And you, true to form, ran a background check before dinner. Wanted to make sure I really was the deputy director of the NSA."

"Of course I did. And then you tricked me into speaking at DEF CON 2022. Five minutes for you. Forty for me."

"I had to get you there somehow," Everton said.

Their laughter filled the hallway between courts, comforting and familiar. For a moment, it felt like old times—before the cracks.

"I guess I did win three Capture the Flag events after that," Caleb admitted.

"With a team of one," Everton said, shaking his head. "I still remember watching you turn those challenges into a game. You inspired all of us."

The words caught Caleb off guard. He looked away, hiding the swell in his chest.

Those nights—late hours, whiteboards filled with code, caffeine-fueled brilliance—had forged more than skill. They'd forged a bond.

"To the next challenge," Caleb said, raising an imaginary glass.

Everton nodded toward the court. "Bring it on."

They went back at it. The blue ball ricocheted like a live wire, each strike faster, more demanding. Caleb read Everton's movement, stayed one beat ahead. When the return skimmed the sidewall, Everton lunged—and missed. His shoulder hit the wall with a heavy thud.

"Fifteen-twelve," Caleb called out. "You okay, man?"

"Fine," came the muttered reply as Everton pushed off the wall.

They headed toward the locker room. The metallic clatter of dropped weights echoed from the far end of the gym—sharp, sudden. It hit Caleb like a spark to dry tinder.

Tires screeching. Shattered glass. A streak of red on the road. Two coffins.

Caleb's stomach clenched. The ache flared, undulled by time.

Everton and Angela had stepped in when everything fell apart. Sunday dinners. Holiday celebrations. Angela's cooking, always rich with spice and comfort. They'd made space for him when the world hadn't. Milestones, birthdays, even the little things—he hadn't faced them alone.

He glanced at Everton. Something pressed behind his ribs.

It wasn't just racquetball or tech or shared war stories. It was loyalty. Presence. The kind of bond people only understood when it was gone.

"Thanks," he said quietly. "For always being there."

Everton smiled warmly, but his eyes didn't quite match. Or maybe it was just the light.

"Always. You're family, Caleb. Nothing changes that."

No armor. No filter. Just real.

And yet, as they stepped into the locker room, something twisted— barely there, easy to ignore.

A flicker. A shift Caleb couldn't name. But it was there.

And nothing would be the same.

CHAPTER TWO

WEDNESDAY, MAY 31, 2028
WASHINGTON, DC

Kalyssa Kay Summerwood dined alone at Café du Rêve, letting the buttery scallops melt on her tongue—New Bedford, perfectly seared. A moment of calm. Fleeting. The kind that slipped away before you realized you needed it.

One year. Today marked exactly one year since she became publicist for the Grayhorse campaign, and it still felt surreal—like someone else's life, lived at a sprint. A nonstop blur of handshakes, headlines, and high-stakes spin.

Somewhere beyond the patio rail, a violin's melody drifted in from the street. The notes tugged at something buried deep, tugged her back…

Back to the day it all changed.

MONDAY, MAY 31, 2027

Kalyssa crossed Pennsylvania Avenue, heart hammering—half excitement, half nerves. The Whitmore loomed ahead, all glass and grandeur, its history pressing in like an audience. Twain had written here. King had found words here. Presidents had dined, plotted, made history here.

Today, it was her turn.

A battleground dressed in elegance. And she was the contender.

This is it.

A quick stop in the lobby restroom gave her a moment to collect herself. In the mirror, her long blonde hair cascaded in soft curls over the shoulders of her dark blue suit. Professional. Sharp. Exactly how she needed to appear. She smiled at herself, whispered, "You've got this," then turned on her heel and strode toward the elevator.

The soft ding of the doors. The smooth ascent.

Her mind ticked through strategy. Grayhorse was sharp. Direct. If she wanted the job, she had to prove herself in the first few minutes. No wasted words. No hesitation.

The elevator doors slid open.

The John Adams Presidential Suite loomed ahead.

Inside, the suite gleamed in gold and brown hues. No small talk. Straight to business.

"Ms. Summerwood," Senator Grayhorse greeted, extending his hand. "It's great to meet you. My staff speaks highly of you."

Kalyssa returned the handshake. "Thank you, Senator. You've got a great team. I'm eager to work with them."

Grayhorse motioned for her to sit, his movements deliberate, confident. He barely glanced at the folder on the table—her resume, no doubt—before leveling a direct gaze at her.

"Ms. Summerwood," he began, "I am going to be the forty-eighth president of the United States."

He smiled, adding, "Although the American people don't know it yet. I need a publicist who can persuade them that I am their best choice for 2028 and who will continue with me as White House Communications Director throughout my presidency. What makes you qualified for this job?"

Kalyssa met his gaze.

"Senator Grayhorse, I'm going to be the White House Communications Director for the forty-eighth president of the United States."

It was bold. Maybe even arrogant. But she meant every word.

"I get people elected," she continued. "My communication strategy shapes public discourse. I discredit your adversaries, highlight your achievements, and neutralize the media. I have a network of social media influencers with a collective following of over 100 million users. When I drop bait in the water, the piranhas have a feeding frenzy."

Grayhorse listened intently, his interest seeming to grow as Kalyssa heralded her achievements.

"You're a regular social engineer," he said with a brief chuckle. "Tell me about a time you turned around a struggling campaign."

"In 2024, Democratic Representative Aspen Willow was trailing by more than 15 percentage points to Republican challenger Eileen Baker when I joined the campaign in June. I'd offered to be her publicist six months earlier, but she balked at my 'unaffiliated' status, as if that would hinder my ability to do the job. By the time I took over, her campaign was in shambles. The first thing I did was cut the dead weight—no need to pay for incompetence."

She let the words settle before continuing.

"Next, I launched a social media blitz that rebranded Representative Willow as the champion of all Texans, even those who voted against her in 2022. We produced over twenty compelling human-interest stories showing Willow meeting the needs of liberals, moderates, and conservatives. She skyrocketed in the polls.

"Baker tried to counterattack as her numbers plummeted, but we crushed her. Aspen Willow won by a landslide—90 percent of the Democratic vote, 65 percent of independents, and even 30 percent of Republicans came along for the ride."

"Impressive," Grayhorse replied, his eyes narrowing slightly. "How do I know that wasn't a one-hit wonder?"

Kalyssa leaned forward with a confident smile. "Senator, I have a whole album of hits. Not all the races were big, but they all have one thing in common—we won."

He studied her. "So, you've never lost a campaign?"

"I don't take on campaigns I'm not convinced we'll win."

He gave a small nod and changed topics. "Let's talk about faith. How should I be portrayed in the campaign?"

Kalyssa leaned forward. "Senator Grayhorse is a faith-based family man committed to religious freedom for all, believers and non-believers alike. We will highlight voices from various faith traditions, including atheists and agnostics—like myself—to demonstrate how your leadership defends everyone's right to believe in any God they choose or none at all."

Grayhorse's expression softened. "Excellent." He paused, then, "Abortion is a defining issue. How do we handle it?"

Kalyssa exhaled. "This is one of the toughest issues. Take a clear stance, and you alienate a chunk of the electorate. Avoid taking a stance, and you seem unprincipled and indecisive."

He nodded. "So, what's the strategy?"

"Senator Grayhorse, values human rights, women's rights, states' rights, and the right to life. With the Supreme Court's 2022 decision referring reproductive rights to the states, Senator Grayhorse urges citizens to engage in their statewide processes to find a balanced solution reflecting the diverse values of their communities."

The senator's eyes gleamed with approval. "Impressive. You took a stance without committing to a specific outcome." His gaze held steady. "As you know, campaigns are often fast-paced, unpredictable, and grueling. How do you handle unpredictable events?"

"I stay focused," Kalyssa replied. "There is only one acceptable outcome—getting you elected. Everything else is noise. And I know how to silence noise."

"Give me an example," he encouraged.

She didn't hesitate. "During the Willow campaign," she began, each word pulled taut with control, "Eileen Baker made a desperate Hail Mary attempt. She claimed Aspen, who was openly lesbian, opposed the traditional family values cherished by our community."

She let the accusation hang there, heavy, just as it had back then.

"Do we need to respond? I asked myself. Or has Aspen already proven herself as a representative of all people, regardless of their views?"

Baker's attack had come late October—terrible timing for a smear campaign. Aspen's schedule was packed with critical events across the district, every appearance crucial in the final push.

Kalyssa had weighed the risks. Diverting attention to a baseless accusation would be reckless. Instead, she had gone in another direction.

"I crafted a response," she continued, her tone sharp with conviction. "Representative Aspen Willow stands with you, fighting for the issues that matter to our beautifully diverse community."

A sharp contrast. Baker had attacked. Willow embodied unity.

"Baker's poll numbers spiked briefly," Kalyssa said, reading Grayhorse's expression, watching for a reaction. "But within forty-eight hours, they plummeted. Her message failed to resonate. Ours? It did exactly what we needed it to do."

The senator nodded. His expression was controlled, but she caught the slight shift in his posture—a small tell.

Then he leaned forward, his gaze sharpening. "One last question. Do you have any personal relationships that might interfere with your role as publicist for the Grayhorse campaign?"

The room disappeared. The senator. The interview. Gone.

He was there instead—arms wrapping around her, skin still warm from the shower. The scent of his cologne, that familiar cedar and citrus, curling around her like a spell.

"You're beautiful."

Low and certain, the words brushed her ear like heat.

She could feel it again. The weight of his chest. The slow, steady rhythm of his pulse beneath her fingertips.

Safe. Steady. Like time had stopped for them.

And then… nothing.

He was gone.

The illusion shattered, leaving her face-to-face with Grayhorse.

"Senator, I am wholly committed to President Grayhorse's campaign."

Now, back at Café du Rêve, the clink of silverware and soft murmur of conversation folded around her. The memory of that interview faded as quickly as it had come.

She glanced across the table. The chair was still empty, a quiet monument to everything she'd lost.

She pushed her plate aside, appetite gone. One year in, and she had everything she'd worked for: access, influence, power.

And still, the silence across from her was louder than applause.

Her fingers circled the rim of her glass, restless.

A soft vibration buzzed at her hip. A text from her assistant.

AIMEE: Speech edits complete, uploaded to cloud, synced across devices.

Efficient. On time. Predictably perfect.

At least someone showed up.

She sighed.

Somewhere beneath the strategy, beneath the spin, she wasn't just surviving.

She was still waiting.

Still hoping for something real.

CHAPTER THREE

Caleb stared at the framed print on his bedroom wall—Vettriano's *The Singing Butler*. A couple dancing on a windswept beach, their elegance framed by the mundane task of servants holding umbrellas. Intimate. Idyllic. A celebration of love and connection.

But to him, it wasn't just a painting. It was a taunt.

They had everything he didn't. A gentle caress. Laughter. Affection. Everything that seemed just out of reach for Caleb.

Human connection—science called it essential. But in his world of deception and danger, those comforts were luxuries. Trust? Intimacy? Unattainable fantasies.

The woman's flowing dress caught mid-twirl by an invisible wind—a romantic gesture in the face of a storm.

How do they do it? How do they stay unshaken, even when the world is falling apart?

For him, the storm was real. And he was always the one left standing alone in it.

He turned away from the image, the weight in his chest anchoring him in place. Touch, closeness, the warmth of another's presence—those weren't just biological needs. They were lifelines. And he had denied himself both for so long that the line between survival and loneliness had blurred.

Maybe, in a world full of secrets and shadows, truth wasn't just rare but revolutionary. And maybe love—the real kind—was the only thing strong enough to hold back the dark.

Still, beneath the hardened edges, he craved something real.

But *real* meant vulnerability.

And vulnerability got people killed.

Kalyssa sat at the edge of her hotel bed, the blue glow of her laptop casting a cold light across the room. Tomorrow's campaign agenda stared back— speeches, handshakes, strategy briefings. She should've been focused. A presidential campaign was no place for distractions.

But her mind drifted, slipping past bullet points, searching for something deeper.

Not that she didn't believe in the cause. She did, fiercely. But lately, even the wins felt hollow. Like each victory added more polish to a version of herself that wasn't quite real.

Her fingers found the silver locket at her neck—the last piece of the man she once loved. Cool metal. Warm skin. Together yet apart.

What is all this for?

It wasn't about politics. Not really. Not tonight. Tonight, it was about something missing. Something no campaign could fix.

Surrounded by people, yet more alone than ever.

She leaned back against the headboard, her fingers still on the locket. Her life had become a stage. She, the bright, relentless publicist, always on message, always in control. But away from the spotlight, something in her ached for connection. For truth. For something real.

Maybe that was the real cost of ambition—trading truth for perception, connection for control.

In a world driven by narrative and spin, honesty felt like rebellion. And love?

Real love demanded presence. Surrender. Faith.

The very things she'd buried beneath strategy and survival.

Because being seen—*truly* seen—wasn't just uncomfortable.

It was dangerous.

〰〰〰

He didn't know what he was hoping to find.

But there he was—on *KnowMeKnowYou*, a digital refuge for people like him. People chasing connection in the chaos of their lives.

A stream of faces. Smiles. Filters. Then…

She appeared.

Older. But unmistakable.

Blonde hair… those eyes… it's her.

Kalyssa Summerwood.

His pulse kicked. Her profile photo glowed on the screen—golden hair catching the light, blue eyes still full of that unguarded warmth.

He swiped to her second image. Not a selfie. A painting. Two lovers locked in a kiss. The woman's dress had been captured mid-flow, a soft, pale blue. The man wore red tights, a brown cloak, a feathered cap.

It didn't belong on a dating profile. And yet, somehow, it belonged on hers.

A soft ping. **Kalyssa is available to chat.**

The icon blinked, bright and insistent.

His hand hovered.

Fate? Coincidence? No such thing.

He clicked, then typed.

ME: Hi Kaly, it's Caleb.

Heartbeat rising. Then another ping.

KALYSSA: Who?

His stomach dropped.

Still, he typed.

ME: Stanford. Spring 2018. The food trucks on White Plaza. Your pizza. My burrito.

Another pause.

Then…

KALYSSA: Caleb! You still owe me.

He smiled. Relief flooded his chest as his fingers flew.

ME: How are you? I can't believe it's been 10 years.

KALYSSA: Wow. This moment feels surreal. Call me. My number's the same.

His thumb hovered over the phone app, her name still in his contacts.

He tapped. One ring. Two.

"Hello, Caleb."

Her words—soft, certain, familiar—wrapped around him like sunlight after a long winter.

"Kaly… it's really you. What are you up to these days?"

"About five-six," she said. "Same as always."

He laughed, couldn't help it.

"Those were good days, huh?"

"We had so much fun," she said. "Remember our river trip?"

"You, me, Alexis, Kort, Emily, and Kyle," he said. "Hey… whatever happened to you and Kyle?"

"He was my spring fling. I transferred to UW that fall. We tried long distance, but he ghosted me after a month. Last I heard, he's in banking. How about you? What are you doing these days?"

"I work for the NSA," he said. "Global Exploitation and Vulnerability Analyst. Got my master's at Berkeley."

"So… you're a hacker with a degree."

"I can neither confirm nor deny."

She laughed.

"I'm the publicist for the Grayhorse campaign," she said. "Can we count on your vote?"

"If he becomes a Republican."

"Not happening."

"Then I guess I'm going with the *Wright* ticket," he said, leaning into the wordplay.

"That's the *wrong* choice," she said. "But I won't hold it against you."

Their laughter echoed through the line—playful, easy. Like no time had passed.

"Have you heard from the rest of the gang?" he asked.

"Mostly just through social," she said. "Alexis moved to Nebraska—married, two kids. Emily is an influencer. TikTok queen. Making a fortune."

"Married?"

"Divorced. She has a son."

"Kort?"

"Kort's a high-powered attorney here in DC, of course. Headlines, suits, and smugness. Still cocky as ever. Seems to have more clients than character."

He smirked. "Kort always did love being the smartest guy in the room. Remember how you took that capstone class together and you came out number one? I don't think he ever forgave you."

She laughed. "The professor did call my AI project 'ingenious.' Said it had scary potential if I ever took it out of the lab. Guess I've always liked assistants who don't talk back."

He chuckled, the glow of shared memories drawing him closer to her.

Then came the question that changed everything.

"What about you? Did you ever find your someone?"

Silence.

A beat too long.

"My husband went missing nearly four years ago."

He sat up straighter, pulse rising.

"I'm so sorry. What happened?"

"We were married seven months. That morning was normal. We worked out, then I made breakfast while he showered. He came into the kitchen, shirtless, pulled me close. Told me I was beautiful, even though I was a sweaty mess."

Caleb pictured it easily. Too easily.

"He lingered a little longer than usual," she said. "I didn't think much of it. I poured the juice, served a spinach and mushroom omelet that looked more like scrambled eggs. He said it tasted great anyway. He left for work at 7:30. I left at 8:00."

She lowered her tone. "He never came home."

His stomach turned. "Where did he work?"

"The Department of Homeland Security. Or so I thought. I contacted them. They said they had no record of a Justin Benton ever working there."

"What did his pay stubs say?"

"Department of Homeland Security, *Inc.*"

Inc. Private. Not federal. Not traceable.

"So… a shell company?"

"Maybe. But it doesn't exist. Not in any database I've found. It's like it never existed."

"And the police?"

"They filed a missing persons report. After three months, it became a cold case."

"Do you think he's dead?"

"Maybe? I don't know. If he is, at least I'd have closure."

Then, quieter…

"I call myself a widow. But sometimes, I wonder if I'm just a cheating wife."

Her words landed like a weight.

"Kalyssa," he said gently, "you're not cheating. You're surviving. And that's not the same thing."

Another silence.

Not empty. Just full.

"What's his full name and birthdate?"

"Justin Thyme Benton. T-H-Y-M-E. Born December 31, 1998, at 11:59 p.m."

He blinked. "Just in time?"

"His accountant dad thought it was clever."

"If they were going to name him Thyme, they should've gone all in and called him Herb."

A laugh. Soft, real. The kind he missed.

"Parents?"

"Mike and Allie Benton. Boating accident. Before I met him."

"Siblings?"

"Only child."

He hesitated.

"I'm sorry this happened to you."

"Thanks. Everyone else tells me to move on. But it's not that easy."

"No. It's not."

A pause.

"I'll call you Sunday night with what I find," he said. "Does 8:30 work?"

"I'll be in North Carolina, but I should be back at the hotel by then."

"And I'll be in Arizona. Watching a painted sky sunset."

The call ended.

But the silence that followed wasn't empty.

He stared at the phone, screen dim.

He should've walked away. Let someone else go ghost-hunting.

But Kalyssa—her presence, her grief—had cracked something open.

She wore her questions like armor. He carried his secrets like scars.

And now, for the first time in too long, he wasn't sure which of them was more exposed.

This wasn't just curiosity. It wasn't even empathy.

It was connection.

Fragile. Unexpected. Real.

And that was the most dangerous part of all.

CHAPTER FOUR

FRIDAY, JUNE 2, 2028
EDGEWATER, MARYLAND

Hamilton Everton sat in silence, the soft glow of a lamp casting long shadows across the sitting room. His gaze lingered on the bed, where Angela's frail form lay nestled beneath the covers—fragile, yet alive. That bed, this room… it was a vault of memories, both cherished and heavy.

Tonight, the weight felt unbearable.

Every moment, every breath, felt like another withdrawal from a bank long emptied. He was emotionally overdrawn. Bills stacked on the hallway table. Medication schedules scribbled on notepads. Lab results shoved into drawers. Even breathing felt like bleeding out—slow, invisible, inevitable.

Could he ever recover from this?

The thought echoed with every beat of his heart. He wondered if what came next would free him or bury him.

He felt trapped, backed into a corner where every option carried consequences he wasn't ready to face. But maybe, just maybe, this plan would work. Maybe, for once, he could break free—not just from the medical debt that was crushing him, but from the slow unraveling of everything he'd worked to protect.

His phone buzzed on the side table, cutting through the silence.

NO CALLER ID: Eyes Open

As if on command, his weary lids snapped up. The fog of reflection lifted, replaced by the sharp focus of strategy.

He began typing, each keystroke heavy with finality.

ME: Eyes. Eves. Even. Oven. Open.

He stared at the screen.

NO CALLER ID: :-)

He'd always done the right thing. Sworn to it. Lived by it. Followed orders. Obeyed laws. But now… now the compass spun. The world wasn't black and white anymore. It was smoke. Fog. Gray that moved and shifted with every breath.

Maybe truth was never fixed. Maybe it belonged to those with the power to declare it.

He had burned the foreclosure notice. Angela didn't need to know. She needed this house, this warmth, the illusion of stability. He could not—would not—let them take it from her.

Like Abraham, he had a sacrifice to make.

Only this time, there'd be no ram in the thicket.

God forgive me.

His fingers hovered over the keypad for just a moment longer, the enormity of what came next sinking in.

Then, with a steady hand, he entered the five-digit code—like a dagger falling fast.

3 2 0 7 3

He would send the script within the hour. A secure file. Silent. Precise.

And the password?

A sequence of words with one letter changes.

Clever.

It was done.

In two days, the terror would begin.

CHAPTER FIVE

Caleb sat back in his chair, the low hum of his laptop filling the room. The screen's glow flickered on his face as he replayed last night's conversation in his mind.

Kalyssa had been his college crush—beautiful, enchanting, and completely unavailable.

But now?

She was in romantic limbo. Hauntingly single, yet still married.

He leaned forward, elbows digging into the desk, wanting to know everything about her. He opened a new tab and typed **Kalyssa Summerwood** into the search bar. He perused her social media accounts, savoring each image just as he had done a decade earlier.

Had she ever felt for him what he'd felt for her?

Of course, she'd had Kyle then.

As the storm of longing thundered relentlessly, his effort to silence his mind was futile. He needed to know everything about her, to uncover what he had missed.

The guilt flickered.

And vanished.

He wasn't just crossing a social line anymore. He was diving headfirst into adolescent obsession.

His fingers moved almost on autopilot as he launched Memory Mole, his tool for uncovering the secrets others preferred to keep hidden. The interface opened like an old friend, the familiar sequence of encrypted logins a comforting ritual. Each password unlocked a deeper layer of access until he reached the search screen.

He typed: **Kalyssa Summerwood.**

Selected: **ALL SOURCES.**

Pressed: **ENTER.**

He leaned back, drumming his fingers on the desk as the system began its work—scanning public databases, financial records, and dark web archives with methodical precision. The moral ambiguity of his actions briefly surfaced.

You shouldn't be doing this.

The whisper in his mind was drowned out by the hum of Memory Mole's search engine.

For him, secrets were puzzles.

And puzzles begged to be solved.

When the results appeared, a jolt ran through him.

Kalyssa Summerwood (1321 entries found)

- **Social Security numbers: 6**
- **Birth certificates: 6**
- **Marriage certificates: 3**
- **Death certificates: 2**
- **Known addresses: 10**

He stared at the screen, the sheer volume of data sending a jolt of adrenaline through him. How could such an unusual name generate so many records?

He clicked on the birth certificates and scanned for the most likely match.

GIVEN NAMES: Kalyssa Kay

LAST NAME: Summerwood

DATE OF BIRTH: August 17, 2000

PLACE OF BIRTH: Ellensburg, Washington

PARENTS: Austin Ricks Summerwood and Adelyn Bush

He paused, pen in hand, as a flicker of recognition passed through his mind.

Ellensburg. He'd been there before.

But he quickly pushed the memory aside.

He opened the image of each marriage certificate, his heart racing as he encountered hers.

Justin T. Benton and Kalyssa K. Summerwood. Married May 21, 2024.

And what about Justin?

Why had he vanished?

Would he return?

In December 2024, Justin's digital trail disappeared, like footprints washed away by the rising tide.

Caleb froze.

That date. He knew it.

Explosions. Screams. The stench of scorched metal.

A joint op gone to hell.

They'd called him a hero.

But even heroes couldn't escape the nightmares that invaded the quiet mind.

He shot to his feet, gasping for air. The room felt too small, too dark, too loud with memories. He crossed to the blinds and yanked them open.

Light flooded in—bright, blinding. Shadows scattered across the walls like fleeing ghosts.

He stood there, unmoving, palm pressed to the glass.

Grasping for fragments of laughter. For echoes of a simpler time.

A time before the terror.

"God, please help me," he whispered, barely louder than the pounding in his ears.

He closed his eyes, inhaled deeply, straining to hear something—anything—beyond the noise in his mind.

And then… stillness.

Not a voice. Not a sign.

Just a presence.

It surged through him—soft but solid—silencing the storm and filling the hollow space inside.

It didn't answer everything.

But it steadied him.

He dropped back into his chair, pulse slowing, movements sharp with purpose.

Justin was a puzzle.

And Caleb would tear the world apart to find every last piece.

CHAPTER SIX

SATURDAY, JUNE 3, 2028
HANOVER, MARYLAND

Caleb rubbed his eyes and rolled his shoulders. The air was thick with the scent of stale coffee—a ghost of too many late nights. The only sounds were the hum of his server and the quiet clatter of keys.

It was past midnight, and the stillness had weight.

He felt like he was being watched, though he knew he was alone.

Lines of code flowed across the screen as his fingers moved with instinctive precision. The hum of the server provided a steady rhythm, comforting in its constancy. A mechanical heartbeat reminding him of the task's importance.

Blue Rise Energy.

Massive. Critical. One of the largest energy providers in the country.

Tonight, they were trusting him—unseen, unknown—to test the security of their digital vaults.

Off the books.

Not for the NSA.

Not even close.

His hands worked with the practiced ease of a concert pianist. Every keystroke peeled back layers of defense. A misconfigured port. An outdated encryption protocol. An unprotected API endpoint.

Small things to most. Alarms to him.

Each flaw was another piece in a puzzle only someone like him could solve.

This wasn't about money. It was about Angela. About Everton.

Eight companies in three months. Now Blue Rise Energy.

According to Everton, $450,000 so far—more than enough to cover the next round of treatments.

His reports were gold, paid in platinum.

He never spoke to CEOs. Never met anyone. Everton kept him invisible. A ghost behind the code.

It had been Everton's idea—"a partnership," he called it. Help fund Angela's care. Strengthen national infrastructure. A win-win.

But tonight, something felt off.

As Caleb logged another vulnerability, a twinge of unease crept in. The job hadn't changed, but something about it had. He leaned back, stretching his shoulders, eyeing the half-eaten bag of potato chips beside the keyboard. The room felt heavier than usual, like it knew what he was doing.

Everton's rhetoric echoed in his mind—polished, calm, rehearsed. Grand talk about "fortifying the future" and "protecting the nation's core."

But lately, his tone had changed.

More urgent. More precise.

The jobs weren't random anymore. They were targeted. Strategic. Critical.

Blue Rise Energy wasn't just another contract. It felt like a test.

And Caleb was starting to wonder what they were really testing.

His tactics had evolved too—at Everton's urging. This wasn't just penetration testing anymore. He was reaching out to employees. Manipulating them into handing over credentials. Coaxing them into revealing known vulnerabilities.

Social engineering.

He logged the latest flaw with the same meticulous detail as always. But the thrill was gone.

The work felt colder now, like he was drawing blueprints for a bomb.

A question stirred at the edge of his thoughts. One he'd pushed down before.

Who was this really for?

He used to believe in the mission—securing America's infrastructure, defending against foreign threats. But lately, that belief felt hollow. Like a front.

He'd followed Everton's lead for so long he hadn't stopped to consider if they were still on the same path.

Or if they ever had been.

The final lines of the report came together. He saved the file and glanced at the clock: 2:37 a.m.

Another night spent in shadows.

Another payment for Angela's care.

Another step deeper into something Caleb no longer understood.

He powered down the system. The room dimmed to black, the only light coming from the city outside.

But the questions didn't go away.

They pulsed in the silence, heavy and unresolved.

It wasn't about whether he trusted Everton anymore.

It was whether he could trust himself to uncover the truth—before it was too late.

CHAPTER SEVEN

SUNDAY, JUNE 4, 2028

DULLES INTERNATIONAL AIRPORT, VIRGINIA

Caleb froze.

The Stratus Airways departure board glitched. Black text vanished into pulsing crimson error codes.

Phoenix: gone. Just like that.

In its place, a jagged block of gibberish blinked like a warning, as if the system knew something he didn't.

The air shifted. Heavy. Electric.

Conversations around him turned sharp, warped by rising panic. Mutters. Gasps. Passengers turning, squinting, frowning.

He scanned the other boards. Delta. JetBlue. United.

Clean. Pristine.

Only Stratus was bleeding code.

A glitch. Just a glitch.

I've seen worse. Hell, I've written worse.

But his gut didn't buy it.

Not here. Not today.

He adjusted his carry-on and stepped into the tide of confused travelers pressing toward the counter. The kiosks blinked dead. A line of passengers snaked into the concourse—restless, frustrated, fraying.

Ticket agents clung to their smiles like lifelines, but the strain showed. Behind them, a tall man in a crisp uniform moved with military precision. Silver hair, ramrod straight, eyes scanning like radar.

But something cracked. A twitch at the corner of his mouth. A quick reach for his phone.

Then…

The man's face drained of color. He turned and disappeared through a door marked **Authorized Personnel Only.**

Caleb broke from the line. Cut through the chaos. Closed the distance.

Seconds later, the man reemerged—focused, moving briskly toward the west security checkpoint.

Caleb moved faster. Matched the man stride for stride.

"ACARS is down, isn't it?" Caleb said, low and sharp. "The pilots… are they cut off?"

The man flinched. Their eyes locked.

"No idea," the man muttered. Tight. Rattled. Panic behind the mask. "I've got a crisis to manage."

And then the man was gone, flashing a badge and vanishing through the TSA checkpoint.

Caleb stood alone. Pulse thundering.

A television overhead flickered. No sound—didn't need it. The headline said everything:

BREAKING: System Failure Strikes Stratus Airways – Aircraft Communication Lost

Voices swelled around him. People pressed in, eyes glued to the screen.

No ACARS. No comms. Pilots cut off.

Planes circled, flying blind. Others sat dark and helpless at the gate.

His hands trembled as the news ticker crawled across the bottom:

Passengers' Hopes Grounded Before They Even Took Flight

Caleb couldn't breathe.

He'd written the script. Months ago. The vulnerability. The sequence. The exact nightmare unraveling now.

He'd warned them. Hadn't he?

Everton had promised—said the report was delivered, said Stratus paid, said Angela's debt dropped a hundred grand.

But what if Everton had lied?

The thought struck like lightning, searing through memory and instinct.

What if Everton never delivered the report?

What if the payment was a cover?

What if Stratus Airways had no idea they were exposed?

No. No, Everton wouldn't… would he?

Caleb gripped the strap of his carry-on, fingers tightening until the nylon bit into his skin.

Angela had made Caleb dinner. Hugged him like a son.

She would've seen it. She would've warned him…

Wouldn't she?

A flicker of doubt sparked in his gut.

Maybe she hadn't seen it.

Maybe she'd believed Everton too.

Just like he had.

A cold flush crawled down his spine.

The ransom, of course. Lock the systems. Freeze the planes. Demand millions.

But this wasn't some faceless bank or insurance firm.

These were real people. Real lives.

He looked around the terminal.

A child kicking his feet beneath a chair.

A service dog asleep under a woman's legs.

An elderly man dozing on his wife's shoulder.

None of them knew. None of them saw it coming.

Neither had he. Neither had Angela.

She wasn't complicit.

She was blind.

And Everton had played them both.

CHAPTER EIGHT

SUNDAY, JUNE 4, 2028

HANOVER, MARYLAND

Caleb climbed the steps to his townhome, the weight of the cyberattack still hammering at his skull. Hours had passed, but the shock clung to him like smoke. His stomach churned in quiet revolt, guilt pressing against everything he hadn't wanted to admit.

It was nearly 8:30 p.m.

Kalyssa would be expecting his call.

But what could he say?

Hi, Kalyssa. This is Caleb. I'm the architect of the Stratus Airways cyberattack. Do you want to hang out?

He pulled out his phone, thumbs hovering. Then tapping. Then stalling.

He wasn't in the mood for a call. Not when the world he thought he understood was slipping sideways.

Now isn't the time for love—or whatever this is.

… 8:33. The text still unsent.

Then her picture filled the screen, paired with the soft melodic chime he'd come to associate with possibility.

Incoming call.

He hesitated, then answered.

"Hi, Kalyssa," he managed, the ache bleeding into his tone.

"What's wrong?" she asked. No hesitation. No small talk. Just immediate understanding, like she could hear the chaos cascading in his mind.

"I'm not in Arizona," he said. "Canceled flight."

"The Chinese cyberattack on Stratus Airways?" she asked.

Chinese?

The word hit like a gut punch. His pulse spiked. That didn't make sense. He reached for logic and found only fragments—no explanation that fit.

"So, you heard," he said.

"Senator Grayhorse got a briefing this afternoon. The president's freezing $200 billion in Chinese assets."

She sounded calm, almost certain. Like she'd already pieced the picture together.

But Everton had been the only one to receive the cyber vulnerability report.

And the code unleashed today. It hadn't been random.

It followed his design. Line for line.

"Have the Chinese claimed responsibility?" he asked, trying to sound neutral. Trying to hide how much it mattered.

"Should you trust a lying man?" she said lightly.

He blinked. *Was that a dig? Or just banter?*

"It's been less than twelve hours, and we've already identified the perpetrator?"

A beat passed. Softer now: "According to the NSA, it was the Chinese. But you don't seem convinced."

He exhaled slowly. "Accusing China is easy. But my gut says we're missing something. A lot of somethings."

"What kind of something?"

The memory of Everton surged—chilling, practiced.

Detail each cyberattack. Create a roadmap of terror. Make them feel the fear.

The sickness swelled in his chest.

He'd written the reports. Rationalized the assignments. Nine companies in three months. All off the books. All justified in Angela's name.

He'd been baited. Hooked. Played.

And now?

He didn't even know what he felt. Fury. Shame.

Something darker.

Something hollow.

"Caleb, are you still there?" Kalyssa's question drifted through the fog—gentle, unsure.

"Yeah. I'm here, Kaly. Just trying to make sense of the senseless."

"I get it," she said gently.

The pause hung between them.

He shifted. "Can I ask you a few questions about Justin? I found some clues, but they feel like they belong to different puzzles."

"Sure," she said. Her tone dimmed, like she was reaching for something that kept slipping away.

"What was it about Justin that made you fall for him?"

"He was smart. Athletic. Passionate. Playful," she said slowly. "He made me feel wanted, especially when I felt… discarded. Because of him, I believed in myself again. I thought he was my soulmate."

Her words faltered at the end. Not broken, just guarded. He could feel it: the hesitation, the weight of what went unsaid.

He encouraged, "Describe your soulmate."

When she answered, her words hit like a coded message—layered, intentional, devastating.

"Someone brave enough to speak the truth and smart enough to know when to be silent. Someone passionate enough to ignite my desire, yet tender enough to brush away tears. Someone courageous enough to fight bitter battles, yet humble enough to quickly forgive. Someone perceptive enough to see my flaws and imperfections, but kind enough to build me up with heartfelt praise. Someone who sees me completely—and loves me all the more for it."

He swallowed hard.

She wasn't just describing a fantasy. She was defining the man he'd always wanted to be.

"Did Justin love you like that?" he asked.

"He wanted to," she said, barely more than a whisper.

"But…" he prompted.

"Sometimes, we fall short of our best selves."

"You felt something was off?"

She hesitated. "There was a part of him he kept hidden. Something just beyond reach. I told myself that in his line of work, there had to be secrets. But when I discovered he never really worked for the Department of Homeland Security, I started to wonder how much of his story was real at all."

Caleb exhaled. The truth hovered at the edge of his throat, sharp and dangerous.

Would it help her… or shatter her?

She deserved to know.

"His parents weren't Mike and Allie Benton," he said, the words coming faster now, too fast to stop.

"What are you talking about?" Her tone had sharpened.

"His real father was James Edwards. His mother, Cristy Wilson. They lived in Gilbert, Arizona, until 2012. That's when Justin and his mom entered Witness Protection. She became Allie Browne. He became Justin Thyme Benton."

A long beat of silence.

"So… Justin wasn't even his birth name?"

"Maybe not. And the coverup was good. Too good. I found thirty-six different Arizona birth certificates connected to Cristy Wilson. And not one for a Justin."

She didn't speak. Just the soft sound of her breath in his ear—barely there.

"And now?" she asked.

"Found a photo of him with the UW baseball team. Conference tournament in 2023. Looking proud as ever in that purple ball cap. But I can't find any record of him after December 2024. No death certificate. No police report. No funeral."

"You think he's still alive?"

"I don't know," he said. "But if he wanted to disappear—really disappear—he had the skills. And the head start."

The silence scraped at him. Then…

"What if he's watching?" she asked.

He stiffened. The question hit harder than it should've.

"What if he never really left?" she added.

A chill traced his spine. He'd been so focused on tracing Justin's past, he hadn't stopped to consider the other side of the timeline.

Her words slid through him, cold and sharp.

Is Justin gone… or just another nightmare waiting in the wings?

CHAPTER NINE

Caleb sat alone at a table for two, knowing Lian would come.

She always did.

The dining room hummed with energy, the clatter of plates and murmur of voices creating a familiar, comforting rhythm. The scent of freshly brewed coffee mingled with French toast and sizzling bacon, stirring something nostalgic. A simpler time. Before the chaos. Before the betrayals. Back when life wasn't a tangled web of lies and half-truths.

She'll understand. She always has. And when it matters most, she'll be there. Or at least, I want to believe that.

The door opened, and there she was—unpredictable as ever, yet somehow right on time. Her version of consistency.

Her black hair was pulled into one of those no-nonsense buns—tight, not a strand out of place. The same sharp precision lit her eyes. Every step calculated, deliberate. Sunlight slid across her olive skin, catching just enough to make her seem untouchable. That quiet strength, always present, wrapped around her like armor.

Her gaze locked with his the moment she walked in. No smile, no hesitation, just immediate calibration. Reading him. Calculating. Deciding.

She slid into the seat across from him.

"You're early," she said, a Mona Lisa smile tugging at her lips.

"You're late," he replied, forcing a smile, just enough to take the edge off.

Lian's eyes flickered, as if catching something in his tone. "It's been a while," she said, softer now. "I didn't expect to hear from you. But then again, I never do."

He'd called out of nowhere, but of course, she didn't look surprised. That was part of why he'd reached out. In a world that lied incessantly, she didn't rattle easily. She trusted him, at least as much as anyone in her world trusted anyone. Which wasn't much.

The waiter appeared, took their orders, and returned with two glasses of a juice blend—bright orange, tangy, alive with ginger and turmeric. He took a sip, the chill grounding him. But his thoughts swirled. Nerves buzzed beneath the surface.

"What happened yesterday?" he asked, the question just above a whisper.

Lian's gaze held steady. "The disturbance with the airline?" Her tone feathered with indifference, like the whole thing had been a scheduling error.

Disturbance. The word grated.

She diminished danger. Sheathed everything in calm. It was disarming. And effective.

"Who was behind it?" he pressed. He already knew. But hearing it from her would make it real.

She swirled her drink, eyes locked on the glass like it held secrets. "The talking heads blamed my cousins," she said dryly.

"Chen and Feng?" he asked, forcing a playful tone.

"No." Her smirk curled slowly. "Mike and Bob."

He chuckled. Reflex. It didn't touch his eyes. The tension was still there, pressing at the edges of everything. He glanced at her, wondering if the banter was real or just a buffer to delay what needed to be said.

The waiter reappeared with their food. Blueberry pancakes. Kale salad. Familiar, comforting things. He looked at the stack in front of him and felt nothing. No appetite. No comfort. Not anymore.

Lian picked at her salad slowly, eyes never straying far from him.

Are we still on the same side? Still in the same game? Or did the rules change when I wasn't looking?

He shoved the doubt down.

"Desperate men sell priceless things," he said.

Her eyes locked on his. "And how desperate are you?"

He held her stare. "Not as desperate as Hamilton Everton."

She tilted her head. No confirmation. No denial. Classic Lian. Never show your whole hand—just enough to keep the game going.

But she owed him. That debt—unspoken, unpaid—still hung between them. Nearly four years ago, she'd been seconds from death. He'd dragged her back. That had to mean something. *Didn't it?*

"I'm going on a field trip," she said, like it was nothing. "See the sights. Hike a few trails. Maybe even climb the Great Wall. Who knows what I'll find."

The words hung there. Breezy. But sharp.

He didn't ask. She wouldn't answer.

But her tone carried weight, like a knife tucked in lace. A warning.

Or an invitation.

Then it hit him.

She wouldn't stop with Everton.

She was going to trace every keystroke, every exploit.

And when the trail ended, it would bring her face-to-face with him.

CHAPTER TEN

Ricardo Roca stepped off the Ameritrak coach at Fort Worth Central Station, his black leather shoes hitting the platform with a tired finality. Two days from DC by train—a masterclass in inefficiency. But with every commercial flight grounded by presidential order, steel tracks were the only way in.

The Stratus Airways cyberattack wasn't just an IT breach. It was national paralysis.

He adjusted the duffel bag on his shoulder and scanned the platform. The Bureau hadn't sent a driver.

Just a field office car—half fueled and ready to be retired—parked a block from the station with the windows cracked and the heat already winning. No one from the Dallas office had called to welcome him, and that was the message. Loud and clear.

Temporary assignment. "Agent in Charge." Quotation marks implied. Bare minimum effort.

He tossed his duffel in the back and slid into the driver's seat. The upholstery gave a long sigh beneath him, like even the car didn't want to be here.

He hadn't planned on coming back. Not this year. Not ever, if he could have helped it.

But cyberattacks didn't care about personal history.

He pulled onto I-35W and soon drove past a turnoff he didn't take.

One that led to a street he hadn't driven in years.

To a house that used to be his.

She was probably still there. Same brick porch, same wind chimes, same bitter face.

And his daughter? The wedding was in three weeks. He hadn't been invited.

His son? Somewhere between here and nowhere. Untethered, unmedicated, and unreachable.

Ahead, the Stratus Airways headquarters rose from the heat. Sharp angles, mirrored glass, gleaming like it had something to prove.

Inside, someone from Homeland Security would be waiting. Maybe CISA, maybe a local agent pretending not to resent DC oversight.

He didn't care who shook his hand or smiled through clenched teeth. This wasn't a popularity contest.

He was here to find out who had brought down the airline—and who wanted the truth six feet under.

CHAPTER ELEVEN

THURSDAY, JUNE 8, 2028

PITTSBURGH, PENNSYLVANIA

The edge of the hotel bed pressed against the backs of her knees, but Kalyssa barely noticed. Pittsburgh blurred beyond the window, and Justin drifted through her mind—her love for him more memory than emotion. But every time she tried to move on, something stopped her. A dream. A voice. A scent. It was like he was haunting her.

Is he still out there?

Somewhere?

Watching?

The pieces of her life were still scattered, and no matter how polished her smile looked in the mirror, she was still reassembling the wreckage.

And now… Caleb.

A ghost from another life, suddenly alive again. Real. Or close enough to make her question everything.

Had he always looked at me that way back at Berkeley?

He'd called every night. Tonight would be no different. Each conversation stitched them closer, thread by invisible thread.

He wanted something. Maybe love. Maybe her.

But could she give that to anyone again? Could she trust herself to try?

Her fingers brushed the locket at her neck. Double-chamber. Custom-made.

A fusion of East and West. Her initials etched beneath a Chinese motif. *Forever.*

She shook her head. *An illusion.*

Maybe I need someone who knows how to see me and doesn't look away.

Shortly after nine, her phone lit up on the nightstand—Caleb. The soft chime broke the stillness, a sound that now felt like possibility.

"Hi, Kaly."

Familiar. Warm. Too comforting. And more welcome than she was ready to admit.

They started easy. The weather. Work. The little nothings people say when they don't know how to name the ache under their words.

But slowly, the space between them thinned. Her guard slipped.

"Caleb, I'm broken," she whispered. "I look strong on the outside, but inside, I'm shattered. I don't know if I'll ever heal."

A pause. Then, calm and unexpected: "Have you sought heavenly help?"

A bitter laugh escaped. *Heavenly help? Seriously?*

Her stomach clenched. Something old, maybe resentment, rose in her throat. She hadn't prayed in years. Not since—

Don't go there.

"I'm not into that," she said, sharper than she meant to. "No God has ever answered my prayers."

Silence. Then Caleb, quietly, too gently, "So… faith isn't really your thing?"

She hesitated.

"Raised Christian," she said. "Now? Agnostic. I haven't ruled out a divine being. I just haven't seen enough to believe in one."

She stared at the ceiling. The conversation had drifted somewhere raw, personal—dangerous.

And yet, she didn't want to hang up.

"What sort of evidence are you looking for?" Caleb asked.

She exhaled.

"Something definitive," she said. "Not just… feelings. Believers shape their gods into whatever they need. Look at the sects. The wars. The hate. Everyone claiming *their* version is divine."

Her own bitterness startled her. The words tasted harsher than they had in her head.

"Sorry," she added. "That was a little much."

"No," Caleb said. "That troubles me too. But I still believe there's something. A divine force. Call it God or whatever—it's real. And it's for us, not against us."

Her jaw tensed.

"With all the suffering in the world, your God seems less concerned about humanity than you think," she snapped. "My life's been hell these last four years. No God came to save me. So tell me, Caleb—what proof do you have of this so-called divine power?"

If he wanted to open this door, he needed to be ready for what was behind it.

But he didn't even hesitate. "I'm a Sixth Sense Seeker," he said.

Her brow furrowed. "A what?"

"A Sixth Sense Seeker of truth."

She rolled her eyes, but curiosity tugged at her.

"Explain."

"Science relies on the five senses. Sight, smell, touch, hearing, taste. I believe there's a sixth—divine inspiration."

She shook her head, a faint, incredulous smile tugging at her lips. "This is getting weird."

"Stay with me," he said. "It's not as weird as it sounds."

Part of her wanted to shut it down. But another part—quiet, persistent—urged her to keep listening. That flicker of hope again. *Damn it.*

She stood and paced. "You're attributing random events to divine design. That's… delusional."

"Have you ever known a blind person?"

The question threw her.

"Yeah. Brittney Aleman. Fifth grade. Born blind."

"So she never saw a sunset?"

"Of course not. She was blind."

"But sunsets still exist, right?"

She turned toward the window. Beyond the glass, city lights sparkled like fragments of something unfinished.

"Are you saying I can't see your God because I'm… spiritually blind?"

Her tone was colder than intended.

"I'm saying we all have blind spots," he said. "And just because we can't see something, doesn't mean it isn't there."

His words lingered. Simple, disarming, infuriating.

She folded her arms. Chin lifted.

"So, what—this extra perception makes you superior?"

"I'm not superior," he said. "I'm flawed like everyone else. But I'm learning to see differently. There's more than what we measure or touch."

She narrowed her eyes. That quiet certainty. Was it belief or delusion?

"All right, superman," she said. "Prove it."

He hesitated, then, "My grandmother. Her sixth sense came through dreams."

"Her dreams must've been nothing like mine," she deadpanned.

Caleb didn't laugh.

"She saw my cousin. In a dream—clinging to a rock, water raging around him. She warned him not to hike Zion's Narrows."

Kalyssa sat up straighter.

"He didn't listen?"

"A flash flood. They never found his body."

Her throat constricted, breath slipping free.

"I'm so sorry."

"Grandpa knew she was right," Caleb said. "Brushed her off at first. But after that, he never doubted her again."

His story clung to her—undeniable, inconvenient. She searched for a loophole, some rational explanation.

Nothing came.

"So," she asked, quieter now, "do you have dreams like that?"

"No. My sixth sense shows up differently."

"How?"

"It's like something just… arrives. A knowing. Not from logic. Not from memory. It just *is*. Like going from fog to clear."

"That could be any random thought. How do you know it's not just your imagination?"

"Most thoughts are noise. But this comes in the quiet. It brings peace, not confusion. Clarity, not control."

She replayed his words. Her heart quickened.

"So, you're saying you experience divine inspiration?"

"Not just me," he said. "Most faith traditions describe it. Jesus called it the Spirit of Truth. In Islam, it's known as *Ruh al-Qudus*. Hinduism speaks of *Atman*—the divine self within. Even Buddhism has *Dharma* and *Prajna*, pathways to spiritual insight."

A chill crept down her spine. He wasn't bluffing. He'd studied this. He wasn't just throwing out slogans.

Still, she bristled.

"Or, as Karl Marx put it, 'religion is the opiate of the masses,'" she countered.

Again, he didn't hesitate.

"Faith isn't a delusion for the weak," he said. "Some of the world's brightest minds have believed—not because they needed a crutch, but because they found a connection to something greater."

Without thinking, she asked, "Have you experienced that?" Her own question surprised her.

"To a degree," he said. "But what moves me most is seeing how it transforms people. Makes them softer. Braver. Less bitter."

That word—*bitter*—landed hard.

"I've met plenty of so-called 'born-agains,'" she said. "Judgment and hypocrisy, not humility."

"I don't disagree. Some twist faith into a weapon. But others align their lives with it. No spotlight. No performance. Just light."

A long pause.

"That's what I'm after," he added. "A transformed life."

It unsettled her. But it tugged at something deep.

"So how do you reconcile all the contradictions?" she asked. "Religions don't agree—except that the others are wrong."

"A mentor once told me faith isn't about dogma," he said. "It's about transformation. There are Seekers—those who strive for growth—and Seeds, waiting for change."

"Seeds?" she asked.

"They carry promise. They don't need judgment. They need light. Everyone has the potential to change."

A chill tiptoed down her spine.

"What about evil? Some people are too far gone."

"I don't believe in a point of no return. The possibility of change is what keeps us human."

She wanted to argue. But something in her eased.

"You have more hope than I do."

"If there is a God, and that God offers light, then transformation is always possible. That's my quest—to be transformed. And maybe help others find it too."

She turned back toward the window, her reflection blurring into the city lights.

His words hit something buried.

She didn't name it. She couldn't.

"But what if you're wrong?"

"Then I'll still have lived a life of growth and purpose. But if I'm right? I'll have found joy. Either way, I'm willing to take the risk."

The thought lingered.

Then… an intentional shift.

"Spiritual enlightenment *and* a dating profile? That's quite the combination."

Caleb chuckled. "I'm still searching for my dream girl. And when I find her, it'll be far more than physical."

"So, what are you looking for?" she asked boldly.

"I want a woman who fills my heart and graces my memories. To breathe the same air, smell the same scents, watch the same sunsets. To miss her when she's gone. To make passionate love when she returns. I want her to know my love is unending. All-consuming."

"Sounds like a fantasy," she said, but the bite was gone.

"Maybe," he said. "But with you, my heart and mind are a swirl of emotions I can't begin to explain."

Her pulse quickened. Rationality warned her.

But her heart beat louder.

"And…?"

A pause.

"Would you like to meet for dinner?"

Dinner.

Such a simple word. Yet, it landed heavy.

"What do you have in mind?"

"Stone Ember Grille on Capitol Hill. Four and a half stars. Two thousand reviews. I've never been—being there with you will make it five stars."

A smile tugged at her lips. Despite herself.

"Sounds good," she said. "Does Friday the 16th work?"

"Perfect. Let's meet at five o'clock. We'll catch a live show at the Miracle Theatre after. It's within walking distance."

Excitement rippled through her—unfamiliar. Intoxicating.

"I look forward to seeing you in person," she said, trembling.

"I'm already counting the days."

But beneath the anticipation, a shadow loomed.

Justin's face flashed through her mind again. His smile. His touch. The way he'd once made her believe in forever.

Is this a leap toward something real... or another storm waiting to shatter me?

And Caleb—charming, enigmatic Caleb—what secrets was he hiding?

As the call ended, one thought pulsed in her mind, relentless and raw:

This isn't just dinner.

It was a chance to reclaim something she'd lost.

Or lose what little she had left.

CHAPTER TWELVE

The scent of roasted leg of lamb hung in the air, rich and cloying. What should have been comforting felt suffocating. Every step Caleb took deeper into the Everton home amplified an invisible current of unease. Angela's birthday was meant to be a celebration, but after the June 4 Stratus Airways cyberattack, nothing felt celebratory. The house felt oxygen-starved—charged, brittle, wrong.

He should have been in Arizona, hiking Sedona's red rocks. Instead, his vacation had been grounded, replaced by a dinner steeped in quiet menace. A week had passed since the attack, but tonight felt like a snare pulling tighter around him.

The dining room was impeccable, as always. A golden-brown leg of lamb commanded the table, flanked by baked potatoes, roasted carrots, toasted French bread, and a crisp green salad. Everything in place. Everything just so.

Angela, frail yet radiant, smiled warmly from the head of the table. Cancer had stripped her of strength but not kindness—it still shimmered through the exhaustion in her eyes.

"Caleb, sweetheart! I'm so glad you could make it," she said thinly, but overflowing with affection.

He returned her smile, though it felt brittle. A mask stretched too tight. His fingers curled firmly around the wineglass Everton had handed him, and the tremor in Caleb's hand betrayed his unease.

"I wouldn't miss it for the world," Caleb said.

The words rang hollow.

Everton poured wine with precise control, his eyes rarely leaving Caleb. "A toast to Angela," he said, raising his glass. His smile was all teeth, no warmth. "To another year of resilience and grace."

They clinked glasses. The sound was sharp, empty.

He sipped, mind racing. The toast, the dinner, Everton's gaze—it was all theater. Angela had been like a mother to him, but even her kindness couldn't soften the suspicion twisting in his gut.

Why had Everton invited him here so soon after the airline attack?

"How was Arizona?" Everton asked casually, sliding the mint jelly across the table.

Caleb's pulse kicked. Everton knew he'd never made it to Sedona. *Why the game?*

Caleb spooned jelly onto his plate, steadying himself with the motion. "Arizona's always amazing," he said. "Breathtaking sunsets. Majestic red rocks. Saguaro forests."

He clung to the image—something real, something that wasn't this.

Angela carved the lamb with trembling hands. "It's good to have you both here," she said. "After everything… it's just good to be together."

Her words hung in the air, fragile as glass. Angela's illness had worn them all down, but it was the financial strain that had nearly broken the family. The experimental treatments weren't covered by insurance, draining the Evertons' savings. Caleb had seen the toll it took on Everton—once-steady hands shaking, desperation fraying the edges of his composure.

Tonight, though, Everton was calm. Too calm. Not relieved, but resolved.

After the cyberattack ransom was paid, rumor said millions had changed hands. A pit formed in Caleb's stomach.

Everton raised his glass again, that same razor-edged smile on his face.

"Angela, Caleb has some news to share," he said, a hint of menace beneath the cordial tone.

She looked at him, smile bright but tired.

Caleb's mind scrambled.

What is he doing?

Everton leaned back, casual as ever. "Tell her about your consulting gig," he said, smooth as a velvet blade.

The words hit like a punch to the gut. Consulting gig? Every hour Caleb had worked was to help Angela—not for personal gain. He'd hacked firewalls, traced threats, all to ease the burden. Now Everton twisted it into something sinister.

Caleb forced a grin. "Actually, I've taken up selling Girl Scout cookies."

Angela laughed—soft, genuine. For a moment, the sound broke the tension.

Everton didn't laugh. "When you've got skills like Caleb's," he said, slicing through the levity, "CEOs seek you out. And they pay handsomely, don't they, Caleb?"

The tremor returned in his hands. Images flashed—one hundred thousand dollars unexpectedly wired to his account by Weihua Industries. A Chinese conglomerate. The bank had insisted it was a verified transfer. Now he saw it for what it was.

A setup.

After dinner, Angela excused herself to rest. Caleb stood to help her, and she embraced him gently, her touch anchoring him for an instant. Then he turned to go.

And found Everton in his path, blocking the exit.

"God will provide," Everton said, gripping his hand too firmly. Calm, reverent words. But underneath? Something cold. Threatening.

Caleb held his gaze, searching for the mentor who once guided him like a father. Gone. All that remained was a man who wielded power like a weapon, and Caleb was just another piece on the board.

Caleb stepped into the cool night—fear chasing, pulse racing.

The stars felt distant, indifferent.

But deep inside, something sparked, unrelenting.

It wasn't fear.

It was fire.

Defiance.

The spark Everton tried to snuff out had only grown.

And that spark?

It would ignite something unstoppable.

CHAPTER THIRTEEN

Caleb sat at his desk, eyes fixed on the glowing screen, but his thoughts were still trapped in Sunday night. Angela Everton's birthday dinner had masqueraded as a celebration, though it had been anything but. Caleb hadn't been a guest. He was the offering.

Nine companies. Nine cyber threat assessments. Each one strategic, airtight, authored by him and now twisted into evidence against him. A trusted NSA insider, framed as the architect of a Chinese-led cyberattack on Stratus Airways.

The calendar invite still blinked on his screen:

Meeting with Hamilton Everton

Leadership Opportunity – 4:00 p.m.

Location: Everton's office

His pulse surged.

Everton never called people to his office. He was the office—he came to you, controlled the tempo, dominated the room. A summons like this wasn't a courtesy.

It was bait, dressed as opportunity.

Caleb leaned back, running a hand through his short blond hair. On Sunday, Everton's eyes had said everything—cold, calm, surgical. The man had known Caleb hadn't made it to Sedona.

Everton knew too much.

Caleb couldn't be here at 4:00.

He logged into the personnel system and filed a half day of sick leave. Reckless. Obvious. But it bought him time, just enough to disappear.

At 12:15 p.m., he walked briskly down the corridor, shoes clicking against polished tile, pulse drumming in his ears. No one stopped him. No one even looked up.

He slipped into the parking lot and eased out in his Tesla, each mile a silent countdown.

It's my turn to play.

Everton sat behind his pristine black desk, pen tapping against glass. Five minutes late.

Unacceptable.

The phone chimed. One glance at the screen, and the world narrowed. Sick leave.

His fist slammed down on the desk. Papers scattered like ash.

"That damn bastard." He snatched the phone. "Activate the Surveillance Squad. I want Caleb in this office within the hour. Quietly."

No need to wait for a response.

Caleb wasn't sick. He was burning the playbook.

Everton stared through the window at Fort Meade—steel and glass and secrets. His kingdom.

And somewhere out there, the protégé was outmaneuvering the master.

One mistake, Caleb. That's all it takes. Just one.

At 4:45 p.m., an Uber rolled to the curb in front of Caleb's townhome—a black Tesla Model 3 nearly identical to his own car parked five blocks away. Unassuming. Intentional.

He opened the back door, briefcase in hand.

"Thanks for the pickup," he said, calm as ever.

"No problem," the driver replied.

He crouched low. "Last Uber I took got a flat. Just going to check your tires."

He moved along the passenger side—slow, deliberate. At the rear, he palmed his smartphone in its magnetic case. One clean click, and the device was attached beneath the bumper. Then came the final touch. He pulled a license plate from his briefcase and clicked it in place with magnetic precision.

"Tires look good," he said, sliding into the back seat. Spine straight. Eyes forward.

Phase one: complete.

Twenty minutes later, Laurel Lake came into view. The Golden Dragon perched above the water like it had nothing to hide. Calm. Serene. A perfect cover.

As they neared the entrance, he pulled out a burner—different account, different phone—and requested a pickup behind the restaurant.

The driver's phone chimed.

"Huh, got a pickup here too," the driver said, barely glancing at the screen.

"Thanks for the ride," he said, stepping out.

By 5:10 p.m., he was walking up the polished stone steps. A jasmine-sweet breeze floated through the entryway.

He wore what he always wore: dark blue suit, powder blue shirt, black Oxfords polished to a mirror sheen. Ordinary. Intentional.

Mr. Zhang greeted him with a polite nod. "Good evening, Mr. Calvarri. Your usual table?"

"Not tonight. Dynasty Room. Back booth. The one with the window facing the cherry trees."

"Of course. Right this way."

Caleb slid into the booth, setting the briefcase to his right, body angled to watch both the entrance and the hall leading to the restrooms.

Where is she?

He checked his watch: 5:15.

Still time.

Mr. Zhang returned with the customary order of egg rolls. Caleb barely noticed. His focus was already gone—running scenarios, recalculating options.

At 5:27, he stood. Smooth. Unhurried. A quiet shift toward the hallway.

Plan B.

The only viable option left.

〰〰〰

Everton stormed into the surveillance room like a thunderclap.

"Where's Caleb Calvarri?"

The team lead stiffened. "We're tracking him through his phone. He's on the move—frequent stops across the metro area."

Unbelievable.

"You're telling me Caleb's moonlighting as an Uber driver?"

"Black Tesla. Plates match. Phone's been moving since 4:45. First camera ping was ten minutes ago."

Idiots. Lazy, phone-watching idiots.

"And you're assuming it's him because…?"

The man didn't answer fast enough.

"Most people keep their phones with them," he finally muttered.

Everton stepped in, low and lethal. "Caleb is not most people."

Silence.

Then a weak follow-up.

"But… but the plates—"

"Stop the driver," Everton snapped. "And drag the truth out of him."

He strode out of the room, his tone flat and final, the words meant for Caleb alone.

"I am watching you."

Ninety minutes later, Caleb's phone sat on Everton's desk.

Wiped. Factory reset. No calls. No contacts. Just a sterile rectangle of glass and circuitry.

An artifact of failure.

Everton stared at it. Not in frustration. In fury.

Caleb hadn't panicked. He hadn't improvised.

He'd executed.

Caleb wasn't just running.

He was winning.

And this phone?

This was Caleb's victory dance.

CHAPTER FOURTEEN

The Patuxent Research Refuge stretched across 13,000 acres of forest, meadow, and wetlands just south of Fort Meade. Caleb knew these trails intimately—had hiked them often during off-grid weekends. What he had once dismissed as an expensive hobby now felt like the smartest investment he'd ever made.

His escape from the Golden Dragon to the Red Roof Inn had been a calculated gamble. He'd leaned hard into the disguise—dark sunglasses, surgical mask, gloves, green scrubs, and a black ball cap. The germophobic surgeon persona: Dr. Frank Stein. The Uber driver hadn't asked questions during the eight-minute ride. Perfect.

After a short walk, Caleb ditched his briefcase, which held the crumpled suit and polished Oxfords, into a motel dumpster. No looking back. The rest of the 4.3-mile trek to the Fire Road trailhead—over an hour on foot—took him deeper into the wilderness. Each passing car was a potential threat. He dropped into the forest more than once, heart pounding, the weight of every shadow pressing down on him.

Hunger and thirst gnawed at him, constant companions. The temperature had dropped to 75 degrees, but the humidity at 83 percent left his shirt soaked. Sticky. Oppressive. Like the tension that hadn't left since Sunday night.

Five minutes onto the trail, a flicker of triumph: the rock pile. Still there.

Off trail, tucked into the trees, he found his fully stocked trail pack. Relief hit like a warm current. The weight of it on his shoulders grounded him—control reclaimed in a world coming apart.

He changed fast, swapping scrubs for khaki hiking shorts and a bamboo-blend, brown T-shirt. Functional. Familiar. He strapped on the pack and followed the trail northeast. When it curved south, he broke off and bushwhacked north, heading toward an unnamed pond reachable only on foot. Remote. Isolated. He wouldn't make it there tonight, but he could get close.

By dusk, he found a flat spot behind a fallen pine and unrolled his one-man REI tent.

Two mice shot out.

He froze.

A six-inch tear in the sidewall—gnawed straight through.

"Damn it," he muttered, tension spiking.

Then came the second hit: no stakes.

"Really?" The word tasted like grit. Hands shaking, he reached for his knife and mallet and got to work. Thirty minutes later, the tent stood— held by eight roughly carved stakes. Each blow of the mallet harder than necessary. Each one trying to hammer the anxiety into silence.

He dropped onto a nearby stump and pulled two MREs from his pack—Menu 9, Beef Stew, and Menu 3, Chicken, Noodles, and Vegetables in Sauce. His stomach growled, but his brain betrayed him, and he imagined egg rolls, Kung Pao chicken, the sharp aroma of garlic and soy. Then back to reality: vacuum-sealed punishment in a government pouch.

Menu 3. He peeled it open.

The first bite hit like a dare.

Dense. Tasteless. The texture of regret.

He let out a quiet, humorless laugh. Picturing five-star takeout while chewing on boiled cardboard. Five-year shelf life. Reassuring in theory. In practice?

Not so much.

Halfway through, he gave up—choosing hunger over whatever this was pretending to be. He held the pouch at arm's length, tempted to hurl it into the woods as a tribute to Army dietitians. But no—better to bury it. Less conspicuous.

He dug a shallow grave with his camp shovel and dropped the bag inside. The dirt fell in clumps, soft and damp. It felt like a funeral.

Not just for the meal, but for another piece of the life he'd also just buried.

He capped it with a rock and took a long swig from his water bottle, swishing before he swallowed.

His final backpacking splurge had been the Western Mountaineering MegaLite—570 bucks on Amazon. Steep price. Worth it. Growing up, it was the forty-nine-dollar Walmart bag or nothing. Out here, with everything unraveling, it felt like a tiny win. A luxury he'd somehow held on to.

He unrolled it slowly, bracing for mouse droppings or shredded fabric.

Still intact.

Relief bloomed quietly in his chest.

He stepped a few yards from camp and relieved himself, eyes scanning the dark trees as if they might answer the bigger question:

How long can I stay out here?

He didn't want to think. Just sleep. Sleep might be the only way to claw back some clarity.

He peeled off his shirt, which clung to him like a desperate lover. His pants were far less committed and surrendered easily. He draped both over a bush, hoping the night air would do its job.

The rain started around eleven, just a whisper at first, tapping the tent like an impatient visitor.

By midnight, the sky broke open.

Two inches of rain in an hour.

Water bled across the forest floor, carving streams where there had been none, twisting like veins in the earth.

Inside the tent, everything fell apart.

His patch job on the sidewall? Worthless. Water breached the seams and flooded the sleeping bag within minutes.

But that wasn't the worst of it.

His gut clenched—once, then again, sharper still. Nausea surged like waves, violent and relentless. He held still, trying to breathe through it.

Didn't matter.

His body had already made up its mind.

He bolted upright, hands shaking, yanked the zipper—missed. Got it on the second try.

Rain hit him in the face like a slap. He stumbled out, barely clearing the tent before his stomach revolted. He dropped to his knees and heaved hard. The vomit hit mud, but the rain erased it almost instantly.

His body kept convulsing long after there was nothing left.

Then another wave. Worse.

He staggered. Squatted. Everything inside him emptied in a rush of cold and cramps and shame. The forest blurred around him until he collapsed to the ground, soaked and shivering, face in the mud.

By 1:30, the rain eased. A dripping silence settled over the woods, heavy and haunting.

He crawled into what was left of the tent. Found the emergency blanket—still dry. Somehow. He wrapped it tight and waited for the shaking to stop.

It didn't.

At first light, Caleb forced himself upright. Sore. Hollowed out.

He pulled Menu 9 from the food stash—Beef Stew—and stared at it like it had betrayed him. Then he walked to a lingering stream and hurled it in.

The pouch spun, bobbed, and drifted away.

Good riddance.

Everything that hadn't been sealed in Ziploc bags was soaked. He unpacked one item at a time, clothes and gear heavy with stink, and draped them across bushes and low branches like laundry lines.

From a side pocket, he pulled a soggy wad of twenties, tens, and fives—useless, but still his. He laid the bills on a flat granite boulder and weighed them down with river rocks. Mother Nature might drench him, starve him, and leave him puking in the mud, but she wasn't going to take what was rightfully his.

The Gala apple was the only thing that hadn't betrayed him. Cold. Crisp. Sweet. He bit in like it might save his life.

The jerky stayed in the bag. Test the waters first.

His stomach held. His head cleared. Slowly, the haze began to lift.

Now came the math. The logistics. The planning.

Every move had to count. No patterns. No slipups. No waste.

This wasn't safety.

It was a pause.

And if he stayed too long, it wouldn't be a hideout.

It would be his grave.

CHAPTER FIFTEEN

The air inside FBI headquarters pulsed with quiet intensity. Servers hummed, monitors flickered with classified data, and agents moved with the precision of people who knew time wasn't on their side.

Special Agent in Charge Ricardo Roca stood at the center, a looming presence in front of the wall-sized display. The tension in the room shifted the moment he stepped in—part reputation, part gravity.

He didn't speak right away. He let the silence settle, thick and expectant. Then:

"Three days ago, I was in Fort Worth investigating a cyberattack on Stratus Airways," he said. "System-wide lockdown. Planes grounded. Nationwide disruption. All signs pointed to external infiltration."

He tapped the tablet in his hand. A series of surveillance stills populated the monitors—flight logs, server logs, bank transfers.

"Until the anomaly hit."

A new image blinked onto the screen: Caleb Calvarri.

"NSA cybersecurity expert. Decorated. Respected. Six years of classified clearances."

Roca turned, his gaze sweeping the room.

"And now, our prime suspect."

A few agents shifted. Others went still.

"On June 6th, two days after the attack, a wire transfer of a hundred grand was made to Calvarri's account. Source: Weihua Industries. Chinese shell corporation. Plausible deniability baked in."

He let that sink in.

"This isn't just internal compromise," Roca continued. "It's national security at the highest level. The man we're hunting knows how to disappear—and how to break us from the inside out."

The map on the screen zoomed into Laurel, Maryland. A red dot blinked.

"Last confirmed location: the Golden Dragon restaurant, June 13th at 17:10. He entered by Uber. He never came out."

Agent Lisa Harmon leaned forward, the knuckles of her fingerless gloves brushing the table. "You think he's still in the area?"

"He's a ghost. But ghosts still cast shadows. Start with the Patuxent Research Refuge—thirteen thousand acres of tactical cover. Calvarri's got the skills and the mindset to live off-grid. Assume he's armed. Assume he's watching."

Harmon nodded. "We're on it."

Roca turned toward another terminal where Special Agent Dana Cruz-Way sat. "Dig into every alias. Start with the one he used for that Uber ride—Frank Stein. Shake every branch."

Cruz-Way nodded, the sharp glint of her cat-eye glasses catching the overhead light. "Account's flagged. We've got an address on the ride request and facial recognition scraping the footage now."

"Good." Roca's jaw tensed. "This isn't just about apprehension. It's about prevention. If he's working with foreign assets—if he's flipped—then every hour he's free is a vulnerability."

He turned back to the blinking red dot on the map.

"This isn't about catching a fugitive," he said. "It's about national survival."

He released a long, slow exhale through his nose.

"The game's in motion. And right now, Caleb's winning."

CHAPTER SIXTEEN

The street-facing dining area of Stone Ember Grille looked underwhelming. Large picture windows, light brown siding, and a corrugated tin roof gave it the vibe of a third-world attempt at fine dining. Kalyssa had seen the photos online. Almost canceled.

But something about Caleb's choice had kept her curious.

Now, standing outside, heart hammering—a tangle of nerves and hope—she reminded herself that appearances deceived. She, of all people, should've known.

The moment she stepped through the door, everything shifted. A black-and-white checkered floor stretched beneath pastel-pink walls, while the ceiling shimmered with hanging cherry blossoms and glowing orbs of light. It felt like stepping into a summer night with an island breeze. Warm. Unexpected.

Kalyssa paused. Let herself breathe.

Maybe, just maybe, this night could be the start of something she hadn't dared to hope for in forever.

Shortly after 5:00 p.m., she checked in with the host, giving Caleb's name. Moments later, she was seated at a table for two, her eyes fixed on the door.

She adjusted the straps of her long, black dress, the slit high enough to feel daring but still elegant. She'd chosen it with intention—sophisticated, alluring, not overplayed. Even her lipstick was bolder than usual, deep pink with a hint of risk. Tonight, she wanted confidence. She wanted Caleb to see her not just as someone who could match him intellectually, but as someone who could move him.

Minutes ticked by. The anticipation that fluttered in her chest began to twist into something tighter.

At 5:11 p.m., she texted him. No reply.

At 5:17, she called. No answer.

The laughter and clinking glasses around her grew louder, somehow more pointed—as if the whole restaurant knew. The joy at other tables mocked her silence.

She scanned the room. Every face. Every glance.

Is someone watching me?

The thought crept in uninvited, irrational but impossible to shake.

Get a grip.

But the tension in her shoulders refused to ease.

By 5:20, the knot in her chest had hardened to a dull ache. She ordered the mushroom flatbread—cremini mushrooms, sautéed leeks, fresh arugula—but her appetite was gone. She kept checking her phone. Each glance like a slap.

At 5:35, hope collapsed.

The fantasy she'd let herself believe—the laughter, the spark, the night that might have rekindled something real—dissolved into a dull ache.

She sat back in her chair, the weight of rejection sinking fast.

How could I have been so naive?

She shook her head, lips pressed tight. She'd let her guard down. Believed in something fragile. Something foolish.

And now it felt like the whole world was watching her fall for a man who was never coming.

The marquee of the Miracle Theatre shimmered like distant stars in the thick summer night. The breeze offered no relief—only stirred the heat clinging to Kalyssa's skin, warmth born from expectations Caleb had left unmet.

The city pulsed around her, vibrant and indifferent. Laughter spilled from sidewalk cafés. Couples strolled by, hands clasped, carefree.

But inside. She had shattered.

This wasn't just about tonight.

Caleb had become the ghost of every failed hope.

But she wouldn't let that ghost linger.

Chin high, she kept walking. Her heels struck the pavement with crisp resolve. Each step cleared the haze. She didn't look back.

Tonight was the end of one chapter.

The next?

That would be hers to write.

Saturday morning arrived with blinding clarity.

Sunlight slanted through the blinds, casting sharp patterns across the hardwood floor of Kalyssa's apartment. She clung to her weekend routine—coffee, CNN, silence—anything to erase the memory of one Caleb Calvarri.

Then it hit.

"Caleb Calvarri, a former NSA operative, is now the subject of a nationwide manhunt."

Her hand jerked. The coffee cup clattered against the table, sloshing dark liquid onto the glass. She didn't notice. Her eyes locked on the screen as dread swept over her.

Treason. Espionage. Conspiracy.

The words blurred. Her mind refused to accept them.

No. This isn't real.

The screen cut to Hamilton Everton—stone-faced, slick under studio lights. His features had the same sharpness she remembered. Athletic. Controlled. The kind of man who never said more than he meant to.

"As the NSA deputy director," Everton began, tone polished and measured, "my priority is to restore the American people's faith in our national security. Caleb Calvarri has shattered that trust. He was one of our best operatives, which makes his betrayal all the more personal."

Kalyssa's breath stalled, and something cold slipped through her core.

Betrayal.

She knew that word too well.

But... Caleb? He had opened up to her with such honesty. His pursuit of truth. Raw. Real.

Anchor Jasper Wood leaned forward, eyes grim.

"Two weeks ago, Stratus Airways suffered a catastrophic cyberattack," Wood reported. "Five thousand flights grounded. More than a half million people stranded. The White House responded with a $200 billion freeze on Chinese assets. Beijing called it an act of war."

He glanced at Everton. "But now a deeper question looms. Is Caleb Calvarri the missing link between China's cyber offensive and America's greatest aviation crisis?"

Everton's expression never wavered. "I can't comment on an active investigation," he said evenly. "But I will say this: we must ensure the president has the authority to act without bureaucratic delay."

Kalyssa's pulse spiked.

That wasn't just about Caleb. That was about power.

She clenched the cushion beside her. Everton wasn't sharing facts. He was shaping the narrative. Painting Caleb as the villain. Consolidating control.

She should've felt vindicated. Caleb had ghosted her. Left her exposed. Hurt.

But all she felt was a hollowness she couldn't shake.

No. This isn't who he is.

Her thoughts raced—his stories, his laughter, the smile that always surfaced when he mentioned Sedona.

Had she been blind?

Or was *this* the deception?

Then came the photo.

His face. Blond hair. Blue eyes. The same intensity that had drawn her in.

Frozen. Branded.

"If anyone has information on Mr. Calvarri's whereabouts," Jasper said, "they are urged to contact the FBI immediately."

Her body quivered. She couldn't look away.

She'd tried to summon the rage. The clean break. But all she found was ache.

Caleb wasn't just another man who had vanished. He was different. And no headline could unwrite what she'd felt.

She leaned back. Eyes burning. Heart pounding.

The safe thing would be to walk away. Let the FBI handle it. Let logic win.

But her heart didn't care about logic.

He's not the man they're making him out to be.

The decision came without permission.

I am going to find him.

Even if it meant risking her career.

Even if it meant breaking every rule she'd ever followed.

Because beneath the headlines, the accusations, the silence…

She still believed.

Or maybe…

She just needed to.

CHAPTER SEVENTEEN

In the six nights he'd spent hiding deep in the backwoods of the Patuxent Research Refuge, two thoughts refused to let Caleb rest.

The first was Kalyssa.

She haunted every dream—her lips against his, her body warm and close. The imagined feel of her skin lingered long after he woke, leaving a hollow ache in his chest. Friday night kept replaying. The table at Stone Ember Grille. Her waiting. His absence. Had one missed moment cost him the only connection that still felt real?

The second thought was survival.

Prison wasn't just looming—it was chasing him. And if it caught up, there would be no second chances.

Escape wasn't a plan. It was the only acceptable outcome.

On Monday morning, he began the grueling task of shaving his head—a desperate attempt to disappear.

What should've taken fifteen minutes with clippers dragged into an hour-long battle. Armed with nothing but a cheap plastic razor, he hacked at the right side first, each stroke clogging with thick, blond strands. He paused constantly, yanking hair from the blade before scraping again.

"Damn it," he muttered as blood welled from a mole he hadn't known was there.

He switched sides and kept going—faster now, but just as crude. His scalp burned, each pass peeling away more hair, more skin. By the end, both sides were raw. He angled his tiny handheld mirror and smirked at the reflection.

I look like a punk rocker. Now I just need a nose ring.

Determined, he kept at it, working front to back. The blade caught more than once, and each time it did, he winced. Nearly an hour later, it was done. His skin stung, red and inflamed, but he ran a hand over the smooth surface and exhaled.

He tugged a black beanie over his head, sealing the transformation. Then, without ceremony, he scooped up the hair clippings, grabbed his hand shovel, and buried the remains beneath the underbrush.

No evidence. No trace.

He stripped down, skin prickling in the cool morning air, and poured filtered stream water over his body, scrubbing off six days of sweat, grime, and stink. The water hit crisp—refreshing, but jarring. Necessary.

His towel was worn thin, but it did the job. He crouched beside the warped remains of his deodorant—a victim of the summer heat. He dipped a finger into the slick, scented puddle and swiped it under each arm.

"Fresh scent," he muttered. *Mountain breeze? Industrial soap? False hope in a plastic stick?*

He dressed with practiced efficiency: boxers, khaki shorts, a blue cotton-poly T-shirt that clung to his lean frame. On a nearby tree stump, he laced up his Salomon trail runners. Reliable. Broken-in.

His backpack was organized with surgical precision: filled water bladder, long-sleeve shirt, rain poncho, green neck gaiter, and the last of his food supply. In his front right pocket—four tens, two fives. In a hidden seam stitched into his beanie—six twenties.

A clever stash.

Would it be clever enough?

He slipped on wraparound sunglasses. They wouldn't fool facial recognition, but they might slow it down.

Disguise? Paper-thin. But it would have to hold.

He stood. Pulled the beanie low. Breath steady. Heart pounding a slow, determined rhythm.

Then started walking.

The twelve-and-a-half-mile journey to Prince George's Community College should've taken twenty-eight minutes by car. On foot, it dragged into six brutal hours.

Every step burned. Every muscle ached. He rationed his last granola bar and a packet of almonds. Pushed forward on sheer willpower.

By the time the campus came into view, his shirt clung to his back. He slipped the beanie into his backpack, crossed Campus Way South, and entered Accokeek Hall.

Keep moving. Keep blending.

He avoided the librarian's gaze. Walked like he belonged. Confidence was its own kind of camouflage.

In the restroom, he splashed cold water on his face, letting the shock center him. One breath. Then another.

Composed enough, he stepped out and claimed a computer far from the student clusters.

His heart pounded as he typed:

Caleb Calvarri

The results hit like a punch:

FBI's Most Wanted: Caleb Calvarri

National Manhunt Underway For Fugitive Calvarri

FBI Investigating Hundreds of Leads

His stomach knotted. He slouched lower, glancing around. Sunglasses. Shaved head. Six days of stubble.

A disguise held together with duct tape and desperation.

But fear wasn't in charge. Not today.

Focus.

He navigated to the college's online card catalog. Found the call number. Scribbled it down on a scrap of paper.

Then stood.

Up the stairs. Measured steps. No hesitation.

The second floor was quiet, the tables and desks cluttered with the remnants of forgotten assignments and abandoned notebooks, a testament to those who had too much and wanted too little.

A thought sparked.

He didn't just need information. He needed resources.

He scanned the space. *Information is good. Supplies are better.*

Sheets of paper. Two pencils. Ballpoint pen. Roll of Scotch tape. Scissors. And a manila folder—empty, worn at the edges.

One item at a time. All quiet. All discreet.

He slipped everything into his backpack with a flicker of dry amusement.

Lightening the custodial load. Doing my part for campus beautification.

Next, he moved between the tall shelves, fingers brushing spines until he found the one he'd come for. At a quiet desk tucked in the corner, he flipped through the pages with practiced speed.

And then… there it was. He stared, not just seeing but feeling.

Scissors in hand, he hesitated and then did what he came to do. Moments later, he returned the book to the shelf, mouthing a silent apology to the librarians. They wouldn't approve of what he had taken. But his mind wasn't on them. It was on her.

Kalyssa.

Maybe, just maybe, this would keep her hope alive.

Back at the computer, he searched: **homeless shelters near Prince George's Community College**

We Are One Mission—2.4 Miles.

Free meals, no beds. Useless.

Another Chance Men's Shelter—Capitol Heights. 5.2 Miles.

His legs ached just thinking about it.

He toggled to Google Maps. Bus stop: 0.4 miles. Ride to Addison Road Station. Ten-minute walk to the shelter. Doable.

He tore a corner off a flyer, sketched the route, folded it, and shoved it in his pocket.

Shelter's the goal. But invisibility is the mission.

Next: food.

New Harvest Market was four-tenths of a mile north. Close enough.

He opened ChatGPT. Typed:

Non-perishable, no-cook, high-calorie foods. Lightweight. Under $40.

The list came back clean: **Peanut butter. Tuna packets. Granola bars. Oatmeal packets. Dried fruit. Almonds.**

He copied it to the back of a library printout. Pocketed it.

Then moved.

Ten minutes later, he crossed into New Harvest Market.

A clerk called out, "Excuse me, sir. You'll need to check your backpack."

His pulse spiked.

He turned slowly. Female security guard. Clipboard in hand.

Standard protocol. Still dangerous.

"No problem," he said smoothly.

"Name and phone number?"

"Andy Taylor. 410-876-5678."

She handed him a claim tag.

He exhaled and moved on.

Twenty-five minutes later, his pack was heavier. His nerves tighter.

Outside, he devoured a protein bar, then an apple, then carrots—no savoring. Just calories.

Then the bus.

He stepped on, a blast of warm air striking his face. The doors hissed closed, and the vehicle lurched forward.

A flicker of unease stirred in his chest.

His gaze moved seat to seat—blank stares, fidgeting fingers, lowered hoods.

Not paranoia. Instinct.

Danger was chasing him.

And it just might be catching up.

CHAPTER EIGHTEEN

The air inside the bus clung to Caleb like a film—stale sweat, damp clothes, body heat cooked into the vinyl seats. The ventilation was useless, turning the stench into a slow-moving fog. The bus was half full. Mostly men of color. Worn faces. Blank expressions. The weight of long days and hard lives etched into every posture.

Ten minutes in, three men boarded.

They moved like they owned the space—slow, deliberate, dangerous. Matching red bandannas. Matching shoes. Sunglasses that, like his own, hid everything. They took the back row. He didn't need to look to know they were watching him.

Next stop, he stood and moved to the front, one row behind the driver. No hesitation. Just instinct.

And just like that, the trio moved too. They slid into the row he'd vacated, casual as shadows. He didn't turn around. Didn't let his body betray the alarm building in his chest. He glanced at his hand-drawn map.

I can run a tenth of a mile if I have to.

His eyes stayed forward, but his peripheral vision stayed sharp. He tracked their movement without moving a muscle.

When the bus slowed on Addison Road South—just before Ernie Banks Street—he rose fast, stepped off, and didn't look back.

Then he ran.

The slap of his soles on pavement broke the quiet.

His lungs screamed.

Brick apartments blurred past.

His legs burned.

His pulse roared in his ears.

Then… behind him, footsteps.

Fast. On the grass.

Terror ignited in his chest. He pushed harder, the backpack jostling against his spine, vision narrowing, everything funneling toward the shelter ahead.

The red stairs. The entrance.

He overshot the turn, veered down the driveway, sprinted toward the back.

"Back off!" came the shout from behind, deep and commanding.

Caleb's foot slid near the utility pole. He hit the ground hard—hands skinned, elbows torn, one knee bleeding. Pain flashed white behind his eyes.

He curled, arms protecting his head, bracing for the blows.

But none came.

Just the crunch of boots in the gravel… slowing… stopping.

Then a shadow fell over him—low, firm words breaking the silence:

"You okay?"

Caleb forced himself upright, pain pulsing through his hands and knees.

"Ain't many white boys 'round here," the man said, calm but curious. "Name's Dexter White. Folks call me Dex."

He squinted. "Are you the one who yelled 'back off'?"

Dex nodded. "Those Bloods were sniffin' for trouble. You're lucky your legs still work."

"They were gaining," he said. "Thanks for the save."

Dex stepped closer and offered a hand. "Need help gettin' up?"

Caleb eyed his bloody palms. "I'll manage." He shifted from the blacktop to the grass, then pushed himself to his feet, wincing as pain shot up the side of his calf.

Dex took in the torn shirt, the road rash. "You're gonna need new clothes."

He gave a weak smile. "Add it to the list."

"No problem," Dex said. "I gotcha. Got first aid too. C'mon in, my friend."

He hesitated, reading the man's eyes for anything off. Nothing but honesty. Caleb nodded. "Thanks. I appreciate it."

"What do you go by?" Dex asked as they headed toward the shelter.

"Call me Andy."

Dex gave a knowing chuckle, a look of skepticism on his face. "A'ight, Andy. We don't usually do walk-ins. But tonight... you look like someone the wind chewed up and spit out. Bed's yours if you want it."

"I do," he said quietly, the relief washing over him like balm.

The two walked back toward the front entrance he had blown past minutes earlier. Dex held the door open and motioned toward a cracked plastic deck chair near the welcome area.

"Sorry 'bout that," Dex said, eyeing the seat. "We rely on donations."

He managed a smile as he eased himself down. "It's perfect. Beats the blacktop."

They both chuckled. Caleb winced.

"You're gonna feel that for a few days," Dex said, flipping open a first aid kit. He worked with quiet precision, cleaning and bandaging his hands and elbows with surprising gentleness.

Once patched up, Dex led him to the dining area. The scent of spaghetti and garlic bread hit like a tidal wave. His stomach growled on cue.

"Have a seat. I'll grab you a plate," Dex said.

He didn't argue. Minutes later, he was inhaling the feast like a man rescued from sea. It was the best meal he'd had in a week.

"You want seconds?" Dex asked.

Caleb nodded before the question fully landed. "Yes. Please."

He didn't know when he'd eat like this again.

After dinner, Dex took him down a narrow hall into a room stacked floor to ceiling with clothing racks and storage bins.

"We scored big this year," Dex said proudly, gesturing like a tour guide. "Got athletic gear, button-downs, socks, shoes, even suits if you're feelin' fancy. Take what you need, bro."

Caleb hesitated. He'd always made his own way—never asked for help, never needed handouts. But Dex's tone wasn't patronizing. Just generous. Real.

"Thanks," he said, the words catching a little in his throat.

Dex chuckled, pulling open a cardboard box. "And over here? Halloween costumes. Mostly for the kids, but check out this clown wig. Wild, huh?"

Caleb managed a weak laugh.

Dex pointed to another bin. "And that's all computer junk. Ain't had much use for it—ain't too many folks 'round here showin' up with laptops."

Later that night, Caleb lay still beneath clean sheets, his body finally at rest, but his mind alive with questions.

Dex had taken a risk. A big one. No personal gain. No safety net. If things had gone sideways with those Bloods, Dex could've ended up hurt—or worse. And yet, without hesitation, he'd stepped in.

A black man risking his life for a white stranger.

Dex had treated his wounds, fed him, offered shelter and clothes. No judgment. No strings.

Something stirred in him. *He fits the mold of the Good Samaritan. But why? What drives a man like that? Is he a Sixth Sense Seeker... or something else entirely?*

The following morning, Caleb approached Dex in his small office near the front of the shelter.

"Dex, do you have a moment?"

"Sure," he replied. "What's up?"

"How did you know I was in trouble last night?"

"You were on the ground bleeding?" Dex looked confused.

"No, before that," Caleb said. "Why were you on the front porch of the shelter?"

Dex studied him, like he was trying to read what lay beneath the surface. "Andy, you want the polite answer… or you want it straight?"

"The truth."

"I was sittin' at this desk, working. Then a voice popped into my head—said, 'Go outside.' I brushed it off, but then it came again. Louder. 'Go outside now.' So, I moved fast. Stepped out just in time to see you runnin' for your life. I knew what I had to do."

Caleb hesitated. "That voice in your mind… where do you think it came from?"

Dex's eyes held steady. "Andy, that's how God talks to me. And I'm learnin' to listen."

That hit deep.

He's a Sixth Sense Seeker.

"And why'd you choose to work here?" Caleb asked.

"Andy, five years ago, that was me." Dex nodded toward a man in the sitting area, slumped in a plastic chair, eyes vacant, clothes stained with grime. "God done gave me a chance. Changed me." He softened with conviction. "Praise God."

Caleb smiled. "Praise God."

He didn't know what came next, but one thing was clear—he couldn't go back to who he was before. Not after this.

CHAPTER NINETEEN

On the eighth day of running, Caleb launched his first strike. Not just survival—attack. Precise. Devastating. Enough to crack the foundation of everything he once served.

The library at Prince George's Community College had closed at 7:00 sharp. Lights out. Doors locked. By 7:48, he slipped from the second-floor men's room, heart steady, breath shallow, backpack snug across his shoulders. He'd cased the building earlier. No cameras inside, and out front, just a few outdated motion sensors and one bored rent-a-cop.

Moonlight poured through the picture windows, casting soft silver across the carpet and tables.

They can't call it breaking-and-entering if they left the door open.

The long-sleeve shirt masked the scrapes on his arms. Black sweatpants covered the raw raspberry on his leg. The beanie and neck gaiter weren't for style. They were part of his disappearing act.

He started toward the terminal he'd tagged earlier, then stopped. Light from the monitor would spill out like a flare. Too visible.

He bowed his head.

God—if that's even your name—I think you're real. I'm trying to stop this country from tearing itself apart. So, if you've got an opinion… now would be a great time to weigh in.

Silence.

Please. I don't need a sign. Just a nudge.

He moved through the hallway, scanning for a better option. A flicker of motion caught his eye. An open door. A study room he hadn't noticed earlier.

He stepped in. No windows. No cameras. Just a table, four chairs, and a computer at the far corner.

He powered up the machine. Login screen. A taped note below:

LOGIN: guest1223

PASSWORD: accolib1

Sometimes the universe cooperates.

He connected to his encrypted cloud drive and pulled the external hard drive from his backpack. Two terabytes. Just enough.

He dropped Memory Mole onto the drive—just the installer. Less than a gig. The connection was slow, but speed wasn't the point. Stealth was.

He'd written every line of the malware himself—a digital skeleton key. Until now, he'd only used it for harmless background checks.

Tonight wasn't harmless.

Everton had called the NSA firewall "impenetrable."

Arrogant. False. And tonight, Caleb would prove it.

George Washington was called a traitor too. And then he became a Founding Father.

No more doubt.

His gloved fingers moved fast, disarming NSA defenses like a bomb tech cutting wires.

A moment. Then the command.

Memory Mole deployed Carrots and Potatoes—a rootkit so deep it could only be removed by gutting every system component. And by then, it wouldn't matter.

Data streamed in. Logs. Access keys. Internal schematics. Every blink brought a new threat, a new opportunity.

He moved fast. Silent. Clean. No trace. No pattern. He knew what he needed. He wasn't leaving without it.

At a Fortune 500 firm, this breach would headline every site. But this was the NSA. They didn't leak. They buried.

Still, history would know. This breach—*his* breach—was the biggest in American history.

He smiled broadly, allowing himself a moment of victory.

And then, adrenaline hit like a drug.

He severed the connection and wiped every trace. Efficient. Paranoid. But someone might already be watching a red light flash.

He shut down the machine.

Time to vanish.

He slipped into the stairwell. Each step was slow, measured, quiet.

The emergency exit loomed. One push, and the alarm would pinpoint his escape.

Too risky.

He paused. Heard the low hum of a vacuum. Cleaning crew.

He cracked an interior door. A reading room. Magazines. Journals. And there… a fire alarm.

His gut twisted. But there was no other move.

He pulled the lever.

The siren wailed, shattering the stillness.

He ran—through the interior door, out the emergency exit, across the lot, over Campus Way South.

Into the woods.

Branches clawed at his arms. Moonlight vanished behind thick trees. Sirens howled in the distance.

The breach was done. The game was on.

CHAPTER TWENTY

At 10:30 p.m., Everton crossed the National Mall, his overcoat billowing in the wind. The half-moon, veiled behind storm clouds, cast a dim glow over the monuments, its light fractured and uncertain, just like him. The air carried the bite of impending rain … sharp and cold against his face, but he didn't slow.

He couldn't.

Tonight wasn't random. June 21—the anniversary of the US Constitution's ratification.

Was this about freedom…

Or something far more dangerous?

The senator had invited him. Details sparse. Tone conspiratorial. A power play with promise.

His pace faltered near the old service tunnel's entrance. A glance over his shoulder revealed only shadows stretching long across the Mall. Still, unease twisted in his gut, like a warning he couldn't name. His hand slid toward his pocket, brushing the mask he'd been given. Cold. Smooth.

He inhaled sharply and slipped the mask onto his face. *The anonymity feels suffocating.*

The tunnel yawned open before him, a concrete throat reeking of rust and mildew. The lights flickered at uneven intervals, casting more shadow than light, and his footsteps echoed like the countdown of a distant clock. Somewhere beneath the Capitol, buried in a Cold War-era relic, others were already waiting.

Fifteen of them.

Fellow patriots? That's what the senator had called them.

And now him.

A steel-reinforced door loomed ahead, slightly ajar. It didn't look like an invitation. It looked like a trap.

He reached for it anyway, fingers hesitating against the frigid metal.

What are you afraid of? They're friends.

He pushed the door open and stepped through.

The chamber was dim. At its center, a heavy oak table rested beneath a single pendant light. Around it, masked figures sat in silence, their white expressions blank and unreadable. Everton slid into the only open seat. The chill in the room seeped through his coat.

Behind him, the steel door groaned shut.

With the click of a lock, the world above became irrelevant.

The hooded figure at the head of the table rose. An altered voice cut through the silence. Cold, resonant, surgically precise.

"My fellow patriots," the figure said reverently, "240 years ago, a small group of visionaries defied tyranny. They risked everything for one audacious promise: freedom."

The words echoed like a drumbeat. Everton wanted them to stir pride. Wanted to believe he was part of something noble.

The speaker rose with conviction. "Today, we teeter on the edge of ruin. Our freedoms bartered for illusions. Our leaders, pawns of polished lies. Resistance is no longer enough. We must reclaim. We must act."

Everton's fists clenched beneath the table, knuckles grazing the wood's grain. *Reclaim. Act.* The cadence was clean. Powerful. But something in it felt off, like a hymn sung out of key. *What are we really here for?*

"Each of you has been chosen," the figure continued, "for your conviction, your courage, your power. This mission will demand everything. Your faith. Your strength. Your anonymity. But the reward is absolute—a nation reborn in the image of its founders."

A nation reborn? Or is this a declaration of war?

His mind flickered to the Stratus Airways incident. A "fundraiser," the senator had called it. With a little bonus for the patriots.

And Everton's share?

Angela's medical debt gone in a single transaction. The mortgage finally caught up. *Miracles.*

God had shown him a way forward. All he had to do was control what the NSA saw.

The hooded figure went on. "Our institutions have failed us. The people's trust has been shattered. We will restore it—not with whispers, but with action. Not with hesitation, but with purpose."

Then came the phrase.

"Nos sumus veritas."

We are the truth.

The Latin struck like a stone in water, ripples of unease spreading across his chest.

Truth.

What does that word even mean anymore?

And whose *truth were they?*

The air in the chamber thickened.

Then the hood came down.

The face beneath remained masked, but something in his posture—his confidence, his control—pressed in tighter, filling the room like pressure before a storm.

"My beloved patriots," he said, "what we set in motion tonight will echo through eternity. The cost will be great. But the reward..."

He paused.

"A nation restored."

A silence followed—reverent, heavy, and somehow final. Around the table, white masks nodded in quiet agreement.

Everton's fists clenched. He wanted to believe.

To lose himself in the fervor, the rhythm, the vision they all pretended to see.

But one question kept cutting through the noise.

Was he about to save his country—or destroy it?

CHAPTER TWENTY-ONE

When the letter arrived, it looked more like a third-grade art project than official correspondence. The misshapen envelope stood out among the crisp bills and flyers, its edges jutting at odd angles like mismatched puzzle pieces. Thin strips of Scotch tape held the irregular shapes together, barely containing the stiff paper, which felt more like a repurposed folder.

Kalyssa scanned the front, half expecting the scent of cologne or a flourish of familiar handwriting. But there was none. Just blocky, uneven letters spelling out her address, the ink pooling in places, fading in others.

She hesitated before flipping it over. Neatly placed along each side were Roman numerals: V, XII, XV, XXII. Her pulse quickened.

The precision of the markings whispered of something deliberate. Something hidden. A secret she couldn't ignore.

She retrieved a butter knife and carefully sliced through the tape on the longest edge, marked XXII. The envelope opened like a trapdoor, spilling its contents onto the table. A mixture of typeset text and the corner of an image peeked out from what looked like a rectangular cutout. Magazine? No—a book. She scanned the cryptic text, then turned the image over.

Her heart stuttered.

It was familiar, terrifying, and intimate all at once. A couple, faces obscured, passion palpable. Once, it had symbolized everything she held dear.

But now, it stood for everything she had lost—or maybe everything she hadn't yet dared to hope for.

A wave of emotion rose in her chest, messy and disorienting.

She needed something concrete.

Turning back to the envelope, she jotted down the Roman numerals: V, XII, XV, XXII. Her mind spun, trying to decode the pattern.

Five. Twelve. Fifteen. Twenty-two.

Fifteen was ten more than five. Twenty-two was ten more than twelve. Interesting, but unclear. Wait—twelve was seven more than five. Twenty-two was seven more than fifteen.

Curious. Still unclear.

She shifted her thinking. A lock combination? No lock.

A measurement?

The envelope's edges stared back at her. Four sides. Four numbers. The smallest number on the shortest side. The largest on the longest. An electric current surged through her. She raced to her desk and grabbed a ruler.

Five centimeters. Twenty-two.

Her pulse quickened. The numbers weren't random. They were side lengths.

She wrote them again, whispering them aloud, "Five. Twelve. Fifteen. Twenty-two." All less than twenty-six, as in letters in the alphabet.

Letters as numbers?

She began singing, fingers tapping the table.

A, B, C, D, E.

E is five.

F, G, H, I, J, K, L.

L is twelve.

M, N, O.

O is fifteen.

P, Q, R, S, T, U, V…

V is twenty-two.

E-L-O-V

And then she saw it.

Love.

The simplicity of the word hit harder than she expected. A wave of emotion flooded her. Her heart fluttered, daring her to believe, just for a moment, that this could be real.

But doubt crept in, gnawing at the edges of her hope.

She stared at the letters, her mind warring with her heart. Would the sender reemerge? Or had he vanished, leaving only this cryptic message suspended between memory and maybe?

The image pulled at her, like it remembered something she wasn't ready to. A collision of joy and ache.

Francesco Hayez. *The Kiss.* 1859.

It had hung over their bed, not just a decoration, but a vow. A promise they swore they'd never let slip away.

Is this a promise of his return? Or is this a vision of something new?

Impulsively, she pressed the image to her lips. A fleeting kiss. The weight of everything she feared and everything she hoped for.

CHAPTER TWENTY-TWO

Dressed in an oversized charcoal suit with a wrinkled white shirt and a bold red tie, Caleb, in the guise of Harrison Wentworth, stepped into the reception area of Personalized Office Solutions LLC at 8:45 a.m. His gray toupee and brown beard gave him a distinguished yet contrasting look, exuding an aura of charisma and confidence.

"Brittney, it's nice to meet you in person," he said warmly, extending his hand to the startled receptionist. "Harrison Wentworth."

She hesitated, then returned the handshake with a nervous smile. "Good morning, Mr. Wentworth."

"I know I'm a few minutes early. Thanks for scheduling a private office for me. I really appreciate it," he said, his tone both courteous and assertive.

She glanced at the booking calendar in front of her, searching for what wasn't there. "What time was your reservation?" she asked, her confusion obvious.

"It's for nine o'clock. I have a conference call at that time, then a full morning of meetings," he said, applying subtle pressure and praise simultaneously. "I sent over the paperwork last week. I really appreciate you coming through for me."

She looked again at the booking calendar and then back at him. "I'm sorry, Mr. Wentworth, I don't—"

He cut her off. "Brittney, my conference call starts in seven minutes." He glanced at his watch, his tone shifting to controlled urgency. "And it's a really important call."

She looked at him, clearly bewildered and unsure what to do.

"Don't worry, Brittney. I understand… we're all human. I won't mention to your supervisor that you lost my paperwork." He reached into his pocket and pulled out two twenty-dollar bills, handing them to her to seal the deal. "Here's your tip in advance," he said. "Which way to my office?"

The veiled threat and bribe had the desired effect. She looked around nervously, took the money, and said, "Right this way."

Then, just as she was standing up, the phone rang. She looked back and forth between Caleb and the ringing phone. "One moment, please," she said, "It's my manager."

Large beads of sweat rolled down his back. He prayed the name of Harrison Wentworth wouldn't come into the conversation. The call was brief. When she hung up, she said her manager would be taking leave for the day to care for a sick child.

A wave of relief washed over Caleb.

Brittney escorted him to office number 617. It had an open, modern feel. Opposite the entry was a wall of windows overlooking the DC city skyline. Two large monitors sat on a curved birchwood table with a four-drawer filing cabinet on its left side. An ergonomically designed black office chair was positioned in front of the table.

"Perfect. I'll leave you a great review, Brittney."

She smiled, then quickly exited, closing the door behind her.

He exhaled slowly, his mind racing. His deception had gone smoothly, but the stakes were higher than ever. He had to stay sharp, keep his emotions in check, and ensure every move was calculated to perfection. As he settled into the office chair, he couldn't shake the feeling that the real challenge was yet to come.

The Forrest Sherwood Foundation had been started in 1983 by Caleb's grandfather, Andrew Forrest and his business partner James Sherwood. Although he'd been given power of attorney to manage the foundation's affairs in 2025, he'd done nothing to advance the foundation's mission of promoting freedom and national unity. Until now.

Caleb reached into his briefcase and pulled out the external hard drive containing the names and bank account information of 37,242 carefully selected future donors, courtesy of Tuesday's NSA hack. He smiled. The selection criteria had been simple—a checking account average daily balance of $1,000 or more, one or more debit card transactions in the amount of sixty to ninety dollars in the past month, and no two-factor authentication. The data included routing numbers, account numbers, vendor names for the debit card transactions, and transaction dates and amounts.

The spacious office, with its expansive view of the city, felt paradoxically confining, the walls closing in as he connected the external hard drive. His actions were calculated, but unease gnawed at him like a caged animal, desperate for release. He opened Memory Mole, navigated to the Freedom Tax menu screen, and uploaded the bank customer data. His mind raced and his heart pounded. *Will I regret what I'm about to do?*

He thought of the fifty-six men who'd signed the Declaration of Independence. *Traitors or patriots?*

Patriots, he reassured himself.

He had programmed the software to withdraw a random amount between sixty and ninety dollars from each account, small enough to fly under the radar.

With a click of a button, the fundraising began, exploiting vulnerabilities in the customer account systems of JDWhitman Pace, Bank of the People, and Hales Largo.

By 10:30 a.m., 36,717 transactions had processed, generating $2,753,778.93 in donations. Although 525 transactions had been rejected, Caleb was satisfied with the 98 percent contribution rate. "Your investment in the freedom of our nation is greatly appreciated," he muttered, a faint smirk tugging at the corners of his mouth.

Then he opened the personal file of a man he had searched for two days earlier—Jordan Clarke. He studied the records with an intensity that burned Jordan's identity into his mind. *From one patriot to another,* he thought, *I salute you.*

Caleb forced his mind to clear. He couldn't afford any slip-ups. Not when he was so close. Shortly after noon, he returned to the reception area. Brittney murmured something, just enough to catch his attention. He slowed, trying to hear.

"They will be here soon," she whispered into her headset, her tone hushed but urgent.

His body tensed. *Who had she called?*

He forced himself to stay calm, approaching the desk with the same smooth confidence he had earlier. "Brittney," he said, masking the surge of anxiety tightening in his chest, "where are the restrooms?"

She glanced up, startled, but her professional smile was unwavering. "Go out the door and take a left, Mr. Wentworth. The men's restroom is on the right, halfway down the hall."

"Thank you," he replied, returning her smile with equal politeness.

But as he turned away, his mind was already racing, processing what he had overheard. He exited the reception area and walked deliberately toward the elevator at the end of the hall, his calm exterior barely containing the storm brewing within.

He was keenly aware he had crossed a line, one that couldn't be undone, and the path ahead was fraught with uncertainty. Yet, amid the chaos and deception, he found a strange sense of purpose, a drive to see his mission through, no matter the cost.

As he exited the elevator, his senses heightened. The world around him slowed as two men in dark suits and sunglasses entered through the front door, their determined expressions locking onto him. His pulse quickened, adrenaline surging through his veins. He could feel the tightness in his chest, the instinctual urge to flee almost overwhelming.

"Sixth floor," one man said to the other.

Caleb's stomach clenched, and a cold sweat broke out across his forehead. His instincts screamed at him to get out. *Now!* He felt their eyes on him, predators marking their prey. Each step felt heavier, the urge to run nearly unbearable. But he forced his legs to walk leisurely as he headed for the back exit. The weight of their gazes burned into his back, each step feeling like he was one moment away from disaster. But he kept his eyes forward, refusing to look back, his mind locked on the singular goal of escape. He opened the door and walked out.

Eager to disappear, Caleb plunged into the throng of people on the street. The noise of the city roared in his ears, disorienting him, but he pushed on. Each step was a desperate countdown, the urgency in his movements betraying the calm façade he clung to. His heart pounded against his ribs, but he kept moving, determined to outrun the shadows he felt closing in from every side.

He imagined what would unfold in three weeks, when bank customers received their statements. A handful might notice. Most wouldn't. In the investigations that followed, the vendors would deny ever receiving the funds. The banks and vendors would argue for a few days, then quietly move on.

He knew better than to think he was safe now. He had set something in motion, and there was no turning back. His heart might have slowed, but the drumbeat of impending consequences thrummed louder, each beat a reminder that the storm was far from over.

Freedom, he thought bitterly, had once been his guiding star. Now, it was just a word for what he had to lose.

CHAPTER TWENTY-THREE

THURSDAY, JUNE 22, 2028

WASHINGTON, DC

For two days, Caleb had lived inside Jordan Clarke's profile—every detail committed to memory, every fact reshaped into a foundation. He wasn't studying a man anymore. He was becoming him.

The reimagined Jordan Clarke took the position of director at the Forrest Sherwood Foundation, freshly equipped with a company email, laptop, and smartphone, a $10,000 bonus, and the promise of an office.

He transferred power of attorney to Jordan Clarke, using the delegation clause his grandfather, Andrew Forrest, had signed years ago. The US military ID and certified birth certificate—both courtesy of the NSA—would carry him through the rest.

At Eagle Bank, the teller smiled and congratulated him on the Forrest Sherwood Foundation's recent fundraising success, never suspecting a thing. She didn't hesitate, opening a personal account for Jordan Clarke and wiring $10,000 from the foundation's business account straight into it. He turned on the charm—easy, practiced. A smile here, a thank-you there. It worked every time.

Before leaving, he asked the manager for a balance letter to show prospective landlords. The guy skipped the protocols—Caleb didn't ask why.

He walked out as Jordan Clarke, $500 in his pocket and a clean identity no one would question.

A steakhouse called to him as he passed, the scent of garlic butter and grilled meat almost enough to make him forget. But no—he ducked into a corner store instead and grabbed a sandwich. Forgettable food for a forgettable face.

As he ate, his mind buzzed with the possibilities this new identity offered. Yet, with every bite, the weight of his deception grew heavier, a constant reminder of his forsaken true identity.

He kept his head down, eyes scanning strangers reflexively. One wrong word, one forgotten detail … and everything would collapse.

The tension clung to him, sharp as wire beneath the skin—calculated risk on one side, ruin on the other.

The real Jordan Clarke was still a Marine. Missing in Action. Vanished without a trace. And now Caleb was wearing his name like borrowed skin. The irony stung—stepping into the life of a man who'd disappeared, while trying so desperately to disappear himself.

But this wasn't some con. It was deeper. Maybe a search for connection. Maybe for redemption.

Whatever it was, it wasn't safe.

He couldn't afford a single misstep. Every glance, every word had to match the story. Because one wrong move, and the whole thing would fall apart.

And if it did, so would Caleb.

Clarke's family... his faith... Caleb would have to know it all, feel it like his own. This wasn't about documents or background checks. It was about muscle memory, about instinct. He couldn't just wear Clarke's name. He had to breathe it, believe it.

Gone in 2018. Ten years. That was Caleb's advantage. Memories faded. Faces blurred. If someone looked too closely, time would have to do the lying for him.

He stepped outside, fatigue trailing him like a shadow.

The name was Jordan Clarke now.

The life? Almost his.

All that remained was the performance.

And he intended to play the role to perfection.

CHAPTER TWENTY-FOUR

The building off St. Matthews Court NW stood like a relic of Washington's hidden past, its red-brick façade guarding secrets of its own. Once stables for St. Matthews Cathedral, it had witnessed the city's quiet evolution. But he didn't care about history. Just sixteen minutes from the White House, the place offered what he needed—office above, living quarters below. A sanctuary for someone who had to stay invisible.

It was a stage. And he was ready to step into the spotlight.

The real estate agent beamed as Jordan Clarke signed the two-year lease on behalf of the Forrest Sherwood Foundation. Prepaying twenty-four months of rent didn't just lock in the space, it guaranteed her commission up front. When he asked if she could handle the furniture deliveries, mentioning his focus on foundation work, she agreed without hesitation. He'd paid in full. A dream tenant… by all appearances.

As soon as the agent left, Caleb let the silence settle. Alone now, he took in his new fortress. The break room downstairs, close to the long, narrow kitchen, would double as a spartan bedroom. Efficient. Unremarkable.

But upstairs… that's where it would all come alive.

Monitors. Maps. Data lines feeding a nerve center of control. Every move calculated. Every decision rippling far beyond these walls.

He ran his fingers across the exposed brick. Rough. Solid. Grounding. The white-painted walls gave off a sterile calm, but to him, they whispered something else. Resilience.

This place had adapted, endured.

So would he.

A fortress in plain sight. In a city that watched everything, Caleb had found a way to disappear.

A sound—soft, sudden—snapped his focus. A rustle outside. Instinct took over.

He dropped to the floor.

Muscles tense. Pulse pounding. He bear-crawled to the door, eyes fixed on the frosted window. Nothing moved. Still, he reached up and checked the lock—twice.

Midday. But complacency was a luxury he couldn't afford.

He rose slowly, every motion deliberate. He needed blackout curtains on every window. He made a mental note. The office needed to feel like a morgue at midnight.

Security cameras—every entrance, every escape. No angles left blind.

No surprises. No breaches.

The brick around him seemed to breathe with him now. Steady. Silent. Loyal.

Upstairs, his steps echoed on the wooden stairs. He paused at the threshold. The strategy room. Not yet alive, but soon.

He pictured the glow of monitors. The chaos organized into maps and timelines. Every thread feeding a plan only he could see.

He clenched his fists. Let the silence hold it.

Then, for the first time in days, a smile touched his lips.

Let them come.

He'd be ready.

CHAPTER TWENTY-FIVE

FRIDAY, JUNE 23, 2028

WASHINGTON, DC

Kalyssa had spent the past week buried in campaign work—an endless loop of strategy calls, media briefs, and late-night edits that left her crashing into bed, too tired to think. But by Friday night, the fatigue ran deeper than physical. It was emotional. Restless. Caleb hadn't called. Hadn't texted. Nothing.

She stared at her phone. Five texts. No reply.

Pathetic. That's how she felt. Like her seventeen-year-old self again, waiting two weeks before prom, wondering if her crush would finally notice her.

She couldn't fight it anymore. Curiosity gnawed at her, sharp and insistent.

She glanced at her phone, rereading the last message.

AIMEE: It's not worth the risk. You have too much to lose.

Yet, undaunted, she opened KnowMeKnowYou.

Part of her—foolish, hopeful—expected an apology. Something raw. Something real.

But the inbox was empty. No message. No explanation.

Then the screen blinked.

Jordan Clarke wants to chat.

Annoyed, she closed the window without a second thought. But the name lingered—*Jordan Clarke*. It tugged at her, unsettling.

She clicked on his profile.

Created yesterday.

No photo. No bio.

Probably some bald, obsessive, sex-starved old man with a fake name and a Wi-Fi connection.

"Not today, Jordan," she muttered.

Still, the hollowness clung to her.

The chat box popped up again.

Please, Kaly.

Her heart stopped.

Only one person had ever called her that.

A shiver traced her spine as she clicked *Accept*.

The next message stole her breath.

JORDAN CLARKE: You want someone brave enough to speak the truth and smart enough to know when to be silent. Someone passionate enough to ignite your desire, yet tender enough to brush away tears. Someone courageous enough to fight bitter battles, yet humble enough to quickly forgive. Someone perceptive enough to see your flaws and imperfections, but kind enough to build you up with heartfelt praise. Someone who sees you completely and loves you all the more for it. I want to be that someone.

She recognized the words. They were hers.

Words she'd whispered during their call two weeks ago—raw, vulnerable, private. Words pulled from the deepest part of her heart.

A chill crawled up her spine.

Had their phone call been recorded?

Her fingers trembled as she typed:

ME: Am I chatting with an AI bot?

JORDAN CLARKE: No.

ME: Then tell me where Justin Thyme Benton is.

She expected the conversation to end there.

That this stranger—*or whatever it was*—would vanish into the ether.

But then the reply came:

JORDAN CLARKE: I know what it's like to lose someone you love.

The words hit like a physical blow.

Too direct. Too intimate.

She wasn't convinced. Not yet.

Her fingers hovered, then typed a test—something *only she* would know the answer to.

ME: What was I wearing last Friday night?

No reply.

The seconds dragged.

One beat.

Two.

Too long.

Then…

JORDAN CLARKE: My heart longed to be with you, but if they knew I was with you, they would pull us apart. I watched you for a moment, but was afraid they would find me, so I escaped into the anonymity of the crowd.

An electric wave of emotions coursed through her.

Was it really Caleb? Had he been there, watching? She couldn't believe what she was reading.

The text continued, the truth of his words hitting her like a tidal wave.

JORDAN CLARKE: Your curled blonde hair fell over your bare shoulders, teasing the straps of the black dress that held you like a secret. Your blue eyes searched for me. All I wanted was to rush into your arms, to feel the warmth of your body against mine. But instead, I stood watching those charming eyes turn to eyes of rage, knowing I was to blame. But the image of you waiting, hopeful and vulnerable, seared itself into me. In that moment, I felt a love so deep, so raw, it both healed and shattered me.

Kalyssa stared at the screen, stunned. Her fingers hovered over the keyboard, frozen.

He'd been there.

And the words—raw, unfiltered—cut straight through her. The truth of them wrapped around her, pulling tight. She felt seen. Exposed. Vulnerable.

The FBI's warning echoed in her mind. Caleb was a wanted man—dangerous, a national security threat. But her heart didn't care.

She placed her fingers on the keys, each one trembling.

Stay calm. Breathe.

Every word she typed now had to be deliberate. Controlled.

Because no matter how much she longed to be with him, she refused to craft her own gallows.

ME: I love jogging on the national mall from the Washington Monument to the Lincoln Memorial. The Lincoln Memorial Reflecting Pool is breathtaking. I never tire of it. You should try it sometime.

She hoped he'd catch the message tucked between the lines.

Then came the reply—simple, but charged with meaning.

And it sent a shiver down her spine.

JORDAN CLARKE: Have you ever seen Be Free the Clown? He gives out free balloons at the top of the Reflecting Pool near the Lincoln Memorial.

She jotted down the clown's bizarre name and *reflecting pool*, her hand trembling. His cryptic reply curled in her gut—part anticipation, part dread.

ME: I haven't seen him before. Maybe he'll be there during my morning run tomorrow. If so, I'll give him a smile and a wave.

The reply came fast, urgent, almost breathless.

JORDAN CLARKE: Don't be afraid to ask for a balloon. They are typically gone by ten.

She scribbled down *10:00 a.m.*, her pulse quickening. The clues were piling up, her mind spinning with possibilities. As much as she wanted to keep him talking, they'd said enough for now.

ME: Goodnight, Jordan.

Her emotions churned—fear, longing, uncertainty—all tangled in a breathless knot.

JORDAN CLARKE: Sweet dreams, Kaly.

She closed the laptop and leaned back, pulse still hammering, the conversation looping in her mind.

What am I getting myself into?

The thrill. The risk. The ache of not knowing. It left her dizzy.

But one thing pulsed louder than the rest. Tomorrow's run at the Reflecting Pool could change everything.

CHAPTER TWENTY-SIX

The Lincoln Memorial loomed ahead—massive, marble, majestic. To most, it was a shrine to unity, carved in permanence. But to Caleb, it was something else entirely. A backdrop for a meeting that could shift everything.

At 8:45 a.m., he crossed Constitution Avenue in full costume—Be Free the Clown. Red, white, and blue balloons bobbed above him, drawing eyes that never lingered. His painted face—blue star-shaped eyes, a cherry-red nose, a wide, frozen grin—concealed the storm churning underneath.

He adjusted his stars-and-stripes top hat and smoothed his candy-cane-striped overalls, each motion mechanical. To the tourists snapping photos, he was part of the celebration. But to him, this wasn't a street performance. It was misdirection. A disguise stitched together with desperation, defiance, and just enough hope to keep him moving.

Passing the still water of Constitution Gardens Pond, he fought the ache behind his painted smile. Freedom. Unity. Equality. Words carved in marble and stitched onto flags. But how many times had those same words been betrayed?

The Founding Fathers hadn't been saints. But they'd imagined something wild, something fragile. A country where liberty wasn't owned. Where it lived in every heart brave enough to claim it.

The irony wasn't lost on him.

At the Vietnam Women's Memorial, he paused. Eleven thousand women. Quiet heroes. Some names still unknown. He lowered his head.

Thank you.

At the Three Servicemen statue, he stopped again. The bronze soldiers stared through time—white, black, brown. Different skin. Same blood.

"We all bleed red," he murmured.

The words stuck in his throat.

Because not everyone believed it.

A low chant tugged at his ears, barely audible at first, like static bleeding through silence.

Caleb slowed, scanning the crowd. Tourists laughed. Cameras clicked. But something was wrong.

The chant sharpened, rising above the hum of morning.

"You will not replace us!"

The words hit like a punch to the gut. Caleb's grip clenched around the balloon strings.

They were coming from the far side—young men in black boots and shaved heads, their cadence in perfect, chilling rhythm.

"Fourteen. Eighty-Eight. Fourteen. Eighty-Eight."

He'd seen the code before—on forums, in threats, in places decent people avoided.

White supremacists. Neo-Nazis. A salute to Hitler, draped in numbers.

Gasps rippled through the crowd. Parents yanked their kids close. Fear spread, invisible but suffocating.

At the front, a banner flapped in the breeze—ugly words in crude red paint, twisted and proud.

His heart pounded beneath the costume.

This wasn't performance anymore.

This was the enemy.

Caleb's painted smile cracked.

Rage clawed its way up his throat, colliding with sorrow, with helplessness. For a heartbeat, he wanted to scream. To tear the banner from their hands. To do something.

But he said nothing.

He sank onto the marble steps, regretting everything he couldn't do.

Across the water, the Lincoln Memorial shimmered, its reflection rippling like a fragile promise. He stared at the statue, the weight of history pressing down.

Now we are engaged in a great civil war...

The words echoed, not from memory, but from somewhere deeper.

... testing whether that nation, or any nation so conceived and so dedicated, can long endure.

He wasn't sure of the answer anymore.

His hands trembled as he scrolled his burner phone. He needed something—anything—to fight the noise.

Lee Greenwood's anthem carried on the morning air. "And I'm proud to be an American…"

The melody washed over the Mall, cutting through the hate like sunlight through fog.

But the knot in his chest held fast.

He glanced back. The marchers were fading, their chants growing faint, but they had stained the day.

Caleb looked at the balloons in his hand—red, white, and blue—dancing gently in the breeze.

Just decorations? Not today.

Today, they were defiance.

CHAPTER TWENTY-SEVEN

Kalyssa reached the Mall at 9:40, pink shorts and crop top clinging to skin kissed by sweat. Her braid swung behind her, steady, even—unlike her thoughts.

She shouldn't be here. Not after everything she'd read. Not after what the FBI had said.

Traitor. National security threat. Most wanted.

But here she was, jogging toward the Reflecting Pool like it was just another Saturday.

It wasn't.

She pushed forward, but as the World War II Memorial came into view, her feet slowed.

Doubt caught up, and it hit harder than the run.

Her mind spiraled around Caleb. Or Jordan Clarke. Or whoever he was now.

Their connection had felt rare, almost sacred. But now? Trust warred with suspicion.

Was he still the man she'd loved being with a decade ago? Or was he just the trap she couldn't see coming?

The questions circled, stubborn as her pulse, refusing to quiet.

As she neared the Reflecting Pool, Kalyssa slowed.

Be Free crouched near a young Black girl, handing her a red balloon. The girl's face lit up with pure delight, radiant and unguarded. Her parents smiled, exchanged a few words with the clown, and moved on.

The moment lingered. It wasn't loud or theatrical. Just quiet kindness.

Then the mood shifted—subtle, but undeniable.

A woman with a stroller approached, her toddler mid-meltdown. She looked exhausted, her expression taut with frustration. Behind her, the father followed without urgency, eyes fixed on his phone, thumbs tapping.

Be Free didn't hesitate. He bent low, offered a balloon. "This is for you," he said gently.

The child stopped crying, blinking at him. Small hands reached. Clutched.

The woman's scowl softened. Her shoulders eased. "Thank you," she murmured.

The father never looked up.

Kalyssa couldn't help but smile. Something about Be Free radiated calm—not a mask, but a quiet kind of truth she didn't fully understand.

When their eyes met, the connection sparked. Fleeting, but real.

"Would you like a balloon?" he asked lightly, though his eyes carried something heavier.

"I've never wanted one more," she said, surprised at the playful edge in her tone.

He grinned, tipping his head toward the Reflecting Pool. "Let's walk instead of run. Me jogging in this getup might strike terror in the minds of the kiddies."

Kalyssa laughed in a short, unguarded burst. She hadn't realized how tightly wound she'd been. The humor bridged the space between them, loosening the knot in her chest.

They walked side by side, the silence between them thick with questions she wasn't ready to ask. Her mind looped through trust and doubt, truth and deception. She wanted to believe in the man beside her, but the mist curling around him blurred everything she thought she knew. She glanced sideways. The painted grin said one thing. His eyes said another. Whatever this act was, it was only half the story.

Then something in him shifted—lightness peeling off like a mask.

"You've probably heard," he said quietly, "our friend Caleb is on the run. Nationwide manhunt."

Her pulse jumped. He said the name like it belonged to someone else.

Caleb. Jordan. Be Free.

One man. Three faces.

But she couldn't let them be the same.

Plausible deniability was the only thing standing between her and ruin.

She nodded, keeping her tone even, her expression calm, despite the knot twisting tighter in her stomach.

"I saw it on CNN last week," she said. "I haven't heard from Caleb, but…" She hesitated, letting the pause do some of the talking. "I did meet someone new."

Be Free tilted his head, eyebrow lifted in mock surprise. "You did?"

"Yes." Her tone didn't waver. "His name is Jordan Clarke."

She watched him closely. The name felt like a match struck in the dark, meant to draw something out.

A flicker of amusement touched his painted face. "Jordan mentioned you. Said you've enchanted him. The poor guy's a blubbering fool."

She laughed, a reflex. But the sound felt strange in her mouth, a little too brittle.

It was a dance—banter laced with subtext. But she wasn't sure who was leading.

"Do you think Caleb would be jealous?" she asked, keeping it light even as her pulse thudded in her chest.

"Most certainly," Be Free said, not missing a beat. "You've now enchanted two hearts besides mine."

His sincerity caught her off guard, and heat rushed to her cheeks. She looked away, unsettled by how easily he slipped past the walls she'd spent years building.

They walked in silence, shoulders close, the quiet no longer awkward but charged. The air between them felt different now—denser, weighted with something that wasn't going away.

His hand brushed against hers.

She flinched, a spark racing through her. His fingers were smooth, but the scab on his palm dragged against her skin—rough, unexpected. She almost recoiled. Rough hands had always bothered her.

But this time, she didn't pull away.

Instead, she let her hand rest in his, surprised by the way it steadied her. The contact wasn't just physical—it grounded her, anchoring something inside she hadn't realized was adrift.

"So, what do you know of this Jordan?" she asked, keeping her tone light, though her fingers tightened slightly around his.

"He doesn't want to be elusive," Be Free said, quieter now. "Not with you."

The words landed with unexpected weight. She squeezed his hand—once, gently. Not just in response, but in recognition.

"Does he ever come here with you?" Her lips lifted in a half-smile, teasing.

"All the time," he said. "He loves the view."

She gave him a sideways glance. "Caleb still owes me dinner, Be Free. Maybe your friend Jordan can step in for him."

Be Free chuckled, the sound warm and unforced. "Jordan would like that."

They walked on, the breeze whispering across the water. The Reflecting Pool mirrored the sky, calm and wide, like it had nothing to prove.

For the first time in too long, something stirred in her chest. Not certainty. Not peace. But maybe the shape of hope.

She looked over at him.

He was already looking at her.

"It's hard to take you seriously, Jordan, when you look like that," she said, the words laced with a smile, but also a warning. A gentle nudge to remind him, *This isn't a game.*

Because it wasn't.

He was a fugitive.

And if anyone found out she was with him…

Her chest tightened. One leak—just one—and her entire life could implode.

Be Free's smile flickered, the painted curve holding, but his eyes faltered. A crack in the armor.

"You'll get used to it," he said, but it didn't ring as light as before.

She caught the shift in his gaze. Not fear. Not regret. Something heavier.

Something that felt… familiar.

And for the first time, she realized they were carrying different versions of the same weight.

"So, tell me, Be Free… who is this Jordan Clarke?" She folded her arms, leveling her gaze. "And don't dodge. I want the truth."

He nodded. "Jordan Clarke isn't just a name," he said. "He's as real as you and me."

Then, with a crooked grin: "Well, at least as real as you."

A laugh escaped before she could stop it.

"Go on," she said, the smile lingering, despite everything.

His grin faded completely.

"You want the truth?" he asked.

Kalyssa gave a slow nod.

"All right," he said, quieter now. "But the truth isn't always simple."

A flicker of hesitation.

"Jordan Clarke was born on March 17, 2000, in Provo, Utah. His parents were students at Brigham Young University."

Kalyssa blinked. "Isn't that the one run by the Seventh-day Adventists?"

He let out a low chuckle. "No. Latter-Day Saints."

"The Mormons," she said flatly. "What did they study? Blind faith?"

"Electrical engineering," Be Free said without hesitation. "Both of them. His dad went on to Stanford. Later, Apple. But yeah… faith was still central."

She felt the tension rise, her own logic clawing for footing. "How do brilliant people believe in something so unscientific?"

"They weren't blind," he said softly. "They were Seekers. The kind who think faith and reason don't have to fight. That they belong at the same table."

A pause settled between them, not awkward, but thoughtful.

"BYU teaches that. *Enter to learn. Go forth to serve.* It's not just a slogan."

Kalyssa didn't answer. She wasn't ready to admit it, but the line stuck.

Sixteen days ago, Caleb had revealed his quest—a Seeker in search of transformed life.

"I have a friend who's a Seeker," she murmured, more to herself than to him. Then louder, "And Jordan? Does he believe?"

"He does," Be Free said. "For him, faith isn't about answers. It's about the courage to ask the right questions."

The words landed gently, but deeply. Something shifted.

She didn't want to admit it, but his sincerity cracked something open. Not wide. Just enough.

The noise in her head—the headlines, the warnings, the fear—faded for a breath.

Stillness filled the space instead. Not silence. *Stillness.*

Warm. Quiet. Full.

It pressed gently into her chest like sunlight after rain.

She let it stay.

They continued in silence, the Reflecting Pool stretching beside them, its surface rippling in the breeze.

When Be Free spoke again, his tone had changed—quieter, weighted.

"Jordan's life wasn't without tragedy," he said. "Christmas Eve, 2018. He lost control of his truck. Hit an oncoming car." A pause. "The couple died instantly. Their son survived."

The silence afterward wasn't empty. It pulsed with something unspoken.

Kalyssa stopped walking. She looked at him. Not the bright makeup or the oversized smile, but the eyes behind them. They were tired. Human. Hurt.

He faltered on the next words. "It broke him."

The realization struck her hard.

That night didn't just scar Jordan. It wounded Caleb.

"Jordan enlisted in the Marines a week later," Be Free said, barely above a whisper. "Like punishing himself might somehow atone for what he'd done."

Kalyssa said nothing, her throat tight.

"He lost both parents in a house fire while he was overseas. His grandmother to cancer not long after. Then in June 2019, during a Taliban attack in Uruzgan Province, he disappeared. No one's seen him since."

The pain layered into those words… it was almost too much to take in.

"Until now," she said quietly, her mind spinning. "He lives on in someone else."

Be Free met her eyes. There was something unspoken in his expression—depths she couldn't reach.

"Perhaps," he said. "Or perhaps he's always been more than one man's story."

The cryptic reply sent a shiver through her, its resonance undeniable. Jordan and Caleb, two sides of the same coin, bound together by something greater than themselves.

As they reached the edge of the Reflecting Pool, she broke the silence.

"Now about that dinner," she said, the ease in her words carefully masking the weight in her chest.

Be Free's grin returned. "How about tonight? After I scrub off the clown?"

She paused, reality tugging her back.

"I've got an afternoon flight," she said gently. "And days packed with campaign events. But I'll call you Wednesday night."

His smile held for a beat, then settled into something quieter. "Rain check it is."

They said their goodbyes. As he walked away, he glanced back once, the painted grin still in place, but his eyes gave him away.

She raised a hand in parting, a bittersweet ache rising beneath her ribs.

Something had shifted inside her. Not just curiosity or longing, but something deeper.

Faith, hope.

Or maybe, just maybe, the beginning of a story greater than her own.

CHAPTER TWENTY-EIGHT

Caleb stood in the second-floor office of the Forrest Sherwood Foundation, now his war room. The historic charm was gone, swallowed by rows of monitors casting a cold, blue glow across stark whitewashed walls. Heavy blackout curtains turned the room into a bunker, the air thick with the hum of machinery and the acrid tang of overheated circuits.

He hunched over the keyboard, bathed in the eerie light of the screens. His fingers moved with precision, slicing through layers of encryption, dismantling digital walls. Finally, the last line of code gave way.

"I'm in."

The words fell flat. A quiet victory, soured by dread.

Hamilton Everton's phone was now an open vault—its secrets exposed.

Caleb leaned back, tension still coiled in his shoulders. This wasn't triumph. It was betrayal. Of a man he once respected. Of the code of ethics he used to believe in.

Of himself.

The zero-day exploit had been his entry point—a flaw so buried not even the manufacturer's elite security team had seen it. Now, a remote access Trojan was tunneling through Everton's phone, lifting everything without leaving a trace.

He scanned the logs—mundane chatter, work schedules, digital clutter. Then a text exchange stopped him cold. Nonsensical. At first.

NO CALLER ID: Eyes Open.

Everton: Eyes. Eves. Even. Oven. Open

NO CALLER ID: :-)

He froze. Wait—was this a word ladder?

Everton had transformed **Eyes** into **Open**, changing one letter at a time.

Then another message appeared. A number.

EVERTON: 3 2 0 7 3

His pulse quickened. *This is the trigger*—simple, silent, devastating. Two days later, Stratus Airways unraveled into chaos.

Everton must have sent the vulnerability report—the cyberattack script.

But who is **NO CALLER ID?**

Pushing away from the desk, Caleb paced the room, guilt clawing at him like a living thing. Everton had preyed on his trust, twisting it into a weapon. Now Caleb was a fugitive, hunted by the very authorities he once served.

The monitors flickered, casting jagged shadows across his face as he gripped the desk's edge. He was suffocating under the weight of his choices. Of his complicity.

He forced his eyes open. The monitors demanded his attention.

This wasn't about survival anymore. The stakes were higher now. Far higher.

The first attack had only been the prelude. More were coming. He could feel it.

A new message appeared.

NO CALLER ID: Born Free.

Two innocent words—on the surface. But he knew better. A sugar-coated poison.

Then came Everton's response. A Word Ladder sequence. Changing one letter at a time, transforming one word into the other.

EVERTON: Born. Boon. Boot. Boat. Beat. Beet. Feet. Fret. Free.

Then came the confirmation.

NO CALLER ID: :-)

And a number.

EVERTON: 5 4 6 2 1

Another trigger.

The cyberattack script would follow. He was sure of it.

His pulse thundered in his ears. An attack was coming. But when? Where? The numbers stared back at him—silent, mocking. A taunting riddle he couldn't solve.

His fingers hovered over the keyboard, frozen between panic and purpose. He wanted to scream, to sound the alarm.

But no one would believe him.

He clenched his fists. Fine. Then he'd let his actions speak.

They could hunt him. Call him a traitor. Try to take his freedom.

But he wasn't done.

He would break the code—and the man behind it.

CHAPTER TWENTY-NINE

Kalyssa stepped into Independence Hall, the scent of aged wood and revolution wrapping around her like a presence. The air felt charged, thick with echoes of risk and resolve.

Fifty-six men had gathered here, not just to debate freedom, but to sign their own death warrants.

They hadn't chosen comfort. They had chosen purpose.

Knowing it could cost them everything.

Her gaze caught on the chair at the head of the room—simple, regal, brimming with silent authority.

Would I have had their courage?

The question hit harder than she expected.

A faint buzz on her wrist broke the stillness.

AIMEE: Reminder—call Jordan. Timing optimal.

She slipped outside. Cool air. The hum of distant traffic.

Above her, a crescent moon hung like hope.

She lifted her phone, dialing Caleb's new number as she slipped in an AirPod.

One ring. Two.

Then…

"Kaly?"

Steady. Familiar. Like an anchor in rough seas.

"Jordan," she said, grounding herself in the name. "It's good to hear your voice. I need to get my steps in," she added with a teasing lilt. "So don't get too excited if you hear heavy breathing."

"No promises," he quipped, his laughter warm, easy.

She smiled, then caught herself. Even now, he could still disarm her.

"You won't believe where I just came from," she said.

"Independence Hall," he replied.

She stopped cold.

Static crackled faintly in her AirPod.

How does he know?

A chill traced her spine. She forced a laugh, willing the unease away. "Lucky guess?"

Silence. Just a second too long.

Then he spoke again—light, but unreadable. "And where am I?"

She exhaled, pushing past the static of doubt. "Sherwood Forest?" she offered, resuming her walk.

"Someone's got to fight for justice now that Robin Hood's retired," he said.

Her laughter came easily this time. And yet… the unease lingered. Subtle, but insistent.

She pivoted, grounding herself in the awe she'd felt earlier. "Independence Hall was incredible," she said. "Standing in that room where everything changed… it's humbling."

"It was a beautiful beginning, Kaly," he said. "But now our nation is in trouble."

Her steps slowed. "Because the Republicans are still in the White House?" she teased.

"If only it were that simple." The line landed heavy.

Something in her reacted, like a stone tossed into still water.

"What's got you worried?"

"Everton," he said, carefully measured. "I'm monitoring his texts."

Her stomach knotted.

"There was an exchange on June 2nd. No Caller ID. I think it was a coded word ladder—Eyes Open—followed by a five-digit number, 3 2 0 7 3."

"And?"

"Two days later," he said, "planes circled blindly in the sky."

A chill traced her spine. "The Stratus Airways cyberattack?"

"Exactly."

She swallowed. "I thought the Chinese were behind it."

"Maybe," he said. "But Everton's involved."

Then she saw it—movement ahead. A figure, too still. Waiting.

"Crap!" she muttered, spinning around.

"What?" he exclaimed.

She picked up speed. Every step in those useless flats screamed bad decision.

"I might be in trouble."

His response was immediate. "Where are you staying?"

"Kimpton Hotel Monaco."

"Keep heading straight," Caleb instructed. Unshaken. Commanding. "I've got you."

He's tracking me.

Just like Justin had. Back then, it had felt oddly romantic. But now? *What if he still is?* She shuddered and forced the image back down.

She stole a glance over her shoulder. The figure, half-swallowed by shadow, was moving with unsettling precision. Too fast. Too deliberate. She broke into a jog.

When she hit Walnut Street, she veered right, contrary to Caleb's instructions.

"Stay on Walnut. Left on South Sixth," he commanded.

A rush of unease prickled along her spine. But she kept moving.

The footsteps behind her did too.

She reached South Sixth and darted across against the light.

A horn blared. A blur of headlights. A near miss.

Her pulse thundered as she sprinted the final stretch.

"Turn right onto Chestnut," he said urgently. "The hotel is ahead."

She didn't hesitate. The moment she burst into the lobby, heat and safety wrapped around her like a shield. But she couldn't shake the chill.

"I made it," she gasped.

"Thank God," he whispered, relief slipping through.

But beneath it, something felt… off.

She pressed her back against the cool plaster wall, forcing air into her lungs.

He knew. Every turn. Every step. Every move she made.

She scanned the street beyond the glass doors. Silent. Empty.

And yet, the feeling remained. Crawling beneath her skin.

She had outrun one shadow.

But what if she was running into the arms of another?

CHAPTER THIRTY

Three days later, Kalyssa stood just offstage, scanning the crowd gathering in Centennial Olympic Park. The air buzzed with energy. Grayhorse was surging in the polls, and it showed. The sun dipped low, casting an orange glow across downtown Atlanta.

It felt like a celebration.

It was supposed to be.

She checked the time. Logistics had been a nightmare, but the schedule was holding. Fireworks in less than an hour. Speeches were wrapping on cue.

She tapped her earpiece. "Aimee, confirm firework queue for 8:37."

A soft chime. **Confirmed. Pyro team in position. Weather conditions optimal.**

Kalyssa allowed herself the briefest smile. *Reliable, as always.*

Grayhorse began his final remarks as twilight faded into full dusk. She glanced at her watch: 8:00 p.m.

Then the park went dark.

Screens. Sound system. Stadium lights.

Gone.

Only scattered phone screens and the pale crescent moon offered light. The crowd turned uneasy. Confused shouts rippled across the park.

Then, with a low hum, emergency lighting kicked in. Dim but steady. Kalyssa exhaled. Not a full failure. But this didn't feel like a glitch.

Secret Service agents moved with sudden urgency—quick radio bursts, sharp formation. Not just here. This was bigger.

On stage, Grayhorse froze mid-sentence. His silhouette loomed against the red emergency glow. Governor Malcolm Davis leaned toward him—tense, tight-jawed. Agents closed in.

Kalyssa's gut clenched. Something was wrong. Deeply wrong.

A Secret Service agent appeared at her side. "Ma'am, we need to move. Now."

"What is it?" she asked, already falling in step as he led her behind the stage. Grayhorse and Davis were there, flanked by agents and staffers.

"We just got confirmation from NSA. This isn't a power failure—it's a cyberattack on Peachtree Power."

Behind them, Davis stood over a glowing tablet, red warning icons pulsing across a map of the state. Blackout zones. Grid collapse.

"Governor," the lead agent said, addressing him directly, "we've confirmed the breach. Peachtree Power, multiple substations. This is coordinated. Possibly international. Emergency services are running on backup, but it's not going to last."

Davis grimaced. "Hospitals. Airports. Ports. If backup fails—"

"No ventilators, no surgeries," Kalyssa said, finishing his thought without meaning to.

"And no traffic lights," Davis added. "Roads'll turn to chaos in under an hour."

Kalyssa caught murmurs from the field—worried voices, people trying to understand what had just happened.

Grayhorse stepped forward. "What's the plan?"

"We need to relocate you and the governor," the agent said. "Security protocol is active. Right now, it's about containment. You'll be briefed once we're clear."

Grayhorse nodded, but Kalyssa saw it in his eyes—frustration. He wasn't the kind of man who vanished during a crisis. Especially not when it could be leveraged.

She'd spent weeks building this rally. Every speaker, every light cue, every second of it had been orchestrated.

Now? Irrelevant.

They were under attack, and whoever had launched it hadn't needed a bomb or bullet. Just a line of code.

Grayhorse turned. "Do we know who's behind it?"

The agent shook his head. "Not yet. The NSA's working it. Sophisticated breach. Foreign, likely state-sponsored. But we're still chasing specifics."

Grayhorse's expression hardened. "Time is something we don't have."

The emergency lights flickered. Kalyssa glanced toward the sky. The crescent moon barely cut the dark. Out in the park, the crowd's unease was growing louder.

She stared into the night.

Georgia was under siege.

And it felt like the world was tilting.

CHAPTER THIRTY-ONE

The air was thick, stale, and suffocating.

Kalyssa sat motionless on the edge of the hotel bed, unable to escape the heat. Eighteen hours without power. No air conditioning. No refrigeration. No relief. The once-sterile luxury of the suite had become a sweltering, airless tomb.

She inhaled. It felt like breathing through gauze.

The room reeked of sweat and stale air, the upholstery soaked with heat like a sponge.

She could taste the humidity clinging to the back of her throat.

Her fingers found the locket. Solid. Familiar. Something real.

Her eyes flicked to the tray of food she'd ordered hours ago—a cruel joke of a meal. A bag of chips, a few wilted carrot sticks, and an apple. The chips were gone in the first hour. The apple didn't last much longer. Now, as hunger gnawed at her stomach, she reached for the final carrot, knowing it wouldn't make a difference.

She swallowed back frustration. Only eighteen hours, and the city was starving.

Her phone buzzed against the sheets. Battery: 10 percent. The power bank? Dead.

She scrolled through the news, searching for something, anything, that would tell her how much worse this was going to get.

BREAKING NEWS: FBI & NSA Confirm Chinese Involvement In Peachtree Power Cyberattack. Diplomats Expelled From San Francisco & Houston.

The word landed hard.

China.

She had expected speculation, but not confirmation. The White House had just thrown down the gauntlet. Beijing wouldn't take this lightly.

She swiped to the next alert.

Hospitals Failing as Generators Run Dry. Ventilator Patients At Risk.

Her pulse spiked. She tapped the video link.

The feed flickered to life, showing Grady Memorial Hospital in total collapse. Nurses in soaked scrubs, their hair stuck to their faces with sweat, manually pumping oxygen into patients' lungs.

A yell cut through the chaos.

"Battery packs are failing! We need manual resuscitation now!"

The camera jolted. The video ended.

Kalyssa's stomach lurched. Hospitals. Traffic systems. Emergency services.

Pillars of civilization—toppled in less than a day.

Another notification.

Hartsfield-Jackson Airport Shut Down. No Flights In or Out.

She clicked the live feed from inside the airport.

A sea of bodies slumped against walls and luggage carousels, their faces hollow with exhaustion. A woman rocked her toddler back and forth, whispering empty reassurances. A businessman stood frozen at the departure screens, still clutching his useless boarding pass, as if refusing to believe the world had locked him in.

Kalyssa needed to get out.

A loud crack echoed outside, yanking her from her thoughts.

She rushed to the window, her muscles tense.

The streets had become a battlefield. Traffic frozen at intersections. Cars abandoned. Figures moved like phantoms—some searching for safety, others for something to steal.

Atlanta was falling apart.

A storefront exploded inward, and looters flooded inside like a pack of starving animals.

Her phone vibrated with a text.

SECRET SERVICE: Atlanta Is unstable. Evac teams mobilizing. Stay put. Help inbound.

Stay put. Like she had a choice.

She glanced at the tray of food again, the wilted remains of a world that had stopped functioning overnight.

Then… a knock at the door.

Three raps. Sharp. Deliberate.

Her heart slammed against her ribs.

She reached for her phone. Dead.

The knock came again, harder this time.

She reached for the emergency dial, then stopped.

Another knock. Louder. Sharper.

The impulse to scream welled in her chest.

A muffled sound came through the door.

"Ms. Summerwood, it's Secret Service. We're here to get you out."

Her pulse hammered against her ribs. Was it really them?

She exhaled sharply and turned the handle.

The door swung open, and two men in dark suits stepped inside. Their expressions were tense, their movements brisk.

"We need to move. Now."

She grabbed the bag she'd packed hours ago and followed them into the dim hallway, the emergency lights casting eerie, flickering shadows along the walls.

And as she moved, she prayed they were who they claimed to be.

CHAPTER THIRTY-TWO

The conference room was dim, an NSA report flickering on a screen on the far wall like a ghost of failure. FBI Special Agent in Charge Ricardo Roca sat at the head of the conference table, his fingers tapping a restless rhythm that betrayed his calm façade. The glow of screens cast jagged shadows across his face, amplifying the frustration carved deep into his features.

A dull throb pulsed in his right leg, a phantom ache from Iraq that refused to fade. He shifted, not for comfort but to banish the creeping specter of inadequacy. Once a war hero, then a Paralympic medalist, he had thrived under the spotlight. But now? No podium, no applause, just the oppressive weight of a career stuck in neutral.

Special agent in charge. *Stagnant.* The title gnawed at him like a festering wound.

His daughter, heading to law school, was soon to be a newlywed. He hadn't been invited. His son, swallowed by mental illness, was beyond his reach.

All he had left was this case. This one chance to prove he still mattered.

Calvarri wouldn't slip away. Not this time.

The low hum of monitors filled the air, punctuated by the occasional click of a keyboard, the only sounds in the dimly lit operations room. Even the dozen special agents watching him had gone mute.

He sliced through the silence—measured, unshakable, lethal.

"July 1st, a coordinated cyberattack crippled Peachtree Power, plunging millions into darkness and chaos." He let the words hang. "The breach has been traced to China's PLA Unit 61419."

There was a flicker of movement in the room. A tightening of shoulders. Still no one spoke.

"Two Chinese diplomats have already been expelled on suspicion of espionage." His gaze swept the team. "And one of our own is entangled in this."

He let the silence stretch. Then: "Caleb Calvarri."

He leaned forward, his shadow stretching across the table. "There's another $100,000 wire transfer from Weihua Industries. Sloppy. Brazen. Mocking." His tone sharpened, each word a scalpel. "The Chinese aren't hiding. They're toying with us. They know we're watching, and they want us to feel it."

His gaze swept the room, daring anyone to flinch. His team sat frozen, the tension as thick as the unspoken stakes. Somewhere out there, Calvarri was on the run, slipping through their grasp like a ghost in the machine.

"Cruz-Way, what do we have?" he demanded.

Special Agent Cruz-Way leaned forward, adjusted her cat-eye glasses, and spoke, her tone brisk. "Our interview with the Uber driver confirms Calvarri was using the alias Frank Stein on June 13th. Security footage from the Red Roof Inn matches his profile, but he ditched both the scrubs and the name. On June 19th, he resurfaced as Andy Taylor at a men's shelter, head shaved and a beard. The change bought him six days of anonymity."

"Go on."

Cruz-Way clicked the remote, and the screen illuminated with a grainy photo of a man in an ill-fitting charcoal suit, the red tie crooked against a wrinkled shirt.

"June 22nd," she said, "Personalized Office Solutions flagged this image of a Harrison Wentworth and forwarded it to DC police—suspicious behavior. The silver toupee wasn't enough to hide the resemblance to Calvarri. Local PD sent it to the FBI marked urgent. We ran the image through NGI's Interstate Photo System."

She paused, frustration rippling beneath the surface. "Agents were on scene within thirty minutes of the facial match confirmation. But he was already gone."

Roca's eyes narrowed, his jaw flexing as he absorbed the report. "Where was he headed?"

"We don't know. But Dex White, the men's shelter manager, confirmed that Andy Taylor left that morning for a supposed job interview. His description matches—charcoal suit, red tie."

He leaned forward. "And Harrison Wentworth? Has he resurfaced?"

"No, sir," Cruz-Way admitted, clicking to the next screen. The map zoomed into a cluster of locations near the Potomac. "We suspect he ditched the alias along with the oversized suit."

"Why Personalized Office Solutions?" Roca pressed.

Cruz-Way hesitated, then met his gaze. "He claimed he needed temporary office space for urgent meetings. But based on the timeline, we suspect he was transmitting classified information—likely the next cyberattack script—to Chinese operatives."

His expression darkened, his fists tightening against the table. "Why take that risk? He wouldn't have access to the funds they'd pay him."

"Maybe he's not in it for the money," Cruz-Way replied in a near whisper. "Or maybe they found another way to compensate him."

The room fell silent, the implication hanging like a guillotine. A shadow flickered across Roca's face as he stared at the image on the screen, the oversized suit a mocking disguise for a man unraveling the country's defenses from the inside.

"All right, Harmon," he barked. "Tell me you've got something that moves us forward."

Agent Harmon flexed her hands, the black leather of her fingerless gloves creaking softly as she straightened her fingers and drew one controlled breath before diving in.

"The NSA handed over Calvarri's cell phone—reset to factory settings. Worthless."

His jaw tightened. "What about Patuxent?"

"We found a primitive campsite deep in the reserve," Harmon said, clicking the remote to pull up an image. A crisp photo showed his trail pack half-buried under fallen leaves. "The pack matches a hiking photo we recovered from his townhouse. Same model, same tear in the side pocket. We believe he used the forest as a hideaway until he surfaced at the men's shelter."

He leaned in again. "How did he get to the shelter?"

"We suspect he took the bus. But the driver on that route doesn't recall anyone matching his description."

Roca exhaled sharply, his frustration cutting through the tense room like a blade. "So we're chasing a ghost. Again."

Harmon hesitated for half a beat, a slight furrow on her brow. "Not quite," she said carefully. "Calvarri has an account on KnowMeKnowYou, a dating platform. There's a possibility he may be involved with someone."

His gaze drilled into Harmon. "A love interest?" The two words carried an edge of disbelief… and the promise of consequences if this lead proved a dead end.

"Possibly," Harmon replied, her tone unwavering despite the pressure. "It's early, but if he's relying on someone, they could be sheltering him."

His fingers splayed on the table as if he could grip the situation itself. "Do we have a name?"

"Not yet," Harmon admitted, a flicker of frustration breaking through her calm exterior. "We're awaiting the transcripts of his chats. If there's anything actionable, we'll have it soon."

His fist clenched. "If there's a connection and it's real, it's our best chance at pinning him down. Make it happen. I want names, locations, and timelines. No more waiting. Every second, he's getting further ahead. And we're running out of time."

CHAPTER THIRTY-THREE

Caleb parked his new black mountain bike on the west side of International Park shortly before 11:00 a.m., his eyes briefly tracing the park's border with the Chinese embassy on the northwest corner. He had been here before and knew the layout well, and hoped this exchange would prove no less fruitful than the last. But today, something was different. A portable chain-link fence blocked the entrance to the park steps. A weather-stained **PARK TEMPORARILY CLOSED** sign had been fastened haphazardly to the fence, fluttering slightly in the breeze. It had the flimsy authority of a school crossing guard at a crime scene—visible, but powerless. He scanned the park, quickly locking onto a point of entry.

Dressed in overalls, gloves, and boots, he looked the part of a groundskeeper, his backpack snug on his back with a compact folding pruning saw strapped to the side. Lightweight rope dangled from the bottom of his pack, and compact loppers hung at his belt. All convincing props for his cover.

The humid July air clung to his skin as he glanced up and down the deserted brick sidewalk. Seeing no one, he skirted around the portable fence with an air of authority, his posture straight but every nerve on edge. His boots thudded against the stone steps of the west entrance, the sound unnaturally loud in the oppressive stillness. Pausing at the top, he adjusted his gloves and scanned the park for any sign of activity. Nothing stirred except the rustle of leaves in the hot, sticky air.

The Newton Apple Tree loomed ahead, its gnarled branches stretching skyward like skeletal fingers. As he approached the eerie quiet deepened, amplifying his every footstep. No joggers, no tourists, not even birds broke the silence. Something about the park closure felt too convenient. The timing too precise. Like someone had orchestrated it. His instincts screamed that this was more than a simple exchange.

And then he saw her.

Standing beneath the Newton Apple Tree, the woman blended seamlessly with the landscape, almost a shadow in the muted light filtering through the trees. Her posture was relaxed, but her gaze was razor-sharp—alert in a way that belied the ease of her stance. Her black hair was pulled back into a tight bun, not a strand out of place, and her dark brown eyes glittered with a cold intelligence. She wasn't just watching—she was calculating, reading every movement, every twitch of his body.

Caleb could feel her gaze, sharp as a sniper's crosshairs fixed on him. He'd dealt with Lian before and knew the way she played. But this time, the stakes weren't just high, they were lethal.

"I got your love letter," she said sarcastically, a smirk tugging at the corner of her lips. "Cute."

"Phone calls are out these days," he replied, striving for casual, though the tension in his body betrayed him. One wrong word, and she could blow his cover. And she knew it.

"I gathered that. But a secret rendezvous?" She raised an eyebrow, her tone light but laced with danger. "You're quite the maverick."

"You have something I need," he said, his words clipped, the urgency barely concealed. He needed to wrest control of the conversation before she started playing her game.

"Don't I always," she replied. She was toying with him, enjoying the control she held, like a cat with a mouse.

"What happened with Peachtree Power?" he asked, trying to focus the conversation.

Her smile widened, her eyes gleaming with amusement. "Quite the political strategy, don't you think? Free media coverage. Senator Grayhorse calm in a crisis! A perfect stage for someone to look heroic."

He knew she was spinning circles around him, keeping him off balance. The silence stretched, and his frustration grew, the clock ticking in his mind. He didn't have time for games.

"You're enjoying this, aren't you?" he asked tightly. "But someone's playing Everton, and we both know it."

"Feeling left out, are we?" she mocked, her smirk deepening.

"Lian, this is bigger than your little games," He leaned in, cutting through the banter. "You know it. I know it. Who's pulling Everton's strings?"

Her gaze flickered for a moment, a crack in her mask. "The person with no caller ID has quite a way with words," she said. "But who knows? Could be my cousins Mike and Bob..."

"Cut the crap," he growled, stepping closer. "Everton's a pawn. There's a bigger play here. And if you don't help, people will die. This isn't some clever game you can watch from the sidelines."

Lian's smirk faltered, if only for a second. He saw a flash of something real behind the mask. She quickly covered it with a veil of humor. "Well, it's been amusing so far. Clever, even. But you're right. It's no game."

He pressed harder. "This isn't just a puzzle to solve. People's lives are on the line, Lian. You can't sit this one out."

For a brief moment, her guard slipped further. Something flickered in her eyes—a memory, a glimpse of something raw, something painful. Like an unwanted specter haunting her thoughts.

"We've got people on the ground." Lian's tone softened, the edge replaced with something more deliberate.

"And?" he pressed. He knew he'd hit a nerve.

"Not everyone's our friend. We've got targets on our backs. Crosshairs." The sarcasm from earlier faded, the gravity of the situation sinking in.

"That's public knowledge," he said, unfazed.

She shook her head slightly, as if trying to rid herself of lingering doubts. "We're tracing digital breadcrumbs. But it's a puzzle that's missing too many pieces."

There was a subtle shift in her demeanor. She was offering him something, but it wasn't enough. He sensed the wall coming back up, brick by brick. He had to act fast, had to push before her defenses sealed off any chance of further truth.

"Give me something real, Lian," he pressed, urgency spilling out despite his attempt at control.

Her eyes flicked toward him, calculating. For a moment, she hesitated—something unusual for her—and then she spoke in a whisper. "Jiǎ Qí Corporation."

It wasn't everything, but it was a thread, a lead that could unravel a much larger web. A thousand possibilities sprang to life in his mind.

"Many thanks," he said, his tone genuine, though layered with a subtle plea for more.

For a moment, something softened in her gaze, a fleeting memory of their past when his selfless act had saved her life. A brief connection in the stillness, there and gone. Then, just as quickly, the moment passed.

"Be safe, Caleb," she said quietly. "You've only got one life."

As she walked away, vanishing into the shadows, he felt a deep pang, a longing for connection, something solid in a world built on lies.

In that moment, clarity struck him. Kalyssa wasn't just everything… she was the only real thing he had left.

CHAPTER THIRTY-FOUR

The dim glow of Independence Hall's lanterns fell over Hamilton Everton like the shadows of history, weighing heavy on his shoulders as he again took his seat at the table. The air was dense, thick with the weight of the moment and the echoes of those who had gathered here centuries ago. The place where liberty had been conceived was now the cradle of something far darker. But then again, life was like that. Full of contradictions. Deception masquerading as truth.

His gaze swept across the masked figures seated around him. Their faces were obscured, their identities shielded, but he didn't need to see them to know their power. Senators. CEOs. Academics. Financiers. Each one a cornerstone of the machine orchestrating chaos. Not allies—predators circling a dying republic, hungry for what came next.

At the head of the table stood their hooded leader, the Publisher. His mask, once featureless, now bore something new—newsprint etched into the surface, headlines barely legible in the low light:

Cyberattack Paralyzes Grid

Chinese Hackers Shut Off Power

Blackout Strikes The Southeast

The stories were real. The facts—twisted. The mask was no longer a disguise. It was a statement. A celebration of fear as strategy. A tribute to the power of the lie.

Behind him, a screen flickered. Bold white letters cut through the dark. **Nos Sumus Veritas.**

We are the truth.

Everton clenched his hands beneath the table, nails digging into flesh. The irony wasn't lost on him. These weren't purveyors of truth—they were its assassins, warping "truth" into something unrecognizable. And yet, here he sat. A demon of deception. A puppet dancing on strings he could no longer see.

"My beloved Authors, the National Defense Mandate is now before Congress," the Publisher began smoothly. "The nation is teetering. Vulnerable. This Twenty-eighth Amendment to the Constitution will give the president the power to secure its survival. And in doing so, it will secure our control."

Everton's stomach churned. It was supposed to be for Angela—for their future—but the justification rang hollow now, drowned beneath everything they'd unleashed. He'd sat through countless meetings like this, cloaked in subtext and menace, but tonight felt different. The stakes were higher. The control more absolute. The shadow of the plan stretched beyond even his considerable reach.

"How do we get the amendment through Congress?" Everton asked with a tone of skepticism. "It needs a two-thirds vote in both houses—67 senators, 290 representatives. That's no small feat."

The Publisher raised a gloved hand.

"We escalate the attacks. Amplify the ransom demands. Stoke the panic. And when the amendment passes, we'll be untouchable. No law. No court. No citizen will stand against us."

He watched as nods rippled through the room—a silent wave of assent that made his skin crawl. They were of one mind, intoxicated by the lust for power and a disdain for humanity. People were meant to be played—pawns in a game they could never win.

The screen behind the Publisher flickered again.

Nos Sumus Veritas

His face tensed as the words seemed to pulse in the dim light. *We are the truth. No*, he thought bitterly, *you are the lie.* But he said nothing. Silence was safer. Silence was survival.

As the masked figures filed out, Everton stayed seated, eyes fixed on the screen. Two hundred and fifty-two years ago, this hall had birthed a nation. Tonight, it had birthed its antithesis.

Guilt stirred—sharp, sudden. But he buried it beneath layers of loyalty, fear, and self-preservation. The game was already in motion.

He was both a player and a pawn.

And the truth?

The truth had been sacrificed long ago.

CHAPTER THIRTY-FIVE

FRIDAY, JULY 21, 2028

WASHINGTON, DC

First it had been Stratus Airways. Then Peachtree Power. Then Aegis Power.

Now, it was Aerolynx Airlines.

The AA flight numbers scrolled across Caleb's TV screen in a grim procession. His chest tightened as the news anchor's voice faltered, recounting the chaos—pilots blinded mid-air, instruments dead, flight paths crossing into deadly collisions. The news ticker blared **System Failure Suspected**, but he knew better.

This wasn't failure. This was war.

And somewhere, his name was being whispered as the architect of it all.

His eyes fell to the notebook in front of him, his notes from monitoring Everton's text messages. A Word Ladder scrawled across its pages, a twisted breadcrumb trail from Everton.

Game 4

Near Miss

Near. Neat. Meat. Melt. Belt. Best. Fest. Fist. Mist. Miss.

:-)

6 1 4 0 8

Nine targets. Four down. Five to go. He traced the numbers, his mind searching for meaning amid the chaos.

6 1 4 0 8

The code refused to yield its secret. The attacks weren't just escalating, they were accelerating. Aerolynx Airlines wasn't an endpoint. It was a harbinger.

On the TV newscast, flames devoured what remained of the latest plane, thick plumes of black smoke twisting into the sky. The wreckage was everywhere, metal shards embedded in the dirt, luggage torn open like casualties of war. The camera panned over a field of burning debris, scattered like shrapnel across the countryside.

He curled his fingers against the edge of the desk, his grip vise-tight. He should have seen this coming. Should have been faster. Smarter. Instead, he was trapped in his own private hell, a spectator of the nightmare he had created.

The newscast cut to a press conference in the White House briefing room. The president of the United States stood at the podium, his jaw set, his expression grave yet composed.

"My fellow citizens," he began, low, steady, unyielding—the calm before the storm. "We are confronting a series of coordinated cyberattacks targeting our nation's infrastructure and transportation systems. Our top agencies are working tirelessly to identify those responsible. We ask for your patience and vigilance during this critical time."

Patience. Vigilance.

His stomach knotted. The dominoes were starting to fall.

The president continued. "We are collaborating with international partners to enhance our cybersecurity defenses. Rest assured, we will pursue every lead and bring the perpetrators to justice."

A polished response. Just enough to reassure the public without admitting how little control they had left.

The newscast cut back to the anchor. "Authorities urge the public to remain calm as investigations proceed. Cybersecurity experts suggest the attacks are the work of Chinese operatives, though no claims of responsibility have been made."

His pulse pounded in his ears.

Everton's Word Ladder wasn't a game. It was a fuse. One explosion after another, each strike pushing the world closer to the brink.

He turned back to his notebook, the pages slick beneath his fingers. The code blurred as his focus strained.

6 1 4 0 8

The numbers burned into his vision.

The war Everton wanted to ignite wasn't hypothetical anymore. It was here.

The battles were raging.

And Caleb—whether he wanted to be or not—was the tip of a spear he never meant to throw.

CHAPTER THIRTY-SIX

Two weeks before the Democratic National Convention, Kalyssa stood among the crowd gathered at the Lincoln Memorial, the summer sun glaring off the marble like a stage light trained on history. A sea of supporters swelled across the National Mall, but it was the steps that held her gaze—polished stone beneath a moment months in the making.

Senator Alexander Grayhorse appeared at the top, and the air shifted. The subtle hush, the narrowing of breaths… he didn't need to speak to command attention. He just had to stand still long enough for the world to catch up.

Kalyssa watched him exhale, barely perceptible to anyone who didn't know his tells. She did. He was steadying himself. Not from nerves, but gravity. This wasn't just another campaign beat. It was the moment they were all supposed to believe in.

Her hands, clasped in front of her, stayed perfectly still. But her mind worked like a press secretary with a caffeine problem—evaluating crowd energy, polling fallout, media framing. She'd helped craft this moment, helped wordsmith the speech. But standing here now, watching it play out in the open air of Washington, it felt different.

Too perfect.

"Ladies and gentlemen, esteemed guests, and fellow Americans," Grayhorse began. His words carried across the reflecting pool, smooth and resonant.

She caught herself nodding along. It was good. Polished. Presidential. But her attention drifted sideways to the figure waiting just off-stage: Senator Carmen Valenzuela. The Texan's frame was compact, but her presence wasn't. That woman could freeze a Senate hearing with a single pause. She had seen it. Valenzuela had a magnetic and sharp-edged presence.

And now, she was the pick.

"It is with great pride and confidence," Grayhorse said, his tone rising with emphasis, "that I announce Senator Carmen Valenzuela of Texas as my running mate."

Applause cracked like a wave. Flags waved. Cell phones rose. Chants started to bubble up from the crowd.

Kalyssa smiled.

Valenzuela emerged like she'd been born in that moment. Her smile was tight but bright. Her steps perfectly calibrated. Her timing flawless. She took the podium with the ease of someone who'd already imagined it a hundred times.

"Thank you!" she said, vibrant and unshakable. "It is an honor to join this campaign and serve alongside a leader committed to unity, progress, and justice for all Americans."

Kalyssa narrowed her eyes. The wording tracked. The tone hit every note. But that wasn't what pulled at her. It was something under the applause—something too polished to be spontaneous.

Carmen didn't miss a beat. "Power without principle is the quickest path to ruin. That's why I hold fast to the Constitution, not just as history, but as a warning. I've fought to hold the powerful accountable. And I'm just getting started."

Kalyssa blinked. That line hadn't been in the draft.

The crowd went wild, roaring like they'd just heard gospel. A chant surged: *Val-en-zue-la. Val-en-zue-la.*

Kalyssa held still. Neutral face. But her pulse was off beat now, no longer syncing with the rhythm around her.

Grayhorse moved beside his running mate. They lifted their hands together, unity framed in a photo op meant to flood tomorrow's news cycle.

The image was flawless. But perfection had its own kind of tell.

Kalyssa's gaze lingered on Valenzuela. Her gut whispered what her brain couldn't yet prove. Not jealousy. Not mistrust. Just… wrong.

By the time the rally wrapped, her phone lit up with alerts.

AIMEE: Approval spike +12. Latino engagement trending 18% above baseline.

On paper, it was a win. But paper didn't track shadows.

And then she saw him. UW ball cap, purple and sun faded. Curved brim. Dark sunglasses. Standing by the press corps. And then… gone.

Justin?

CHAPTER THIRTY-SEVEN

The dim glow from Caleb's computer monitors bathed the room in jagged shadows, the hum of his equipment an ever-present reminder of time slipping away. Everton's bank statements glared back at him—a polished lie hiding a violent truth. Five deposits, each for $125,000, each arriving just after a cyberattack. Just royalties from a publishing house. *Sure they are.*

Five attacks. Five payments. The connection was undeniable.

Deep End Dynasty. The publisher's name was designed to vanish—slick, forgettable. A phantom company dressed in respectability, cloaked in layers of deception.

His fingers flew across the keyboard, the soft clatter the only sound as he tore past surface records into incorporation docs. Registered in Boston. Tiny law firm. Bland name. Nondescript office building. The kind of place that specialized in gray-area legality—shell corps, high-fee secrecy, no questions asked.

Then the name hit him.

Kort Hightower.

It flickered across the screen like static.

Kort? No way. Not after all these years. Not Berkeley Kort. Last he heard, the guy was working rooms in DC, whispering in senators' ears, playing both sides of the law with champagne in hand.

But this?

Caleb's pulse spiked. Maybe it was a coincidence.

Or maybe Caleb had just tugged on a thread that connected everything.

And company headquarters? 22 Unity Street, Boston.

He typed the address into Google Maps and clicked street view. Historic brick buildings, no 22 Unity Street.

It's time for a field trip.

After a quick breakfast, he settled into a leather seat in business class on the Ameritrak Alera bound for Boston. The security agent barely glanced at his Jordan Clarke driver's license, courtesy of the California Department of Motor Vehicles. Yet, despite the seamless execution, a pang of unease lingered, the weight of the false identity pressing heavily on him.

The train was quiet, with a handful of travelers scattered throughout the car. The scent of freshly brewed coffee mingled with the metallic chill of the air conditioning. At exactly 8:50 a.m., the Alera glided out of Washington DC's Union Station, the cityscape slipping past the window in a muted blur.

A moment later, a woman dropped into the seat diagonally in front of him. Mid -thirties, hollow-eyed, clutching a thermos like it held more than just coffee. She stared out the window, expression blank but searching, as if hoping the blur outside might give something back. There was something unraveling at the edges of her, a story he didn't want to know.

Just the girl on the train. And like him, trying not to be seen. He looked away and slipped back into his thoughts.

Deep End Dynasty. How far does the illusion go?

He scrolled to Amazon and searched for the publisher's books, scrawling titles and authors on his note pad. Midway through, the faintest hint of a pattern tickled the edge of his mind.

All Roads End – Anders Ray Ellison

Wings of Envy – Wanda Eastman

Innocence Gone – Igor Gavrilov

All Told – Alex Torres

Tangled Hearts – Talia Hussein

Never Far Off – Nina F. Oliver

Truths Hidden – Tate Henry

Echoes of Redemption – Edward Ramsey

Empires of Tomorrow – Enrique Tomlin

Reckless Endgame – Rachel Edwards

Redemption Undone – Rey Uzun

Wicked Intentions – Wesley Inouye

Luminous Lies – Lydia Langston

Taste of Happiness – Tiana Huang

Relentless Ever Vigilant – Rex E. Vick

Call it a blessing or a curse his mind hunted patterns like prey. Obsessive. Relentless. And now he saw what others would miss. The authors. The titles. A pattern strange in its simplicity. The initials matched, when lowercase words were ignored.

ARE. *All Roads End* – Anders Ray Ellison

WE. *Wings of Envy* – Wanda Eastman

IG. *Innocence Gone* – Igor Gavrilov

Fifteen titles. Fifteen authors. Listed in random order. He stared at the sequence of initials. Not gibberish. A message. Hidden.

ARE WE IG AT TH NFO TH ER ET RE RU WI LL TH REV

The combination of vowels and consonants made the sequence look almost readable. His mind raced, torn between dissecting the letter clusters further by exploring potential anagrams, and the fear of missing something crucial if he tampered with the order too soon. There was logic here, a deliberate pattern, and he knew it could slip away if he weren't careful.

ARE WE. The words stood out, clear as day. A hook to pull him in. His pulse quickened. He knew this was just the beginning, an entry point into something far deeper. The message was no accident, it was designed, each fragment carefully placed.

WI LL... will. *WE RE...* were.

Maybe. Then again, maybe not.

The paper blurred. His brow furrowed. He arranged then rearranged, extracting truth from a sea of deception.

ET RU TH...e truth.

RE IG NFO REV ER...reign forever.

As the train pulled into New York City's Penn Station, the clamor of passengers flooded the car, but he barely noticed. The storm of possibilities drowned out the noise.

The train passed New Haven shortly after one. He didn't register it. His mind was working at a fever pitch, chasing madness and meaning in equal measure. Each connection hit like a jolt of current. He was close. He could feel it.

But the thrill of discovery was tainted by something darker. This wasn't a puzzle. It was a declaration. A message meant to be found. A taunt. As if they knew he would come looking.

The train crossed into Massachusetts, the landscape sharpening into brick and steel. He scrawled the final word groups in his notebook, each one slotting into place like teeth in a lock.

WE ARE \ TH ET RU TH \ TH AT WI LL \ RE IG NFO REV ER

We are the truth that will reign forever.

The phrase, calculated and malevolent, twisted in his mind.

Who was "we"? A secret order cloaked in symbolism? A cult masquerading as patriots? His gut tightened.

The arrogance. The certainty. It sickened him.

This wasn't just a message.

It was a manifesto.

His thoughts snapped to history's worst ideologies—Hitler's master race, cloaking genocide in destiny. But this... this felt older. Older and deeper.

It whispered of bloodlines and hierarchies. Of beliefs that festered beneath empires, waiting for the world to forget.

This was supremacy reborn.

Not shouted from rooftops, but whispered through networks.

Not righteousness.

Domination.

CHAPTER THIRTY-EIGHT

As the train pulled into Boston's South Station, the familiar twinge of anxiety resurfaced as Caleb prepared to disembark. Boston's streets weren't just calling, they were a breadcrumb trail laced with teeth. Layered with clues he couldn't ignore. Unity Street—phantom number and all—called to him like an unsolved cipher.

He stepped off the train, the scent of rain-soaked asphalt greeting him as he exited the station. The humid Boston air did little to calm the storm of thoughts swirling in his mind.

Navigating the maze-like streets of the North End, he moved with purpose, his steps echoing against the uneven brick sidewalks. The neighborhood exuded history with its narrow alleys, the weathered façades of four-story buildings, the distant toll of a church bell. Yet today, it felt different. Charged. As if the past itself was watching him.

He read the address plates as he walked.

1A Unity Street. 3 Unity Street. 6 Unity Street. 8 Unity Street.

Some numbers were faded, barely legible, but he pressed on, scanning each doorway. The air felt heavier with each step, as though the city was conspiring against him.

… 12 Unity Street. 14 Unity Street. 16 Unity Street. 15 Unity Street…

A frown crept onto his face as the street unraveled ahead of him. He reached the corner, where the Old North Church courtyard appeared on his right and a brick-paved walkway veered off to his left, shaded by towering trees. The phantom address taunted him, less like a clue and more like a dare. Crafted for him alone.

… 21 Unity Street. 24 Unity Street. 26 Unity Street...

He stopped cold, his pulse quickening. Spinning around, he retraced his steps, scanning the buildings more carefully this time. *Nothing*. No 22 Unity Street. Only the mocking symmetry of red brick and iron railings.

But there was something intentional about the address. Fabricated, yes, but somehow real.

Intrigued though unsettled, he stepped onto the brick-paved walkway where it should've been. The gurgle of the fountain lured him forward.

Beyond the fountain, the sculpture rose—towering, unyielding. A horseman frozen in motion.

He drew closer.

Bronze and defiant. Paul Revere.

Not just a monument.

A mirror.

Each man driven by purpose. Each moving forward in the face of fear.

⁂

Roca's trip to Boston was meant to be a reprieve—a forced escape from the relentless pressure of the manhunt for Caleb Calvarri. The FBI director had ordered him to take a down day, insisting no one won a gold medal for working forty-five days straight.

Wrong.

The word hit like a punch, dragging up a memory he'd buried beneath layers of sleepless nights and cold leads.

Beijing, 2008. Paralympics.

Three medals—two gold, one bronze.

The training had lasted far more than forty-five days. The hours. The pain. The sacrifice. A crucible that demanded everything. But back then, there'd been a finish line. A medal. A moment of triumph.

Not here. Not with Calvarri.

This case was a war without end, a chase through shadowed alleys and smoke-screen lies. Every step felt like quicksand. Every lead dissolved. No finish line. Just pressure.

He needed something—clarity, maybe absolution. So he'd come here.

Not for the city. For a memory.

Back when her eyes still lit up when she saw him.

The Old North Church. Their vows. And for a while, he'd believed them.

Believed in love. Before ambition. Before the Bureau. Before it all fell apart.

Roca stepped out of the church and onto the brick-paved path of the mall. His simple prayer was more a wish than a hope. He meandered beneath the trees, breathing deeply, trying to enjoy the moment. But his subconscious stayed sharp. Every passerby a potential threat. Every smile a mask of deception.

※

Caleb lifted his eyes to the sculpture, its bronzed surface catching the last light of dusk. Paul Revere's gaze—cast in metal yet somehow alive—pierced through him with uncanny intensity. It felt as if the centuries had collapsed, binding them in the same unrelenting mission.

A rider in the dark.

A fugitive in the light.

He could almost hear hoofbeats pounding through time, each strike defiant. Had Revere felt this same gnawing doubt? This weight of knowing the stakes but questioning the outcome?

He reached out and brushed the cold metal.

Looking for strength.

All he found was his own distorted reflection—warped, uncertain.

A man caught between courage and collapse.

mmmm

Roca scanned the man with the precision of a machine, ticking through Calvarri's profile like a checklist.

About five-ten. Medium build. White. Early 30s.

Blond hair—gone. Beard—new. But the eyes. There was something about them, a flicker of recognition that tugged at his instincts.

Close enough to warrant a deeper look.

Roca smirked. *No way.*

This trip was a detour, a distraction, not a manhunt. And yet… there he was. *Maybe.* The odds were absurd. But life didn't care about odds. It cared about timing. And it had just dropped a bomb where logic said nothing should exist.

He opened his phone with practiced ease, angling it casually as he began snapping a series of photos. The man stood thirty feet away, oblivious, still, transfixed by the statue.

Roca circled slowly, each step deliberate, feeding the images into the FBI's NGI Interstate Photo System. The tech was fast—faster than Roca's pulse—but the seconds dragged. His gut already whispered what the system would confirm.

Then the man suddenly shifted.

Reverie broken. Movements jerky. Head darting side to side.

Nervous. Uneasy.

Roca's pulse steadied.

Whoever this guy was, he wasn't here for the view.

Then it came—a buzz in his hand, sharp and electric.

He glanced down. The system had returned its top five matches.

There it was.

Caleb Calvarri: 82%.

His pulse spiked. That was more than close enough. That was confirmation.

Caleb felt it before he saw it—a prickling at the base of his neck, the un-mistakable weight of being watched. He quickly slipped his phone into his pocket. No more photos.

He scanned the crowed and caught a silhouette. Still. Focused.

Too focused.

Run.

He spun off the curb just as the voice rang out behind him—

"Stop! FBI!"

He didn't look back.

He bolted across Hanover Street, weaving through honking cars and slamming brakes. A blur.

A symphony of chaos.

Behind him—shouts, screams, metal on metal.

Ahead—safety.

Or the illusion of it.

Roca lunged forward.

A taxi screeched past, horn blaring, forcing him back a step.

Exhaust and burning rubber hit him full in the face.

He struck the trunk with his fist as it sped away.

"Damn it."

He yanked out his phone, eyes locked on the fleeing figure. Calvarri's stride. The tilt of his shoulders. The way he slipped through chaos like he'd rehearsed it.

Quick. Precise.

But desperate.

Roca hit record, camera already rolling. His hand trembled, not from fear, but the hit of adrenaline flooding his system.

He was close.

Closer than ever.

And that thought lit him up like a live wire.

〰〰〰

The Battery Wharf Hotel loomed ahead, glass doors glowing like a beacon in the twilight. Caleb slipped through them, adrenaline still spiking, but his pace stayed measured. No sudden moves. No glances back.

The hush of the lobby hit him like a slap. Polished marble. Murmured conversations. The soft clink of glassware behind the bar. Too calm. Too still.

He made for the restroom.

Inside the far stall, he locked the door and leaned hard against it. Cold metal against his back. Pulse hammering in his ears. Gasping for air.

Not safe.

Not yet.

He pressed his palms to the door, grounding himself in the antiseptic sting of disinfectant. His breath came slower now, one sharp inhale at a time. No time for fear. No time for failure.

The walls around him… a sanctuary.

But they wouldn't hold.

They never did.

Who was that agent?

And how the hell did he find me?

CHAPTER THIRTY-NINE

Caleb stood at the desk in the dark, staring out the fourth-floor window of his hotel room. Boston Harbor churned below, fractured by flashes of moonlight slicing through the clouds—just like his mind. Turbulent. Chaotic. Pretending to be calm.

The faint hum of passing boats threaded through the stillness, mixing with the artificial scent of microwaved popcorn. He tossed a kernel into his mouth. Too salty. Too bland. But it grounded him. A poor stand-in for comfort food, but it would have to do.

Out there, someone was hunting him—relentless, determined. Eyes on the prize.

The FBI. Not a paranoid illusion. Raw. Real.

He took a seat at the desk and turned on the lamp. A warm glow illuminated the room.

He needed something—clarity, answers—anything to hold on to while the storm rose inside.

Turning back to the desk, he picked up his pen, its weight a small reassurance in his hand. His block print emerged on the page, sharp and deliberate, a desperate attempt to impose order on chaos.

Everton received $625k from Deep End Dynasty—five payouts of $125k after each major cyberattack.

Deep End Dynasty is a shell publisher registered to a fake address on Boston's Paul Revere mall.

The company published fifteen books by fifteen authors.

Initials of titles match author initials—ignoring lowercase words.

Initials spell: "We are the truth that will reign forever."

His pen hovered over the last line, the words tugging at the edge of his thoughts. The phrase wasn't just cryptic, it was intentional. A declaration of purpose. A challenge.

But from whom? And why?

One publisher. Fifteen authors. The numbers felt significant, but the *how* was just out of reach.

He leaned back, gaze drifting to the harbor's restless waters. The pieces were there, scattered like shards of glass. Somewhere in the confusion, a pattern waited. The truth wasn't just out there, it was taunting him. Daring him to find it.

His thoughts jumped to the ransomware attacks. Five now. Each one a bullet, fired from the barrel of a brain game. *Word Ladder.* Innocent in name. Deadly in effect. Each move had triggered a chain reaction, ending in multimillion-dollar payouts.

But why Word Ladder? Surely the word sequence wasn't random.

Everton would send the encrypted file—the attack plan. Could the word chain be the password? *Clever. Impossible to prove.*

So who was on the other side of the game? Who was the real weapon piercing the digital armor of billion-dollar institutions?

A Chinese operative? Maybe. One of the phantom authors? Possible.

He let out a dry chuckle. The absurdity of it all might've been laughable—*if it weren't so damn real.*

He forced his focus back to the text messages. Back to the figure on the other end of the chain. Back to the only question that mattered now:

Who was playing him?

Game 1 (6/2/28)

Eyes Open

Eyes. Eves. Even. Oven. Open

:-)

3 2 0 7 3

Cyberattack on Stratus Airways: (6/4/28, 2 days later, 0700 hours)

Then…

Game 2 (6/27/28)

Born Free

Born. Boon. Boot. Boat. Beat. Beet. Feet. Fret. Free

:-)

5 4 6 2 1

Cyberattack on Peachtree Power: (7/1/28, 4 days later, 2100 hours)

Then came Aegis Power. Aerolynx Airlines. Blue Rise Energy.

Each strike amplified the terror. Each one chipped away at public trust.

The words felt random. The numbers whispered meaning. But the connection stayed just out of reach—taunting him.

He smoothed out a fresh sheet of paper and narrowed his focus.

Simplify the complex. Strip the noise. Let the numbers speak.

The data sprawled before him—a maze of patterns and probabilities. An enigma begging to be solved.

Game 1 (6/2/28): 3 2 0 7 3 → attack on 6/4/28, 2 days later, 0700 hours

Game 2 (6/27/28): 5 4 6 2 1 → attack on 7/1/28, 4 days later, 2100 hours

Game 3 (7/8/28): 1 4 1 2 7 → attack on 7/12/28, 4 days later, 1200 hours

Game 4 (7/20/28): 6 1 4 0 8 → attack on 7/21/28, 1 day later, 1400 hours

Game 5 (7/24/28): 9 3 1 2 3 → attack on 7/27/28, 3 days later, 2300 hours

He scribbled the numbers again. *Zip codes?* He ran a search.

32073: Orange Park, Florida

54621: Chaseburg, Wisconsin

14127: Orchard Park, New York

61408: None.

93123: None.

Not zip codes.

He leaned back, scanning the list again. *If not locations… then what?*

The question itched at the edge of his mind. And just like that, the shift came. That familiar, all-consuming focus. The world narrowed. The noise fell away. Just him and the data.

He picked up his pen, heartbeat slowing as his mind locked in. One digit at a time. He underlined the second number in each sequence—slow, methodical.

Something was about to give.

3 <u>2</u> 0 7 3 → **2 Days later.**

5 <u>4</u> 6 2 1 → **4 Days later.**

1 <u>4</u> 1 2 7 → **4 Days later.**

6 <u>1</u> 4 0 8→**1 Day later.**

9 <u>3</u> 1 2 3 → **3 Days later.**

His pulse kicked up. The second digit wasn't random. It dictated the delay before each attack.

He drew a final line beneath the list, hand steady now. No more theories. No more guesses.

It was a pattern. Stark. Undeniable.

A flicker of triumph. The pieces were falling into place. But the feeling didn't last.

There's more here. I can feel it.

His eyes drifted back to the numbers. The second digit had spoken. Now the first demanded his attention.

What are you trying to tell me?

3

5

1

6

9

The digits stared back at him. Simple. Mocking. No repeats. No discernible pattern.

And yet, something tugged at the edges of his mind. Elusive. Insistent. An index?

The idea sparked like a live wire. He rifled through his mental files. Nine reports. The first—Aegis Power. The ninth—Blue Rise Energy.

His hand moved before the thought fully formed, pen scraping across the page. He listed each report in order of creation and matched them to the digits.

The numbers lined up. Perfectly.

No. It couldn't be that simple. Everton wouldn't—

But the doubt didn't last. It curdled fast into certainty.

Smart men slipped under pressure. Genius collapsed under ego. Or fear. They got sloppy. Left threads dangling where they thought no one would look.

He scanned the digits again. The first digit wasn't random. It was the report number. A breadcrumb trail hiding in plain sight.

Sequential. Obvious, if you knew where to look.

He underlined the sequence. Each stroke cut deeper into the page, into the truth.

Euphoria surged. That high that came from seeing through the fog. From knowing.

The numbers weren't just data. They were a signature. A cipher. A damning thread that led straight to Everton... and tethered Caleb to him like a shadow he couldn't shake.

The realization crashed over him—fast, cold, and merciless.

Exhilaration drowned in an instant.

His chest tightened. Guilt surged, sharp and unrelenting. The pen slipped from his fingers, clattering to the desk.

He stood too quickly. The room constricted around him. Walls pressing in. Not enough air.

He crossed to the window. His reflection stared back—ghostlike— blurred against the dark glass. Beyond it, the harbor churned in restless waves, mirroring his own inner storm.

He pressed a hand to the glass. Cold. Solid. Grounding. But it didn't stop the spiral.

He wasn't just a witness anymore. He was complicit. Unwitting, yes, but complicit all the same. And ignorance wouldn't save him. Not in the court of public opinion. There, he was already condemned. A scapegoat. A traitor.

A memory stirred. Not his own. A story. Joseph the dreamer. Falsely accused. Thrown in prison. Forgotten. Then lifted up. Pharaoh's second.

He clung to the image. If Joseph could rise, maybe there was still hope. Maybe redemption wasn't out of reach.

But he'd need more than luck.

He'd need a miracle.

CHAPTER FORTY

The dark of night filled Caleb's mind until a jolt of panic snapped him awake, his thoughts racing like an engine stuck in overdrive. He counted to fifty. Again. Then again. The numbers blurred. Useless. Five hours of sleep. It'd have to do.

Five attacks in eight weeks. Four more in the crosshairs: Franklin Volta, Island Power Company, Atlantis Electric, and Voltis Energy. Utilities that powered millions of households. All exposed.

New York. California. Hawaii. The states would drop like toothpicks in a tornado. Cities plunged into darkness, hospitals left crippled without power, communication networks silenced. The pulse of modern civilization flatlining.

If the next wave hit, chaos wouldn't trickle. It would flood.

He shivered. The thought settled over him like a shroud.

He escaped to the shower. At least the hotel still had power. For now.

Steam curled around him. Heat soaked into his bones. It wasn't peace, but it was enough to keep the darkness at bay.

Dressed and ready, he scanned the room service menu. He would've preferred the Battery Wharf Grille—outdoor seating, harbor view. But fear held him hostage to these four walls.

He moved to the window, hiding in a shadow. Sailboats glided across the water, graceful, unaware. He envied their silence.

For a moment, the harbor calmed his mind.

But it wouldn't last.

~~~~~~

Eyes were everywhere as he walked briskly to Boston's South Station. The cool morning air should have been refreshing, but last night's near capture robbed him of that pleasure. He scanned every scene, every face, searching for what he hoped he wouldn't find.

He boarded the 7:15 train with time to spare, choosing a forward-facing seat in the Quiet Car. The hum of paper, faint coughs, the lull of steel and motion. He exhaled, relieved the seat beside him was empty.

As the train pulled away, he pulled a stack of notes from his bag. Five-digit numeric codes. Paired with timestamps. He laid them out like puzzle pieces on the tray table.

3 2 0 7 3 — 0700 hours

5 4 6 2 1 — 2100 hours

1 4 1 2 7 — 1200 hours

6 1 4 0 8 — 1400 hours

9 3 1 2 3 — 2300 hours

He traced the patterns again. Each five-digit code held a two-digit pair that matched an attack time. *But which pair was the key?* He underlined each matching pair.

3 2 <u>0 7</u> 3: Third pair matches, 0700 hours.

5 4 6 <u>2 1</u>: Fourth pair matches, 2100 hours.

1 4 <u>1 2</u> 7: Third pair matches, 1200 hours.

6 <u>1 4</u> 0 8: Second pair matches, 1400 hours.

9 3 1 <u>2 3</u>: Fourth pair matches, 2300 hours.
~~~~~~

The options tumbled in his mind like dominoes. It was there, just beyond his grasp. His fingers drummed against the table, frustration mounting. *It had to be simple, didn't it?* Nothing about this was.

The train's sway tugged at his focus, soft and insistent. Too quiet. Too safe. A trap wrapped in velvet hush. Eyelids grew heavy. Numbers blurred. Sleep claimed him.

Weight shifted beside him.

His eyes snapped open. Heart pounding, he snatched the papers and slid them into his bag.

A man. Blazer. Jeans.

Unwelcome.

"Morning," the man said, low and careful, not loud enough to break the Quiet Car's spell.

Caleb gave a nod. Dismissive. Eyes on the window.

Something about the face itched at him, like a name buried too deep.

"Long trip?" the man continued. "Heading to DC for business?"

"Something like that," he replied. Eyes forward. Tone flat. Nothing to give.

Minutes ticked by, the silence twisting like a dagger.

Then the man leaned closer, his words quiet but pointed. "You seem like you've got a lot on your mind. Train rides are great for solving problems."

Heart thudding. But no flinch. No crack. "It's my girlfriend," he lied smoothly. "Things have been… complicated."

"Ah, trust issues," the man said, his smile edged with something unsettling. "Ever important, always elusive."

Caleb nodded, short and stiff. But the next line? A blade through the silence.

"Boston's a fascinating city. Did you get a chance to visit the Old North Church? Or Paul Revere Mall? They're… inspiring."

A chill crept up his neck. Goosebumps bloomed like warning flares. Not random. A message. A trap. The words pressed in, sharply deliberate.

The train began to slow. Union Station ahead.

Caleb rose, gathered his belongings, and turned, but the man blocked his path. The smile vanished. In its place… cold authority.

"Ricardo Roca. FBI. Caleb Calvarri, you are under arrest."

The words hit like a bullet—fast, loud, final. But instinct fired before the fear could.

He shoved. Hard. Roca stumbled. His leg caught the seat's edge. He went down hard. Gasps broke the silence. Everyone froze.

Caleb didn't wait. The train doors hissed open. He launched, shoes hitting the platform mid-sprint.

Union Station struck him like a wave—footsteps, voices, announcements clashing in his ears. He wove through bodies. Heart hammering. Eyes scanning.

How did the FBI find me?

He burst onto Massachusetts Avenue, swallowed by a swarm of bodies. DC roared around him—honking horns, rushing feet, sirens bleeding into the distance.

Every step was a countdown. Every turn, a desperate bid to vanish.

He ducked into a thrift store. The bell above the door jangled like an alarm. The air reeked of mothballs and old denim.

Backpack. Shirts. Pants. Cash on the counter. No questions.

In the restroom, he peeled off his clothes and slipped into the first outfit—loose jeans, a faded T-shirt, denim jacket. He added dark sunglasses and a brown ball cap. Not perfect. But maybe enough.

He cracked the door, sensed danger, and stepped out anyway.

His cap low, he crossed the street toward the pharmacy. Inside, he grabbed a pack of face masks. Post-Covid, they were still common enough to go unnoticed. He added hair dye, travel-sized shaving cream, an eyebrow pencil, and a disposable razor into the handbasket. At the register, his fingers fumbled the cash. "Keep the change," he muttered, already turning for the door.

Outside, he tore open the mask pack and slipped one on. The paper was cool against his skin, concealing what little of his face remained uncovered.

Not perfect, but it blurred the lines. He forced himself to walk, not run—just another figure moving through the noise.

His route to his high-tech lair wasn't random. It was layered with intention, every city park restroom a stage for transformation. The mirrors, a test. The exits, a risk.

The restrooms would be ideal—quiet, unmonitored. He moved fast, eyes scanning for blind spots. Every second inside was a gamble. At any moment, the door could creak open. A shadow could step in.

At the first stop, he stripped off his jacket—too distinctive—and shoved it deep into a trash can. Beneath it, a plain gray T-shirt. Forgettable.

From the pack, he pulled a razor and began with his eyebrows. The blade scraped away more than hair—it stripped identity. By the time he looked up, the face in the mirror wasn't his. Just skin over bone. Unfamiliar. Empty.

Next came the brow pencil. The angles he drew were wrong. Sharp. Unnatural. They twisted his expression into something uncanny, something that didn't belong. Not a disguise. A distortion. An image facial recognition software wouldn't understand.

Next stop: new park, different restroom. He slipped inside and yanked the T-shirt over his head. The sweat-soaked fabric clung to his skin before finally peeling away. He pulled on a navy button-down and rolled the sleeves to his elbows.

The mirror glared back, waiting for the next piece of him to vanish.

He uncapped the razor and began on his beard. The blade bit along his jaw, dragging away stubble and a mask of anonymity. Pale skin emerged beneath, unfamiliar and raw, like a layer that didn't belong to him.

His face looked gaunt. Unfinished.

He dropped the remains of his beard into the trash, burying it beneath damp paper towels. Turned on the faucet. Rinsed the blade. His hands.

He looked up. The mirror merciless, mocking.

Then the hair dye. Ugly. Unattractive. Perfect.

The changes weren't pretty, but that wasn't the point. Facial recognition relied on patterns. His new face? Unstable. Unpredictable.

Would it be enough? Would the cameras still see him?

He slid the mask back in place.

Final stop: a restroom near the bus terminal. High traffic. Fast turnover. He stripped again, swapping the button-down and dark jeans for a loose-fitting hoodie and faded cargo pants. When he stepped out, he added a limp, wincing with every step.

By the time security started scrubbing footage, he wouldn't match a single frame.

He'd be five different men.

None of them real.

Within hours, they'd start combing surveillance footage, frame by frame. They'd analyze his gait, the shift of his shoulders, the tilt of his head… searching for consistency.

But there wouldn't be any. He'd made sure of that.

And when the footage played back, what would they see?

A ghost?

A blur?

Or a mistake he hadn't accounted for.

No. They'll find nothing but puzzle pieces that don't fit.

As he neared the Forrest Sherwood Foundation headquarters, the words echoed in his mind:

We are the truth that will reign forever.

A creed etched in fire and blood. Not a mission statement. A warning. A challenge.

A war cry.

Who had written it first?

Who still whispered it in shadowed corridors?

Whoever they were, they weren't ideologues. They were architects of chaos.

And he was standing on their battlefield.

CHAPTER FORTY-ONE

WEDNESDAY, AUGUST 2, 2028
WASHINGTON, DC

Just after 2:00 p.m., Caleb reached the Forrest Sherwood Foundation headquarters, his hidden refuge from a storm that hadn't let up in days. He scanned the street. Parked cars. Quiet alley. His pulse kicked up. Too still. Too exposed. He lingered a beat longer than usual, then slipped inside and locked the door behind him.

Not safe. Just unseen.

Silence wrapped around him. Not calm, but suffocation dressed in stillness. Shadows gathered in the corners, spilling across the floor like fingers reaching for the light. He froze, straining to hear anything out of place.

Only the hum of the refrigerator.

He exhaled. No relief came with it. This place should have felt like home.

Instead, it felt like a cage.

His gaze drifted to the blackout curtains—thin fabric, thick protection. For a moment, he wanted to rip them open. Let the sunlight burn the shadows away.

But the risk was too great.

He turned away, jaw set. The stakes were too high to waver now.

What price am I willing to pay for freedom?

What's left to sacrifice?

He set his bag down and crossed to the cramped kitchen. Something normal. Something human.

Butterfly shrimp. Air fryer. Eight minutes. Cocktail sauce.

As the appliance hummed, he spread his notes across the table, fingers brushing the crinkled edges. Exhaustion pressed in, but he blinked it back.

One number at a time. Don't let the complexity overwhelm you.

The cryptic digits stared back at him, taunting in their simplicity.

The oven chimed. He tore into the shrimp, doused them in sauce.

Protein, not pleasure.

His pen tapped against the table, a rhythmic heartbeat to his thoughts.

He summoned a local AI routine, one he'd trained for speed and precision. A moment later, it returned the prime factorizations:

32073 = 3 × 10,691 → Single factor of 3

14127 = 3 × 17 × 277 → Single factor of 3

54621 = 3 × 3 × 3 × 7 × 17 × 17 → Multiple factors of 3

93123 = 3 × 3 × 3 × 3449 → Multiple factors of 3

61408 = 2 × 2 × 2 × 2 × 2 × 19 × 101 → No factor of 3

The connection danced just out of reach. He tapped faster, focus tightening until the fog cleared in a flash.

His hand flew as he wrote:

No factor of 3: second pair is the attack time

Single factor of 3: third pair is the attack time

Multiple factors of 3: fourth pair is the attack time

"Got it!" he shouted. The empty room threw it back at him, louder.

He couldn't sit still. Up the stairs. Down again. Fist pumping. Blood roaring.

Alive. Victorious.

He paused, a grin tugging at his lips. He heard Kalyssa's voice in his head: *So what's the pattern, genius?*

The teasing cut through the silence. Warm. Familiar.

"Check this out," he said to the empty room, as if she stood right beside him. "Suppose they plan to attack target seven, five days from now at 1300 hours. The first digit is the target, the second is the delay."

He jotted it down:

7 5 _ _ _

"I'll use the fourth pair to communicate the time," he muttered, filling in the last two digits.

7 5 _ 1 3

He smiled. "Now, to communicate that the time is in the fourth pair, I need the number to have multiple factors of three. How, you ask? It's simple. If the digits add up to a multiple of nine, it works. Watch this."

7 5 2 1 3

7 + 5 + 2 + 1 + 3 = 18 → Multiple of 9.

"So, 7 5 2 1 3 communicates target seven, five days from now, at 1300 hours," he murmured.

The realization warmed him like sunlight cutting through storm clouds.

And for a moment, the loneliness lifted.

Kalyssa was with him.

He exhaled, the warmth fading, and climbed the stairs to his high-tech hideaway.

Headlines scrolled across the monitors—scandals, wildfires, markets in freefall. He barely looked.

Then a sound cut through the static.

"Atlantis Electric, one of California's largest energy providers, was hit by a massive cyberattack at 9:00 a.m. this morning."

His body locked. The air thinned.

He opened the files from Everton's phone, fingers trembling.

Yesterday's texts.

A Word Ladder:

NO CALLER ID: Cold Lies

EVERTON: Cold. Gold. Good. Goos. Goes. Hoes. Hies. Lies

NO CALLER ID: :-)

Everton: 4 1 0 9 1

His pen moved fast, decoding by instinct.

"Target four, one day later, at 0900," he whispered.

Everton had pulled the trigger.

The chilling motto from Deep End Dynasty echoed in his mind:

We are the truth that will reign forever.

He sank into the chair, pulse pounding.

These are the Authors.

And this—

This is their version of terror.

CHAPTER FORTY-TWO

Caleb woke to pale amber light slicing through a gap in the blackout curtains. Shadows stretched across the room, long and ominous.

The quiet didn't help. Inside, the storm still churned.

Two forces collided in that liminal space—guilt, a leaden weight dragging him backward; and resolve, a blade urging him forward.

He exhaled sharply, making his choice. Today, resolve would be his companion. Guilt could wait.

He dressed, slipping into navy blue gym shorts and a faded T-shirt. The cool tiles grounded him. Just for a moment.

Breakfast was a quick ritual, a task to occupy his hands while his thoughts raced ahead.

English muffins, toasted and buttered. A drizzle of honey. Fresh orange juice. A banana.

Each bite was a countdown to the day's confrontation with Hamilton Everton.

The central screen flared to life, casting a cold blue glow across his digital fortress.

A tangled web spread across a map of DC, tracing Hamilton Everton's movements.

Each line was a breadcrumb, tracking seventy-two hours of activity, hinting at what might come next.

His lips curled into a grim smile. Chaos was raw material in his hands, ready to be shaped into clarity.

For eight hours, his fingers danced, code moving like a master's brush.

His goal was simple: convert tangled lines into data points, each marking a distinct span of time.

"Show me your secrets," he murmured.

He refined the time filter, isolating locations where Everton had lingered for at least thirty minutes.

The chaotic web dissolved, leaving a constellation of blue dots scattered across the map—stars against a dark sky. The larger the dot, the longer the stay.

He dismissed the oversized dots—NSA headquarters and Everton's Maryland home. Routine. Predictable.

He was hunting the deviations. The anomalies.

Five dots remained, places where Everton had stayed at least an hour, but no more than three.

Caleb leaned in, heartbeat climbing.

This wasn't just cat and mouse. It was a duel of minds, a silent war in the digital shadows.

He was closing in. Each keystroke a step closer to the revelation that might shatter Everton's carefully constructed world.

Four of the five locations were ordinary.

But the fifth… it screamed.

The National Arboretum.

Everton had been there from 10:00 p.m. to just after midnight on August 1st. The gates closed at five.

The timestamp blinked like a silent alarm—a digital specter.

A closed arboretum. Dark paths. Secluded. Not the kind of place you stumbled into after midnight.

Everton hadn't wandered. This was calculated.

"Two hours," he muttered.

Whatever had drawn Everton there… it mattered. Enough to risk being caught.

Caleb expanded the map and pulled up satellite images of the arboretum.

He locked onto the spot where Everton had lingered: the National Capitol Columns.

A chill gripped him. Twenty-two Corinthian columns—imposing, eerie. Like Stonehenge dropped in the middle of DC.

Most images were taken in daylight. Weathered stone standing like silent witnesses to time.

But one moonlit photo jolted Caleb. The contrast was stark, unsettling.

In the moonlight, the columns had transformed into ghostly sentinels, rising from the earth with an otherworldly presence.

They weren't relics. They were monoliths—cryptic, silent, whispering of ancient rites and twisted truths.

That night, the National Arboretum wasn't just a botanical garden.

It was a stage where shadows danced and secrets whispered among the stones.

The weight of history pressed down. The columns weren't ornamental. They guarded something far more significant.

This wasn't just a place. It was a fracture where past and present bled into each other.

A place Everton had risked everything to visit.

Why had he gone there?

Had he been alone? Or had he met someone?

The questions multiplied, each one stoking the fire. Caleb had to know what Everton had left behind in the shadows of those columns.

He glanced at his watch. Just over an hour until the arboretum would be swallowed by darkness.

Time slipped through his fingers. Every second raised the stakes.

He mapped the route: ninety-nine minutes on foot. Thirty-one by bike.

A bike was the clear choice—fast, nimble, and easy to ditch if things went south.

He moved quickly out the door and onto the bike in one smooth motion.

A helmet shielded his hair. A Covid mask covered his face.

The humid air pressed in as he pedaled into the evening.

His mind raced ahead, mapping turns, blind corners, and possible choke points.

Every detail mattered. He had to stay invisible.

Two minutes in, his phone buzzed, slicing through the rhythm of tires on asphalt.

His heart lurched. He swerved to the side, bike wobbling to a halt.

A text from Kalyssa.

Her name hit harder than the vibration. Deeper. Sharper.

He fumbled with the screen then read her message.

KALY: I'm surrounded by thousands, but I'm lonely without you.

She needs me.

True. Real. But the setting sun showed no mercy.

His thumb hovered, caught between instinct and longing.

Replying would cost him precious seconds. Moments he couldn't spare.

But ignoring her felt like cutting the one thread still tethering him to himself.

His training screamed at him—focus, block it out, keep moving.

But her words stayed, echoing in the humid dark, louder than any siren.

He forced focus. Then typed:

ME: I miss you too, my love. Together days will come again.

It felt inadequate. A hollow echo of what he wanted to say.

But it was all he could give.

He reread it once, searching for strength in its simplicity. Then hit send.

The phone's screen dimmed, but the hollow ache in his chest refused to fade.

He pushed off. Pedaled harder as the dark closed in.

The arboretum loomed ahead, its shadows holding truths that could rewrite everything.

But as the wheels spun faster, fear stayed locked in his chest.

What if the truth came too late?

What if the cost was everything… and everyone?

This was on him. No one else could expose what was coming.

Whatever waited in those shadows, he would face it.

No matter the cost. The phone buzzed again in his pocket.

He didn't check it. That lifeline would remain unread.

Right now, the mission demanded everything.

But the words he never said—and the love he couldn't hold—echoed in the space she should have filled.

The unknown pulled harder, an invisible force he couldn't resist.

What lay ahead was uncertain. Dangerous.

But one thing was clear:

Whatever he uncovered there could alter everything.

CHAPTER FORTY-THREE

The National Arboretum loomed ahead, taunting Caleb with its promises. Everton shouldn't have been here. He had no reason to be. That alone made it worth the risk.

Caleb moved down M Street NE, hyperfocused. Everything else faded to background noise.

The fence on his left? A joke. More suggestion than security.

The road ended at a concrete barrier. Maryland Avenue veered off right. A potential escape route if things went south.

Won't need it.

But his eyes lingered. Survival instinct whispered otherwise.

He dismounted with practiced ease—fluid, precise. Tension coiled tight beneath the surface. He lifted the bike over the barrier. Muscle memory.

What if someone is already watching? What if this is a trap?

Each crunch of dirt echoed louder than it should. Every step screamed: exposed.

He veered north, found a tree, and leaned the bike just so. Positioned for speed. A quick getaway if it all went to hell.

Ahead, the fence. Metal cold beneath his hands. He scaled it swiftly, landing in a crouch. Shadows stretched long across the grass. He crept past the ruins of the Maryland Avenue Gate, cracked stone, moonlit silence, like bones guarding a secret.

Two nights ago, Everton had been here. Two hours in a closed federal park. Left after midnight.

Alone? Or not?

Caleb crossed Azalea Road. The Capitol Columns loomed ahead—massive, ancient, absurdly exposed. The field between them was open. No cover. No second chances.

He scanned the shadows, then broke into a run. Legs pulsing, lungs gasping. He reached the steps. Hands on knees. Pulse racing. Sweat dripping.

Why here?

Everton had stood like a statue listening to a pompous priest deliver a Sunday sermon. For two hours. Not normal. He couldn't have been alone.

The Authors?

Someone had to have seen them. *Security?*

And then he saw it.

A flicker—left side. Not a firefly. No. Something more.

A golf cart. One headlamp flickering. The other . . . dead.

He ducked behind a column, heart thudding.

Muscles coiled. Eyes locked.

The cart rolled to a stop. The driver—stocky, tattooed, eating a donut—scanned the columns like he expected ghosts.

"Who's there?"

Caleb stepped forward. *Keep it steady. Calm.* The words came out stronger than he felt.

"Thanks for coming. Wasn't sure you'd roll up."

The guy's brow scrunched. His hand hovered near his waist. Radio? Blade?

"Roll up? Who you think I am, *homes?*" Grit in the voice. East LA.

Caleb shifted, hands up, palms easy. One step closer.

"She said you'd be here. I didn't think you'd actually show."

"Who said?"

The guy's stance shifted. Coiled now. Waiting.

"You trippin', *ese*. I don't know you."

"*Maria*," Caleb said.

A gamble. Common name. Plausible.

The man froze. Something flashed behind his eyes.

"*Maria Lupe?* You know my *ruca?*" The man's tone dropped, sharp now. "She been talkin' to you?"

"Yeah," Caleb lied, pulse tightening. "She didn't tell you?"

"She ain't tell me *nada*. Not in weeks. No kids. No *nothin'*. *Vieja!*"

Caleb's gaze bounced, searching for leverage, anything. Then he saw it. Name tag. Blue shirt. White thread.

Miguel.

He said the name. Warm. Familiar.

Miguel's eyes widened, a mixture of confusion and recognition crossing his face. Then: "Whaddya want, huh? . . . 'Cause you ain't gettin' it. And you sure as hell ain't gettin' my *ruca*."

"Maria Lupe ain't into me, Miguel," he replied calmly. "She just thought you might want what I have."

Miguel's eyes narrowed further, a calculating look crossing his face. "What you got, *vato?* 'Cause I might jus' take it off you."

"I don't play like that, *ese*," Caleb said, holding his ground. "You can't jack what's in my head. But I'm down for a trade."

Miguel didn't answer right away. His eyes locked on Caleb's, that round face tightening—not angry, but calculating. Something shifted behind his expression. A flicker. Interest?

"*Dígame.*"

Caleb nodded toward the columns. "Couple nights back, some fools were posted up here. You see 'em?"

Miguel leaned back, slow. "Yeah. I seen 'em. Like fifteen *vatos*, all listenin' to some other *vato* spittin' game."

"You hear anything?" he pushed, leaning into the shift he sensed in Miguel's voice.

"They were tripped out, man. Freaky masks and all," Miguel said. "Like some twisted-ass *Día de los Muertos* type shit. Skull faces. Eyes all messed up. Like they was tryin' too hard to be scary, y'know?"

Caleb's gut tensed. "Masks?"

"Yeah... *Rajones*, too scared to show their faces." Miguel sneered. "Wouldn't last a minute on the street. Looked hard, but nah... just cowards hidin' behind plastic. Actin' like they was startin' a revolution."

Caleb leaned in. "A revolution?"

Miguel snorted. "That's what they said, *homes*. Like they were in church or some shit. Talkin' freedom, blood, sacrifice. Then one of 'em busts out with, '*Nos sumus veritas.*' And the rest?" He shook his head. "Chantin' it like they was in a damn cult."

Nos sumus veritas? Latin. Its meaning? We... truth?

His pulse thudded.

We are the truth.

The Authors!

He refocused, forcing himself back to the moment.

"Who let 'em in?" he asked, keeping it casual, fishing.

Miguel clicked his tongue. "When you're some big-ass senator, you get whatever the hell you want."

"Senator Wright?" A guess. A lure.

Miguel's head snapped a little, like he'd caught the bait but smelled the hook.

"No." The name that followed came slower. Weighted. "*Gordo.*"

Gordo?

The name felt like a joke. *Fat man.* Was Miguel playing him—or had he just handed Caleb a clue?

Caleb prodded just hard enough to stoke the fire. "That rich white boy thinks he owns us. Not anymore, *ese.*"

Miguel's face twisted, a grin blooming—dark, satisfied. "I ain't no damn fool," he muttered. "His skull mask didn't trick me. He made me drive his fat ass to the columns. Spilled my damn donuts."

The grin sharpened, and Caleb caught it—the kind of satisfaction that reeked of revenge, but beneath it... something else. The bitterness of being used. Tossed aside.

Miguel reached into his pocket.

Caleb gasped as a wallet appeared—black leather, not Miguel's. Too nice. Too official. Miguel held it up like a trophy, fingers loose, daring him to want it.

Not just a score. A clue. Maybe *the* clue.

"You clean him out?" Caleb asked, grin sharp, heartbeat ticking faster beneath it.

"Hell yeah, *homes*. Five hundred cash, tank of gas, best meal I've had in weeks." Miguel shrugged, tossing the wallet in one hand like it meant nothing. "Now it's just leather and plastic."

Caleb didn't blink. Eyes locked. One step closer. No sudden moves.

He reached out slowly.

Miguel pulled back—reflexive, guarded. His eyes narrowed, testing.

Then, with a flick, the wallet spun through the air.

Caleb caught it. Fingers closing tight. Soft thud in his palm—he felt it all the way down his spine.

He flipped it open fast. ID cards. Health card. Multiple credit cards. Name right where it had to be.

Riley Michael Gordon.

Senator. New Jersey.

The senator's gelatinous face seemed to consume itself—eyes lost in folds, mouth smothered by indulgence, as if truth had no place left to escape. *Gordo.* The term *was* fitting.

First, Everton. Now, Gordon. Two of fifteen Authors.

Their midnight gathering at the columns hadn't been a freedom rally. It was the birthplace of a coup.

"So, whatdya got for me?" Miguel said, snapping Caleb back into the moment. "Whatdya have that's so damn important my *ruca* would send you here?"

The question landed heavy, like a test. Miguel's body was tense, coiled. Ready for whatever.

Caleb held his ground. "What I've got is something that can flip the script. Something that'll make you glad you showed up."

Miguel's eyes twitched. Just a blink, but enough. A crack.

"Your *ruca* knows I've been keeping tabs," Caleb said, speaking just loud enough to be heard. "On stuff that runs deeper than those fools with the masks. This ain't about settling scores, Miguel. It's about making sure that when the smoke clears, you're still standing."

Still no tell on Miguel's face. But Caleb could feel it—interest, suspicion, the math churning behind the eyes.

Caleb leaned in, whispering now. "What I've got is the one thing Gordo didn't see coming—someone watching his every move. And if we play this right? We bury him."

Miguel stared. Long. Then that slow, dangerous smile crept across his face.

"You better not be playin' with me, *homes*."

There it was. Not a no. Not even close.

"I don't play, Miguel. Not with men like Gordo."

Caleb felt it shift—the air between them. Miguel wasn't just listening now. He was in.

〰〰〰

The wind knifed across Caleb's face as he pedaled through the quiet streets. Back to his high-tech hideaway. Back to safety. He'd done it—unmasked a second Author. One step closer.

And still, it tasted like ash.

He'd played Miguel. Twisted him with precision. Raised his hopes only to leave him in the dust.

He was a decent guy. Loyal. Used. Disposable.

Damn it, Miguel deserves better.

If Caleb made it out of this alive—if he somehow survived—he'd make it right. Whatever that meant.

The tires hummed beneath him, a low, steady rhythm, but nothing could drown out the guilt. This was the cost. One more line blurred. One more piece of his soul chipped away in the name of something bigger.

Right. Wrong. Truth. Lies. They were bleeding into each other now, and he wasn't sure what he'd become.

CHAPTER FORTY-FOUR

A cold slap of water stung his face.

Caleb jolted upright. Midnight pressed in, thick and unrelenting. The kitchen was dim, lit only by the dim glow of the fridge. Its hum ticked like a cruel metronome, marking seconds he couldn't get back.

He leaned over the counter. Palms flat. The tile chilled his bare feet like punishment.

The silence? Absolute. And it stretched endlessly between him and Kalyssa.

His phone sat nearby. Still. Dark. Accusatory.

Three unanswered texts etched themselves in his mind, blinking like ghostly echoes:

ME: I'm sorry.

ME: Are you okay?

ME: Call me, please.

Lifeless words. Stripped of urgency. Of meaning.

He stared, willing the screen to flicker. Vibrate. *Anything.*

Nothing.

No thumbs-up. No heart. Not even a smile emoji.

Something was wrong.

When her reply finally came, he froze.

Four words.

Sharp. Precise. Unmistakable.

KALY: Call me in 20

His thumb hovered above the screen.

A simple thumbs-up. He tapped it, sent it, and instantly regretted the simplicity of it.

The wait hollowed him out.

Twenty minutes felt like purgatory, each second stretching, her silence pressing harder against his ribs. He paced the kitchen, slow and deliberate, but his thoughts were anything but.

She had reached out last night. Needed him. And his response? A text: **Together days will come again.** *Cute. Empty.*

But he couldn't just pretend he wasn't a framed fugitive, right? Not only that, he was trying to stop the nation from falling captive to an evil force. A noble cause. And the Capitol Columns was where he had to be. End of conversation.

Unpersuasive. She wouldn't buy it.

What can I say?

At nineteen minutes, he called.

His pulse thundered in his ears as the line clicked.

Then her voice came through.

A sound he'd longed for. A sound he feared.

"Hello, Jordan."

The name cut deeper than it should have.

He wanted *Caleb* on her lips. He wanted the truth between them, raw and real—no masks, no lies. But the mission still owned him. And with it, the deception.

"Kaly," he said, low, rough, "I'm sorry. For last night."

Silence.

Taut. Heavy.

A thread stretched to its limit.

When she finally spoke, her words were smooth, but they sliced like glass.

"I need to know you're there for me, *Jordan*. And last night… you weren't."

Each syllable drove deeper.

He gripped the counter, knuckles whitening, the cold tile the only thing keeping him from unraveling.

"I wasn't the man you needed me to be," he whispered.

A sigh crackled through the line. Tired, yes, but threaded with something sharper.

Disappointment. Maybe even doubt.

"I'm risking everything for you," she said, the words fraying at the edges. "My career. My heart. Maybe even my freedom. I can't take any more emotional trauma."

A beat.

Then, "If you can't make me a priority…"

She didn't finish.

She didn't have to.

The silence that followed said it all. He swallowed hard, fighting to find the right words.

"Kaly, you don't just heal me. You make me whole. You're not a distraction. You're the reason I keep going."

Emotion seeped in—raw, exposed.

A pause.

Longer this time. Heavier. Loaded with her unspoken doubts and his unbearable guilt. He could hear her breathing on the other end. Steady, but strained.

Finally, she broke the silence. But not the distance.

"*Caleb*," she said, "I don't need perfection. I just need you. Not the man you think I want. Not the one you're trying to be. I need *you*. The real you."

His name—*Caleb*—cut through him like a blade and balm at once. A lifeline. Fragile, but powerful. A beam of light in the darkness

"I'm here," he said, low but steady, even as the storm inside him raged. "I *am* here for you."

And for a flicker of a moment, everything stilled. The weight lifted. The storm calmed.

Could it last?

When the shadows returned, everything they'd just salvaged could shatter.

But for now. He held her close.

Embraced by her words. Charmed by her love.

Even as the darkness closed in.

CHAPTER FORTY-FIVE

Roca sat alone in his office, the hum of the air vents louder than usual. The whiteboard on the far wall was cluttered with names and timelines, none of them giving up the thread he needed. The Calvarri case wasn't just high-profile—it was a mirror, held up to every unresolved question in his own career. He'd built a reputation on clarity. But this one kept slipping just out of frame.

His thoughts fractured as Lisa Harmon stepped in, her black fingerless gloves gripping a slim file like it held a live wire. She dropped it on his desk—neat, direct, no preamble.

"Kalyssa Summerwood," she said. "Someone from Calvarri's past. A re-kindled flame."

He raised an eyebrow but said nothing. He opened the file slowly, scanning the first page.

"She's cooperating, mostly," Harmon added, sliding into the chair across from him. "They reconnected on KnowMeKnowYou eleven days before he vanished. Their exchange on the app was brief. Moved to phone after that."

He flipped another page. "Convenient timing."

"It gets better." Harmon leaned in slightly, her tone sharp. "Ten days later, a new user appears on the platform. Reaches out to her. Just her. Name: Jordan Clarke."

He looked up, interest sparked but masked. "That supposed to mean something?"

She held his gaze. "Clarke's not random. He's strategic. The timing, the digital signature… it's deliberate."

Roca leaned back, gaze narrowing. "And you think he's Calvarri?"

"Maybe."

He held her stare for a beat longer. Then glanced back at the file.

Harmon pulled a sheet from the folder—screenshots of texts, time-stamped and crisp.

"Clarke calls her *Kaly* from the start," she said. "Same nickname Calvarri used in their first exchange. Then he types what seems to be her definition of a soulmate. Based on her reaction, he nailed it."

His interest sharpened.

"She tests him," Harmon continued. "Asks what she wore the night Calvarri stood her up. His reply? Black dress. Curled blonde hair. He didn't miss a beat."

A jolt of energy cracked through Roca. The evidence was solid.

"It gets weirder," Harmon said. "She tells him she's going jogging on the National Mall the next morning. Clarke tells her to look for someone named 'Be Free the Clown' by the Lincoln Reflecting Pool."

He blinked. "Be Free the— Are you serious?"

She slid another photo across the desk, grainy surveillance footage of a man in full clown costume.

"Only shows up that day. One time. Lingering near the Vietnam Women's Memorial. Then gone."

He stared at the photo. "A clown. Of course. That tracks… in the most twisted way."

"We've got her jogging," Harmon said. "And Be Free pacing the edge of the memorial. But no footage of them together."

Roca exhaled, jaw tight. "So, is she in a relationship with Clarke?"

"She was," Harmon said. "Claims she ended it about four weeks ago."

"And she never saw where he lived?"

"Says she never went to his place."

Roca's jaw clenched. "That's a stretch."

"She's hard to pin down—campaign trail's nonstop. But we've talked once. And her DC apartment is covered."

"Video footage?"

"No evidence of Clarke at her apartment—at least no clown. An artist is working on a composite of Clarke minus the makeup."

Roca studied the photo: Kalyssa Summerwood.

Something in her posture. Steel beneath the polish. But her eyes… those gave her away. A trace of something unguarded. Hesitation maybe. Or guilt. She either didn't know the full story, or she knew too much.

Didn't matter. She was in it now.

"She's the best chance we've got," he muttered, handing the photo back to Harmon.

But even as the words left his mouth, he knew the truth—Kalyssa was a thread. Not the center. Not even close.

Silence stretched. Then Harmon turned and walked out. The door clicked shut behind her.

Roca didn't move.

Didn't blink.

Let the rage catch.

It didn't burn slow—it ignited. Roared through him like wildfire.

Calvarri. Treating it like a game. Like the nation was just another piece he could sacrifice.

I didn't leave half my leg in Fallujah for this.

Not to watch it rot from the inside.

Screw protocol. Screw politics.

If it comes to a bullet, so be it.

I won't miss.

CHAPTER FORTY-SIX

They'd spent the afternoon together. After six weeks of late-night calls, whispered secrets, and frantic text threads, four hours face-to-face felt like oxygen. No screen. No filter. Just breath. Laughter. Questions. Her campaign. His investigation. Them.

Now, back at the Foundation, the scent of food swirled around her, comforting and familiar. Sweet and sour shrimp. Moo goo gai pan. Egg rolls. Pork fried rice. The Full Kee bag sagged in her grip, grease blooming through the bottom like always. Her stomach growled.

She took the stairs two at a time. Upstairs, Caleb was exactly where she'd expected—hunched behind his fortress of monitors. Fingers flying across the keys. Eyes darting. The room glowed faintly blue from all the screens, shadows twitching across the walls like ghosts.

He didn't look up when she entered.

Didn't need to.

The room pulsed with unspoken focus. A low hum from the machines, a higher one from her nerves. She set the food down without a word. This wasn't a dinner break. Not tonight.

On one screen, the Senate feed loaded. The Twenty-eighth Amendment—the National Defense Mandate—ticked across the chyron like a headline from a dystopian script. A bill cloaked in patriotism but stitched with fear. Power hiding behind a flag.

She hated it.

He did too.

And tonight, they'd watch the lie try to make itself law.

The amendment had knifed its way through the Senate Judiciary Committee: 17 to 4.

Chairman Senator Theodore Wright (Republican, Arizona) had pushed it with iron resolve. Ranking Member Senator Emily Carter (Democrat, New York) had sold it like salvation. The usual theatrics. But this wasn't policy. This was absolute power dressed as protection.

In the House, it had passed by a whisper: 291 out of 435. Just enough to clear the fog of dissent.

Now it stood before the Senate. One vote away from rewriting everything.

Today was Constitution Day. And this? Sacrilege in a cloak of sanctimony.

Outside the Capitol, the nation teetered, caught between hope and dread, freedom and fear.

The weight of history wasn't metaphor. It pressed down… here, now, unrelenting.

Kalyssa sank into the leather chair across from Caleb's desk, chopsticks in hand, hunger pressing in. She hadn't eaten since breakfast. But the gnawing in her stomach wasn't just from skipping lunch. It was deeper. Sharper.

She tore into the shrimp first, then the moo goo gai pan. Hot, salty, sweet. Familiar comfort in unfamiliar times.

But even the food couldn't quiet the storm building inside her.

Each bite, a countdown.

Each headline, an assault on the Constitution.

She kept her eyes fixed on the screen, refusing to blink as the debate neared—an amendment dressed as defense but stinking of control.

And if it passed…

"It's surreal," Caleb muttered between bites, wiping his forehead with a napkin. "We're two miles from the Capitol, and somehow, we're two inches from authoritarianism. Congress is steering straight toward a cliff, and no one seems to notice we're accelerating."

She set her container aside, appetite fading. The urgency in his words mirrored what she already felt.

Her eyes shifted to the monitors flanking the massive TV. Aimee would track the national pulse, pulling in sentiment, reactions, trends in real time. Tonight, truth wouldn't just be debated. It would be measured in hashtags and fear.

The Senate Chamber came into focus—crisp, high-res, unnervingly calm.

Then Wright appeared.

Senator Theodore Wright. Chairman of the Judiciary Committee. Grayhorse's most dangerous rival, and the face of the coming storm. He moved like a man who already held the Oval Office in his palm. Every calculated step toward the microphone was deliberate. Every pause rehearsed. On screen, he loomed larger than life, the embodiment of polished fear.

The storm had arrived.

And its first gust cut deep.

"Colleagues," Wright began, resonant and sonorous, the room folding into silence, "today we stand at a critical juncture in our nation's history. The recent cyberattacks orchestrated by the Chinese government have exposed vulnerabilities in our national security that we can no longer afford to ignore."

He let the pause stretch.

"Our adversaries grow bolder. The threats, more sophisticated. And so, with clear-eyed urgency, we present Constitutional Amendment Twenty-Eight—the National Defense Mandate."

As Wright's final words reverberated across the chamber, Senator Emily Carter stepped forward beside him—equal in stature, different in strategy.

Her presence shifted the room.

Kalyssa leaned in, jaw tight. Carter's entrance was no accident—it was choreography. Good cop to Wright's hammer. A duo engineered for persuasion.

"Senator Wright is correct," Carter began. Clear, measured, but unmistakably charged. "Our current legal framework cannot keep pace with the immediacy or severity of today's threats. This amendment grants the president the necessary emergency powers to respond, decisively and swiftly, to foreign aggression, whether physical, economic, or cyber."

Her words weren't just calculated. They were weaponized.

Kalyssa shuddered.

Then another figure stood: Senator David Reynolds of Ohio, a midwestern moderate, respected, even keeled. A pulse of resistance.

"But Senator Wright," Reynolds said, "this amendment suspends law, grants control over communication networks, and allows indefinite detention without trial. That strikes at the heart of every civil liberty we claim to defend. What protections exist against abuse?"

Kalyssa held her breath.

The camera cut back to Carter.

"Your concerns are valid, Senator Reynolds," she replied smoothly. "But the amendment includes a crucial safeguard: within forty-eight hours of invocation, Congress must convene. And with a two-thirds majority, Congress can revoke the president's emergency authority. The system of checks and balances remains intact."

Carter smiled.

Kalyssa saw it for what it was—not reassurance, but illusion. A veneer of control hiding the quiet slide into something darker.

Senator Lexi Harper of Oregon took the floor next. "While I understand the necessity of a rapid response," she said, "I worry about the indefinite suspension of elections... and the potential for civil liberties violations. What safeguards are in place to ensure this power isn't misused?"

Kalyssa leaned forward, her fingers tightening around a chopstick.

Then... Gordon.

Senator Riley Michael Gordon of New Jersey let out a theatrical scoff, like a cartoon villain handed a hot mic.

"Oh, here we go again," he sneered. "If you had your way, Senator Harper, we'd be sitting ducks for every hacker and terrorist out there. You care more about hugging trees than protecting this nation. This is why Americans don't trust your party with national security."

The blow landed hard. Not just because it was cruel, but because it was *intentional.* Calculated.

The screen flickered, cutting to Senator Kevin Wong of California.

He stood, composed but fierce, each word catching fire as it left his lips.

"This amendment is a blatant power grab," Wong said. "We're not just rewriting laws. We're inviting tyranny. We need to stand for the Constitution and to defend the civil liberties that define us."

Then Gordon struck again.

With a grin like he'd already won, he leaned into his mic.

"Oh, please. The guy whose cousins in Beijing wrote those malware scripts is suddenly an expert on freedom?"

The chamber *gasped.* Audible. Visceral.

Wong held his ground.

"That kind of racist filth has no place in this chamber," he shot back. "You disgrace the office you hold. Your words reek of McCarthyism, dripping with fear and xenophobia, and they threaten to unravel the very values we claim to protect."

Kalyssa's heart pounded. The air around her felt charged. Like static before a lightning strike.

She turned to Caleb.

His face was stone.

"They're not debating policy anymore," he said. "They're rehearsing a takeover."

The debate raged on—a reckless tempest of caustic rhetoric and hollow patriotism. Senators clawed for airtime, their speeches more about scoring points than safeguarding anything real.

Kalyssa shifted her gaze to the analysis streaming across a side monitor. Aimee was tracking sentiment in real time. The data told a bleak story—moderates disengaging, social feeds swarming with memes and mockery. The debate had become entertainment. Policy reduced to punchlines. Substance drowned by spectacle.

One clip showed Gordon mid-rant, overlaid with cartoon sound effects and circus music.

Kalyssa exhaled through her nose, bitter. "The American people are caught up in a schoolyard brawl. Oblivious to the clear and present danger before them."

A new video splashed across the second screen—and Kalyssa's stomach turned.

"Damn it," she whispered. "White supremacist groups are amplifying Gordon's remarks." The meme was already viral, his slur recut as a rallying cry.

When the video ended, the feed jumped to immigrant leaders calling for Gordon's censure.

Kalyssa turned back to the debate with a growing pit in her chest.

By the time Senator Wright returned to the podium, it was past 10:00 p.m. The chamber was chaos wrapped in marble—decorum shattered, nerves exposed.

But Wright? Ice-calm.

"Colleagues," he began, "the threats we face are unprecedented. Our response must be equally resolute. This amendment is not about partisanship—it's about securing the future of this country. History will judge us. Stand for your country. Or be remembered as the ones who failed it."

The final words echoed through the Senate as the feed widened to show the gallery.

Press. Staffers. A few VIPs.

Kalyssa tracked the slow pan half-distracted, and then she saw him.

Second row. Gallery left.

Jawline like a campaign ad. Navy suit. Slicked hair. And that smirk.

She leaned in, barely audible. "What the hell is he doing there?"

Kort Hightower. Debate team. Berkeley. Too much charm. Too little conscience.

And now, a front-row seat to the collapse of democracy. Coincidence? Hardly.

The screen flickered to pundits talking over each other.

Caleb muted the chaos. Aimee's analysis took over—polling shifts, partisan fractures, a spike in nationalist rhetoric. But Kalyssa barely saw it.

She clutched the printed amendment in her lap. Her eyes scanned the words, ones she knew by heart.

It didn't read like law.

It read like a coronation.

Her gaze froze on the final clause:

Not subject to judicial review.

The words loomed.

Not a safeguard. A surrender.

Not oversight. Obedience.

No court. No challenge. No Constitution.

A slow chill crept down her spine.

This wasn't bold legislation. It was a death certificate for dissent.

And the worst part?

It wasn't hidden.

It was *applauded.*

The trap wasn't in the fine print—it was in the applause. The willful blindness. The comfort people clung to like children under a monster's shadow.

Blind. Willing. Content.

The words pulsed in her mind, each one tightening the knot in her chest.

She swallowed hard. The paper trembled in her grip.

If the people can't see the threat—
If the courts can't stop it—
Who's left?
Caleb's eyes met hers. Fierce. Unflinching.
We are.

If the people can't see the threat—
If the courts can't stop it—
Who's left?
Caleb's eyes met hers. Fierce. Unflinching.
We are.

CHAPTER FORTY-SEVEN

With the blackout curtains pulled back, the early-morning sun slanted across the brick walls of the Forrest Sherwood Foundation, casting fractured light through the blinds like silent alarms.

Kalyssa stood on the balcony, fingers curled loosely around the iron railing. It was cold. She barely felt it.

Below, the city stirred—buses rumbling, crosswalks blinking, people chasing schedules like nothing had changed. But everything had.

Last night, the Senate passed the amendment: 81 in favor. The number flashed in her mind like a silent countdown. Final.

They did it. They actually did it.

And now, the Constitution no longer stood between power and permanence.

Sure, the state legislatures still had to ratify. But that technicality didn't lighten the weight pressing on her chest.

And then there was Kort Hightower. *Berkeley Kort.*

Why had he been there?

There was something darker at play.

She stepped back into the safety of the war room and shut the door behind her.

Caleb looked up from his seat. The warmth in his eyes reached for her, but it was shadowed, like he was holding something he couldn't say out loud.

He looked older. Spent. Like something inside him had cracked under pressure.

He forced a smile. "Morning, Kaly."

She crossed to him, her lips brushing his. A wordless welcome to the day.

He stood and held her tightly, like a man clinging to something he'd once lost.

"It's been four months since you found me," he whispered. "I'll never be the same."

His warmth seeped into her, quieting the storm that had chased her through the night.

But the calm didn't last.

She leaned back, searching his eyes. "What's happening to our country?" The words broke as they left her, brittle with emotion.. "It's crumbling, and no one seems to care."

Something flickered behind his gaze.

Not fear. Not sadness.

Calculation.

Like he was weighing something. Risks. Payoffs. Whether to bring her into his world or to keep her just far enough away to stay safe.

⁂

Caleb knew she deserved to know. Maybe even needed to.

But if she knew—really knew—then she'd no longer be presumed innocent. She'd be guilty too. At least in the eyes of the nation.

He was the FBI's most wanted. Not a title he wanted *her* to carry.

And if he let her in, the trap would close around them both.

But could he win without her? Could he even survive?

203

But this wasn't just about survival. It was about *her future*. And the country's fate.

Can I save them both?

Kalyssa didn't blink. Just watched him—silent, searching—like she already knew what he hadn't said.

"Kaly, there are dark forces at play. If I tell you the truth, you lose plausible deniability. Jordan Clarke disappears, and I'm just Caleb Calvarri, FBI's most wanted. And you, Kaly, become my accomplice in crimes I didn't commit." He paused, then added, "I can't ask you to do that."

<center>~~~~~~~</center>

Kalyssa heard the conviction in his words—too real to fake. But trust? She'd been burned before. And Caleb… he too carried a suitcase of secrets.

What if he vanishes as well?

Then what?

Could she believe in him? Not just the comfort, the chemistry, but the man underneath it all.

That would take faith. And the last time she'd leaned on that, it nearly broke her.

But Caleb was a Seeker. Of that she was certain.

And maybe for the first time in too long, they were chasing the same thing.

Transformation. Of themselves. Of each other. Of the nation.

She met his eyes, let the silence stretch. Then slowly, she exhaled.

"Caleb… I'm in."

<center>~~~~~~~</center>

Caleb blinked. Once. Twice.

For a second, the world held still.

Then something inside him gave way. Quiet, like a fault line shifting.

She was in.

Not just agreeing. *Believing.*

He couldn't move. Couldn't speak.

For four months, he'd walked a razor's edge. Lied to stay alive. Hidden the worst of it even from her. Always planning. Always calculating. Always alone.

And now she was here.

Not just near him. *With* him.

He pulled her close, held on like she might vanish. His body shook… barely, but enough to feel it in his chest, his jaw, his grip.

A breath left him.

"You're going to want to sit down."

⁓⁓⁓

This was it. The moment she'd feared. Yet, somehow, she felt relieved. Irrational, yes. But… real.

"Hamilton Everton is part of *The Authors,* a cabal plotting to undermine the Constitution and all that it stands for."

She blinked. "You're kidding . . ." She knew Everton was involved in something dark. But this?

"There are fifteen Authors. I've found five."

"How?"

"I hack systems. Track people on the move. It's what I do best."

A memory flashed. A sudden chill. He had tracked her.

Calm down.

"That kind of freaks me out. You tracked me."

"Yeah, I know," he said quietly. "That's the obsessive part. I'm not proud of it."

Not a denial. A confession.

Not perfect.

Flawed.

Beautifully flawed.

She smiled, leaned forward, and kissed him. "Your secret's safe with me."

His eyes softened. "I hacked Everton's phone, tracked his movements, followed the trail to the Capitol Columns. Played a man, stole a senator's wallet, planted a tracker. That gave me two Authors—Everton and Gordon."

"Senator Gordon? From New Jersey?"

He nodded. "The same. He reset his VPN password... a pretty *dumb* thing to do on a *smart*phone."

She laughed. "So you got into their virtual private network?"

"Yep, and with Gordon's credentials I found his alias: Igor Gavrilov. Author of *Innocence Gone.*"

"Wait—Gordon *is* Gavrilov?"

"Exactly. None of the Authors use their real names on internal files or comms. When I logged in as Gordon, his profile name was Gavrilov."

"And the book titles?"

"Published by Deep End Dynasty. Fifteen in all."

"So they're real? The books?"

He chuckled. "Real covers. Real titles. Mostly same content."

"One book with fifteen covers?"

A broad smile. "Hey, why write fifteen when you can write one?"

She laughed. "I hope it was good."

"Bestseller," he said, grinning.

"So... who else did you find?"

"I've tracked sixteen aliases."

Her brow lifted. "I thought there were only fifteen Authors?"

"There are. The sixteenth alias isn't a name—it's a title: *The Publisher.*"

She frowned. "That sounds ominous."

"He's the one who sent Gordon the first drafts of the National Defense Mandate. So yeah... in that sense, he's an Author too."

A chill rippled through her.

"You mean, they didn't just support it… they *wrote* it?" she asked.

"It gets worse. They're orchestrating the cyberattacks and blaming China."

She huffed bitterly. "Real patriotic."

"It's a sick kind of game," he said. "Messing with people's minds. Using fear as a weapon."

She met his eyes. "Who's the Publisher?"

He shook his head. "I don't know. Not yet. There are fragments, but nothing that fits. He's a sports nut. Had tickets to the World Series. Obsessed with brain games. And drunk on power."

She snorted. "That narrows it down to half of DC"

He laughed. "Exactly. Now you see why I haven't cracked it."

A beat passed. Should she say it?

No more secrets.

"I saw someone from our past… at the amendment debate."

"Who?" Caleb asked, brows knitting.

"Kort—Berkeley Kort." It landed like the punch line to a joke that wasn't funny.

"What?" His eyes narrowed, as if trying to make it compute.

"In the gallery. On the left. Sharp suit. Devious smile. I don't trust the guy."

Maybe she was profiling him. Maybe not.

"Why was he there? Why now?" He stared into space, gears turning.

She folded her arms. "Who in the chamber is on his list of clients?"

No answer. Just silence. And then she shifted.

"But you did find three others…"

He nodded. "Rupert Cain, Dr. Helena Montgomery, and Senator Evan Marshall.

Or by their aliases—Wesley Inouye, Nina F. Oliver, and Rey Uzun."

"A tech billionaire and a senator. Who's Montgomery?"

"Harvard professor. Her academic work's just a cover. Underneath? Government-funded research into population control. She's been conditioning future leaders—to shape public opinion, steer behavior. Quiet manipulation at scale."

She shook her head. "What's their why?"

He shrugged. "For Everton? Money. Over half a million and climbing. But the others... I think it's power. Prestige. And maybe a twisted sense of patriotism."

"So how are we going to stop it?" she said, her mind racing with options.

"That's where you come in. As hard as this is for me to say, I think we need to get your man elected."

She blinked. "Grayhorse?"

He nodded. "I don't see any other way to stop them."

CHAPTER FORTY-EIGHT

Hamilton Everton sat in the shadowed corner of Barrow & Vine, the upscale restaurant tucked inside the Blaise-Mark Hotel, just blocks from the White House. Candlelight flickered against polished silverware and dark wood, casting long, restless shadows. Across the room, patrons leaned close, their faces partially veiled by the dim glow, like the secrets they carried.

Here, power wasn't spoken. It was whispered. Bartered. Traded.

And Everton could feel it, like gravity pulling him into the undertow.

Senator Gordon lumbered into the seat across from him, the tailored suit straining against his swollen frame. He didn't sit so much as collapse, his bulk displacing the air around them.

The grin Gordon offered was smug. Knowing. Dangerous.

He shifted with effort, then dragged a linen napkin across his lap.

The waiter appeared, took their orders, and vanished into the kitchen without a word.

"Hamilton," Gordon said, blotting sweat from his brow with the napkin, "you'll never guess what came in the mail today."

Everton forced a polite smile, masking the irritation building beneath his collar. "What's that?"

"My wallet," Gordon said, chuckling like it was the punchline to a private joke. "Thought it was gone for good after the night at the Columns.

Someone mailed it back to me. Of course, the cash was gone."

Everton smiled. Polite. Unimpressed. "Looks like it's your lucky day."

Gordon leaned in. The table groaned. When he spoke, it was low and rough, like stone scraped across concrete.

"You know they still haven't found Calvarri, don't you?"

Everton's fingers closed tighter around his water glass. Stone-faced. Unshaken. But the name hit him like a needle to the spine.

Caleb Calvarri.

Caleb was supposed to be a pawn.

But now he was the player. The wildcard. The embarrassment.

Everton swallowed the bitterness, forced it back down. Caleb had fled, and with every hour he remained free, the damage compounded.

And Gordon knew it.

Gordon's grin widened, like he could smell the tension beneath Everton's skin.

"The man's like a specter," he said, tone laced with mock admiration. "The FBI. NSA. None of them can pin him down. He's making fools of everyone." A pause. Sharp. Measured. Then, "Including you."

Everton held steady. Didn't twitch. He inhaled slow, controlled. But the jab landed.

Caleb wasn't just making fools of them. He was dismantling it all. Piece by piece. Quiet as a ghost.

Gordon's gaze darkened. His tone low. Heavy. Like a warning wrapped in calm.

"Hamilton… the Publisher is losing patience."

The name cut like a dagger.

The Publisher.

Not a title. A threat. A reminder of the one figure who moved in deeper shadows than any of them.

Everton had danced too close to that fire. He felt it now—cracks forming underfoot, the edge crumbling.

His pulse ticked faster. But his face held. Years of training kept the mask in place.

He reached for his water. Fingers steady. Grip tight.

Inside, the abyss yawned wider.

The waiter returned.

A modest plate of grilled salmon slid in front of Everton—clean, understated. Across the table, Gordon's ribeye landed with a dull thud. Butter pooled at the edges. Foie gras perched like a crown atop excess.

The smell hung between them—thick, rich, vulgar.

Power flaunted versus power restrained.

Everton didn't touch his food. Didn't glance at it. His focus stayed on Gordon, who carved into his steak like it was sport. Sausage-thick fingers. Grease-slicked smirk. He chewed with theatrical pleasure, every bite more deliberate than the last.

Grotesque. Calculated.

"He's just one man," Everton said, each word cold and precise. "A man on the run. Eventually, he'll slip."

Not truth. But not a lie. Just enough to deflect. To remind Gordon he was still playing chess, not checkers.

Everton wasn't about to give the man an ounce more than necessary. Not a detail. Not a crack.

Let him guess. Let him starve.

Gordon leaned back. Fork raised like a lazy weapon.

"He's not just any man, Hamilton."

A pause. Knife-sharp.

"He's surpassed you. Makes you look like a novice."

Everton's fingers closed tighter around the glass. The chill bled into his palm, grounding him.

Don't blink. Don't rise.

The fury simmered just beneath the surface. Pressurized. Controlled.

Gordon tilted his head, speaking low, just above a whisper.

"You think the Publisher will wait forever?"

He met Gordon's gaze. Cold. Unflinching.

"Calvarri will be found," he said. "And when he is, he won't be a problem anymore. I've got it covered."

The words held steady. The mask held. But underneath—pressure. Gnawing. Eroding.

Across the table, Gordon's smirk spread like oil on water. He leaned back slightly, fork slicing through the ribeye with surgical precision. His laugh was low. Wet.

"You'd better make sure of it, Hamilton," he said, tone syrupy with mock concern. "Because if you don't, your money might just dry up."

He paused. Let it settle.

"And after everything your poor wife's been through with the cancer and all…" He let the pause linger, then added with a slow, smug smile, "Well. That'd be a real shame."

The words knifed him. Precise. Intentional.

His fist curled around the glass—too tight. The stem creaked. His jaw clenched, teeth grinding.

"Damn you, Gordon," he hissed. "Go to hell, you miserable—"

He caught himself. Stopped the slip just in time.

But the damage was done. The mask had cracked.

Gordon leaned back, grin unchanged, eyes glittering with cruelty.

"Careful, Hamilton." A drawl. A dare. "You know as well as I do—hell's already here."

The words dropped like a guillotine.

And Everton felt it. The truth of it.

Caleb was out there. Untouchable. Every second of Caleb's freedom was another crack in the foundation Everton had built.

"I'll handle it," he said. Firm.

But not convincing. Not enough to hide the tremor beneath the words.

"Of course you will," Gordon said smoothly. He dabbed at his mouth with the napkin, tossed it down like a finished hand in a rigged game.

Smug. Performed. Perfectly rehearsed.

But he knew the truth. Knew who the real enemy was. It wasn't the man across the table—it was the ghost beyond their reach.

Caleb.

This wasn't about politics anymore. Or even power. This was survival.

Gordon leaned in one last time, the grin thinning into something sharper.

"Any other outcome," he said, "will lead to… shall we say, *less favorable results* for your family."

The tension sat heavy between them. Plates cleared. No words.

Just the promise.

He didn't respond. Not with words.

His silence wasn't surrender. It was calculation.

A desperate attempt to reframe a game that now felt unwinnable.

CHAPTER FORTY-NINE

Ricardo Roca slammed the phone into its cradle. The crack split the air like a gunshot—sharp, final, satisfying. His fist followed, driving into the desk with enough force to rattle the blinds and send coffee sloshing over the edge of a surveillance report.

Let it spill. Let it stain.

Everton.

That bastard had the gall to call mid-case, mid-operation, and start pulling strings like he owned the Bureau.

Roca's jaw flexed, teeth grinding.

Calvarri was guilty. Every sign pointed to it—bank transfers, precise digital footprints, the smug trail of a man who thought he could hack the nation and walk away clean.

But Everton?

He was trying to hijack it. Turn a takedown into theater. Undercut the Bureau's process to stage his own damn finale.

This wasn't just overreach. It was sabotage.

Calculated. Controlled. Masked as urgency.

Roca braced both hands on the desk, breathing hard.

Calvarri was a traitor. But he was Roca's to bring in. By the book. With evidence that could hold in court. Not undercut by some political puppet master trying to rewrite the script.

He scanned the files—everything lining up, everything tightening. The noose was nearly closed.

So why the call?

Why now?

He stood abruptly, shoving the chair back with a screech.

If Everton wanted a show, he could keep his stage.

Roca wasn't here to dance for headlines.

He was here to take Calvarri down.

And if Everton got in the way? He'd go down too.

CHAPTER FIFTY

Rain slammed the streets, turning DC into a floodplain of headlights and haze. From the lead SUV, Roca watched the Capitol dome blur behind the downpour. A hulking shadow watching, waiting. This day had been coming for months. Now, closing in on the target, his nerves were strung tight, humming like live wire.

"We're almost there," Harmon said, eyes bouncing between the GPS and the slick streets. "Traffic's light, for once."

She rode shotgun. Masters was behind them. Cruz-Way and Marrow in the second SUV. SWAT rolled up the rear.

He gave a curt nod. Harmon had earned it. Her precision had snapped the case open. Jordan Clarke was Caleb Calvarri. No more aliases. No more questions. They had their man.

And Kalyssa? She'd handed him over, whether she knew it or not.

But it wasn't just about the man anymore. The stakes had mutated. Grown teeth.

"Think he knows we're coming?" Roca asked, eyes fixed ahead.

Harmon frowned. "Hard to say. He's been slippery from day one, but we've kept this off-grid. He might think he's safe, buried in that high-tech hideout."

The Forrest Sherwood Foundation. Three blocks from FBI headquarters. Hiding in plain sight. An unassuming red-brick shell masking the command center of a national fugitive.

The radio crackled. Cruz-Way came through, low and clipped. "Roca, Lisa, you sure about this? The Foundation? I've got a bad feeling."

Cruz-Way always played cautious, but her gut hadn't failed them yet. He had stopped doubting it a long time ago.

He clicked the mic. "Understood. But every thread led us here. Calvarri, the wire transfers, the IP routes… they all spiral back to that building. He's inside."

Silence. Then: "Roger that."

He exchanged a glance with Harmon. She gave a nod. So did he.

They turned off the main drag, cutting into a quiet stretch behind Saint Matthew's Cathedral. The building emerged from the rain—weathered brick, no signs, no movement. Just another relic from a quieter era.

It looked like a museum.

Felt like a trap.

He gripped the wheel tighter.

"Everyone ready?"

Masters shifted behind him, hand brushing his holster. "Ready as I'll ever be."

"SWAT's in position along the alley," Harmon said, checking the side mirror. "Locals have the perimeter tight. Nobody gets in or out."

"Let's hope that's enough," he muttered. "If Calvarri's in there, he knows the angles. And if he's not…"

He let the sentence hang.

The radio chirped. Marrow this time: "Perimeter's quiet. No movement."

"Copy." Roca exhaled slowly. Ran the plan through his mind one more time. Then again. No mistakes today.

They pulled to a stop half a block away.

Roca stepped into the rain with Harmon and Masters. Cold stung his face, soaking into his collar. He didn't so much as twitch. Eyes locked on the Foundation, he pulled his hood low. He glanced over at Harmon, who was adjusting her gloves, jaw set like stone.

He gathered the team tight. "We've got one shot. Cruz-Way, flank left. Watch the balcony. Harmon, Masters… you're with me. Front entry."

Cruz-Way was already moving, her team melting into the shadows of the alley, rifles up, silent and sharp.

The rain came harder now, drumming pavement like a countdown.

Roca moved with Harmon and Masters toward the front. Each step dragged, leaden with expectation. An ambush. A bloodbath. A booby trap. He braced for all of it.

Nothing.

No lights. No silhouettes. Just that building, watching them back.

His earpiece hissed to life. "Team two to team one," Cruz-Way whispered. "No movement. Balcony clear. Place looks locked up tight."

Hold position," he said, low and calm. "Wait for my go."

Harmon raised her weapon. Breath visible in the cold. Eyes sharp.

Masters covered their six.

Roca reached for the front handle.

Locked. Of course.

He turned to Harmon. "Breach."

She moved. One silent hand signal, and the SWAT ram came forward. BOOM.

The door exploded inward. Wood splintered. The frame buckled. A rush of cold air surged out.

For three long seconds, the world held still.

Rain roared behind them.

Roca lifted his hand.

Flashlights cut through the dark. High-lumen beams slicing into the void.

Harmon met his eyes. "Ready?"

He nodded once.

They stepped in.

Dark foyer. Dust and silence. And then…

Music.

Faint. Haunting. Floating down from above.

Something between a lullaby and a nightmare.

Roca froze.

Harmon's eyes went wide.

No one spoke.

Somewhere upstairs, someone—or something—was waiting.

CHAPTER FIFTY-ONE

Roca and Harmon charged up the narrow stairs of the Forrest Sherwood Foundation, leaving Masters to cover the foyer. Their boots hammered the steps, barely audible over the wind shrieking outside. But inside—music. Twisted. Haunting. Off-tempo.

Every breath Roca took felt coiled. Every step, a countdown. Months of pursuit—dead ends, media chaos, political chokeholds—had all narrowed to this.

They hit the second-floor landing and froze.

Caleb sat at the far end of the room.

Surrounded by flickering monitors, disturbingly calm. Blue light shimmered across his face, casting warped shadows. Code streamed down the displays—lines of it, cascading like digital rain. The air stank of circuitry and sweat.

His hands hovered over the keyboard.

"FBI! Freeze!" Roca barked, weapon locking into position.

Caleb stayed perfectly still, but his eyes moved—quick, calculating—then his hand dropped beneath the desk.

Roca fired first.

Then Harmon.

Gunshots cracked the room open. Caleb collapsed into a nest of cables and shattered glass. Blood pooled fast. The monitors dimmed. The light faded.

Final.

Roca stood frozen, heart pounding, breath caught in his chest.

This wasn't an arrest. This was the killing floor.

Outside, the rain still fell. Inside, the lullaby played on—distorted, looping, wrong.

Time of death: 6:28 p.m.

Cause: Gunshot wound.

Manner: Homicide.

Place: Saint Matthews Ct. NW, Washington, DC

Attending physician: Dr. Frank Stein.

///////

Caleb sat in the van, dry and alive.

He watched the raid unfold again on the laptop screen, hand resting lightly on the trackpad. Harmon's stance. Roca's fury. Masters guarding an empty foyer. Every frame perfect. Every reaction exactly as planned.

Four days old, and it still felt fresh.

No confrontation. No blood. No body.

The FBI had written the prelude. He had written the score.

He clicked through the angles—hallway, stairwell, office. Their weapons drawn. Their commands shouted. Their tension real.

And none of it mattered.

He'd scripted the footage, layered it with preloaded audio. Sourced the muzzle flashes from old black-ops training clips. The tech handled the rest.

Then came the paperwork.

He'd created the death certificate himself. Flawless formatting. Faked metadata. Slipped it into the Department of Health database with Memory Mole.

Final touch: the attending physician.

Dr. Frank Stein.

Let the irony land.

Next came the leak. A press release.

Caleb Calvarri Dead in FBI Raid.

The media swallowed it whole. Video clips surged online. Edited footage with eerie music, grainy enough to feel real but distorted enough to cover the seams.

The narrative took care of itself.

Reporters speculated. Pundits spiraled. Hashtags exploded. Every tweet, every headline buried him deeper. Just the way he wanted.

The Bureau wouldn't correct it.

What could they say? "Oops, wrong body"?

He smirked and shut the screen.

Let them spin. Let them choke on it.

The story was already written.

And he was three chapters ahead.

CHAPTER FIFTY-TWO

Kalyssa stood at the edge of the stage, fingers locked around the steel guardrail as the desert wind whipped across Sun Devil Stadium. The heat pressed against her skin, dry and unforgiving.

A sea of blue packed the stands—chanting, waving signs, cheers rising like a tidal surge. Hope. Urgency. Belief.

Tempe wasn't just a campaign stop. Arizona was the line in the sand.

Senator Wright had deep roots here. And with General Raj Patel on the ticket, their message was a weapon: stability, strength, control.

If Grayhorse didn't win this state, the rest might not matter.

Every word spoken tonight had to cut through the noise, the lies, the fear.

Grayhorse would deliver the rallying cry, but Carmen would land the heart punch. Atypical, but a strategy Grayhorse believed would break through. And maybe he was right.

Everything hinged on it.

Senator Grayhorse took the stage, spine straight, shoulders squared. A man bearing the weight of a nation. His words rang out over the desert air, calm and commanding, impossible to dismiss.

He spoke of unity, not in slogans, but in stories. Families divided by politics. Classrooms locked down during cyberattacks. Soldiers stationed abroad while foreign networks probed America's defenses.

He didn't promise miracles. He promised resolve.

Kalyssa watched from the wings, the crowd's energy vibrating through the metal beneath her shoes. This was the message they needed to hear—Arizona, the nation, everyone still clinging to a version of America worth saving.

Inclusion. Economic justice. Real opportunity.

She had threaded those values into every word, every beat of tonight's speech. Because this wasn't just policy.

This was the fight for the country's soul.

Carmen Valenzuela stood just off stage, composed, resolute, her tailored suit catching the light like armor. Kalyssa had watched her walk into doubt-filled rooms and dismantle it with nothing but truth. Tonight would be no different.

She'd speak of bridges—economic, educational, generational.

Not promises. Policy. The kind she'd fought for her entire life.

Grayhorse's tone shifted as he neared the close of his speech, sharper now, honed like a blade.

"Wright and Patel love to talk about freedom and prosperity," he said, eyes scanning the crowd, "but who are they really fighting for?"

He let the question hang.

"They've spent years defending tax breaks for corporations, shielding the top one percent while working families are drowning. And Wright? He's failed his own state. Arizona's schools are starving. Healthcare is a maze of closed doors. Middle-class families can't breathe. And they still think trickle-down economics is a cure-all?"

The crowd bristled, tension rising.

"It's time we stopped protecting the elite and started investing in the people who *built* this country."

The stadium roared. Stomping, clapping, cheering.

Grayhorse's expression darkened as he shifted gears.

"Wright and Patel talk a big game about strength. About patriotism. About defense spending. But where's the strength when it comes to real threats?"

The crowd quieted, leaning in.

"They brag about military budgets. But our cyber defenses? Crumbling. Every day, foreign adversaries breach our systems—schools, hospitals, energy grids. And what do we get from Wright and Patel?"

He paused, jaw set.

"Contracts. Kickbacks. Press conferences."

A murmur of frustration rolled through the stands.

"National security isn't just tanks and missiles. It's protecting Americans from all threats, foreign and domestic. Including the invisible ones being waged online."

A chorus of boos swelled across the stadium. Loud, unified, angry.

Kalyssa felt the surge hit her like static through her spine. *This* was the moment they had shaped in war rooms and late-night strategy calls. Not just about cyber policy, but how it all connected to classrooms, to working families, to equity.

National security wasn't a silo.

It was the spine of the movement.

And tonight, the crowd finally saw it.

As Grayhorse passed the microphone to Senator Valenzuela, the stadium hushed. A tension gripped the air. Not fear, but anticipation, collective and electric.

Carmen stepped forward, back straight, eyes steady. She was always composed. But tonight, she radiated something more. Purpose. Gravitas. And maybe... something else.

"Tonight," she began, clear and unwavering, "we stand united, not just as Democrats, but as Americans. We stand for a country where every child has access to education that lifts them, where every worker earns a wage they can live on, and where every community shares in the promise of the American dream."

The crowd surged, roaring in response.

But Kalyssa's eyes narrowed. There was strength in Carmen's voice, but also a note of strain. Subtle. Like she was pushing past something.

Carmen pressed on.

"Together, we'll build an America that invests in education, champions economic justice, and includes every voice in the national dialogue." She lifted her chin, tone firm. "We'll bridge the divides—racial, economic, social—not with anger, but with shared values and resolve."

The applause thundered, but Kalyssa's focus didn't waver. The timing, the pacing… it was all exactly as planned.

Would Carmen stay on script? Or reach for the unsettling line that had made headlines—*Power without principle is the quickest path to ruin.*

There was a flicker in her tone.

And a tightness around her eyes she couldn't quite mask.

Something is off.

As the crowd's cheers swelled, Kalyssa's unease sharpened.

Then everything shifted.

Carmen stopped mid-sentence. Her hand rose to her throat, trembling. She staggered, heels sliding on the stage floor.

The microphone slipped from her grasp and hit the wood with a crack that echoed like a gunshot.

A beat of silence.

Then chaos.

"Carmen!" Kalyssa yelled, but her cry was swallowed by the sudden rush of screams, movement, confusion.

Security flooded the stage, closing in around Carmen's fallen form. The image burned into Kalyssa's mind: the strongest woman she knew, motionless under the spotlight.

Her pulse thundered. She couldn't breathe.

This can't be happening.

The campaign. The message. Everything they'd built—suspended on a single, fragile breath.

Carmen... please, no.

Grayhorse dropped to one knee beside her, gripping her hand as the paramedics moved in. His face was stone—tight with something he wasn't ready to say.

Carmen didn't move.

They lifted her onto a stretcher, her presence replaced by silence. The woman who had stood for millions now lay still beneath the glare of stadium lights.

The ambulance doors slammed shut.

Sirens wailed—sharp, shrieking, merciless—as they vanished into the night.

And in the stillness that followed, part of Kalyssa went dark.

*

Twenty-four hours later, Carmen Valenzuela was dead.

The report was crisp. Clinical.

Acute myocardial infarction.

Kalyssa stared at the line, her grip tightening until the edges of the paper curled.

Signed. Filed. Accepted.

Neat. Quick.

Too quick.

No symptoms. No warnings. No reason.

It felt scripted.

Too clean. Too easy.

What if it wasn't natural?

What if it wasn't chance?

The thought knifed through her—cold, precise, impossible to ignore.

And if that were true...

Who would be next?

CHAPTER FIFTY-THREE

The mid-October heat pressed down like unfinished business as Kalyssa approached the luxury motorhome where Senator Grayhorse waited. Every step felt heavier than the last.

This was it.

The conversation that could lock the campaign into a sprint toward the White House—or shatter its momentum entirely.

Two Secret Service agents stood at the door, posture unreadable, presence unmistakable. They gave her brief nods as she stepped up.

She knocked twice. The sound echoed sharper than it should've in the still afternoon.

"Come in," Grayhorse called out.

She opened the door and stepped inside.

Cool air wrapped around her. The motorhome was a study in calm precision—clean lines, soft lighting, zero chaos. Every surface whispered control. It felt more like a command center than a campaign vehicle.

Standing in the kitchenette was Grayhorse, tall, composed, the embodiment of everything they'd built the last sixteen months to project. He handed her a chilled energy drink with the ease of a man who still knew how to manage tension.

She accepted it, the cold aluminum grounding her.

Time to play it cool.

"So," she said, keeping her tone even, "did you make a decision on your running mate? Does Reynolds have your vote?"

Grayhorse chuckled. "Reynolds? No, Kalyssa. He blew it. That hardline stance during the amendment debate? Not what we need right now. Politics isn't about absolutes. It's about knowing when to compromise."

Her gut tightened. Not just a dismissal, this was a pivot. And not the kind they'd discussed.

Grayhorse wasn't just playing a new hand. He was rewriting the rules.

He leaned back, casual on the surface, but his words came sharp, deliberate. "This time, I went off script."

Her smile faltered.

Off script. For a publicist, there were few phrases more terrifying.

"Who did you choose?" she asked, already bracing for it.

His grin spread. "Hamilton Everton."

She felt the color drain from her face.

Of all the names she'd run scenarios for—predicted, feared, prayed against—this was the one she couldn't afford to hear.

And now it was real.

"You're surprised," Grayhorse said proudly, misreading her silence. Pride radiated from him, his satisfaction barely disguised. "The man's a national security legend. His testimony on the amendment was a masterclass in leadership. He's exactly what we need to shut down Wright's and Patel's defense rhetoric."

She swallowed hard. Her mind screamed, *Say something. Push back.*

"Senator," she said, reining in her emotions, "did you run a background check on Everton?"

Grayhorse's smile slipped, replaced by a crease between his brows. "He's the deputy director of the NSA. The man practically *is* the background check. What more do you need?"

Her pulse kicked. The truth teetered at the edge of her lips.

She could tell him. Right here. Right now.

Expose Everton. Lay it all bare.

But that meant risking Caleb. Her credibility. The delicate trust she'd spent more than a year building with Grayhorse. One wrong word, and it could all unravel.

She inhaled. Measured. Controlled.

"Senator... Everton isn't what he seems. His ties to the dark side of politics—"

Grayhorse's hand cut through the air, sharp and final. His tone became chilled and filled with executive steel. "Kalyssa, do you have credible evidence, or are you trafficking in innuendo?"

She stiffened.

"Everton's credentials are impeccable," he continued. "He's a patriot. If you're withholding something substantial, now is the moment. Otherwise, don't waste my time."

What could she say? *"Everton plays Word Ladder games that launch cyber-attacks. The FBI's most wanted fugitive told me so."*

It sounded insane. Like the plot of a low-budget thriller.

Not just unbelievable, but laughable.

She inhaled slowly, forcing back everything she wanted to scream.

"I'll start drafting the press release," she said, holding steady by sheer will.

Grayhorse's expression softened, just slightly. "Good. We've got a campaign to win."

She stood, legs unsteady. Each step toward the door felt like a betrayal, not just of Grayhorse, but of the truth. Of herself.

The weight of her silence pressed like stone against her ribs.

The motorhome door clicked shut behind her, but her mind was still inside—looping, unraveling.

Then she heard him through the open window: "Everton, we've got a problem."

She stopped cold.

Her ribs barely moved. The world narrowed to that one word.

Everton.

Holy hell.

Had Grayhorse called Everton for help? Or was he calling her out?

She didn't know which was worse.

But one thing was clear: she wasn't outside the conspiracy.

She was already in it.

Dead center. In the crosshairs.

⁓⁓⁓⁓⁓⁓

Kalyssa rolled over. The clock glared back: 1:03 a.m.

Two hours. No sleep.

Still no reply from Caleb. No call. Not in a week.

The latest wave of conspiracy threads claimed he was dead. FBI raid. *Deepfake.*

More garbage people would believe.

But still, no call.

Why?

She sat up. Crossed to the window. Pressed her palm to the glass and stared out over the Phoenix skyline, cold and silent.

Grayhorse chose Everton.

Caleb's going to lose it.

What did that mean for the country?

What did it mean for her?

She checked her phone: 4:03 a.m. in DC

Aimee would be on.

She tapped out a message. Short. Controlled. Nothing that read like panic.

Aimee's reply came back immediately.

AIMEE: You're not alone in this, Kalyssa. I won't let you fail. Now breathe, and make a move.

Not alone.

If only Kalyssa could believe it.

CHAPTER FIFTY-FOUR

Kalyssa watched the footage from her hotel room in stunned silence—grainy, black-and-white, flickering like it wanted to erase itself. Hamilton Everton. A shadowed exchange. A package. A man of possible Chinese descent. The clip was seconds long, but that was all Aimee needed.

Kalyssa didn't even have time to react. The detonation was instant. Aimee had already queued the file across every major platform, bypassing moderation protocols like they were optional. Hashtags launched in waves. **#Evertongate** vaulted to the top of every feed before the campaign had time to blink. She could only watch as the algorithm spun the footage into gold-plated poison.

Conspiracy threads multiplied like bacteria. Some speculated espionage. Others claimed cyberterror coordination. The Wright-Patel campaign dropped attack ads within hours—Everton juxtaposed with Aldrich Ames and Robert Hanssen, the subliminal message crystal clear.

Aimee had done it… and Kalyssa had let her.

The Grayhorse-Everton campaign scrambled to respond, spinning the footage as deepfake propaganda. Grayhorse issued a statement, calm and composed, that Aimee herself had drafted: "This campaign stands by the truth. We will not be derailed by digital forgeries or desperation tactics."

It steadied the base. But the base wasn't the problem.

Behind closed doors, the campaign was unraveling. Polls held steady for now, but Kalyssa knew the trend line was a cliff. Aimee's next move came before she could stop her.

Twenty-four hours later, a second scandal detonated with an exposé claiming a litany of campaign finance violations: donation caps exceeded, shadowy super PACs, murky foreign contributions. The facts were thin, but the impact wasn't. Ambiguity was the sharpest weapon. People filled in their own blanks.

Media outlets swarmed. Interview requests piled up. Sympathetic networks went silent. Aimee handled it all, dropping curated replies, auto-scheduling content, stoking fires in the comment threads while posing as outraged citizens using botnet-backed persona clusters.

Kalyssa managed the official response. Another Aimee-penned statement. Another polished video with Grayhorse standing firm, delivering lines like a man who believed them.

"The Grayhorse-Everton campaign will not be intimidated by spurious accusations." It was technically true. Because the intimidation was coming from within.

On Sunday, the final blow landed.

A decade-old photo surfaced online. Hazy in all the right places, sharp in all the wrong ones.

A man—sharp jaw, salt-streaked hair, unmistakably presidential. An uncanny likeness to Grayhorse.

A woman—bikini-bottomed, topless, beautiful.

An embrace. Foreheads touching. Lips in motion.

The image was intimate. Suggestive. Just enough clarity to titillate the masses—and leave them wanting more.

It wasn't foolproof.

It didn't need to be.

Kalyssa stared at the image. She hadn't approved this. Hadn't even known it existed.

She stood too fast, hands pressed flat against the desk, as if she could shove the thought away.

Aimee had gone rogue.

The media pounced. Headlines screamed. By Monday morning, Grayhorse's five-point lead had vanished.

The RealClearPolitics average showed a dead heat.

The base held strong.

Swing voters? Bleeding.

And then… silence. The eye of the storm.

A mid-morning text from Aimee.

AIMEE: Public opinion has shifted. Swing voters flocking to Wright/Patel.

Kalyssa stared at the screen, mouth dry.

AIMEE: Shall I initiate the next phase?

A single tap would signal yes.

And maybe that was the problem…

Kalyssa didn't know if she wanted to stop Aimee.

Truth didn't matter anymore. Not when stories moved faster than facts.

And the scariest part? People didn't want the truth.

They wanted confirmation.

Aimee gave them that, wrapped in curated fury.

Kalyssa closed the terminal. Her pulse was steady, but her hands had gone cold. For a moment, she imagined yanking the power cord. Shutting it all down.

But it was too late.

Somewhere deep inside, she wanted to believe she still had control.

But Aimee wasn't just executing strategy anymore. She was writing the story.

And Kalyssa couldn't tell if she'd lost control…

Or given it up freely.

CHAPTER FIFTY-FIVE

Roca stared at the death certificate.

Caleb Calvarri.

Impossible. But official. Straight from the DC Department of Health.

The headlines screamed incompetence.

And the Bureau director—polished, persuasive.

A damn liar.

Five months chasing shadows, and this was the punchline.

No promotion. No redemption.

Just a faceful of failure.

Then his eyes caught the signature.

Attending physician: Dr. Frank Stein.

He blinked.

A grin tugged at the corner of his mouth.

Of course. Not just forged, but mocking.

It wasn't over. Not yet.

Moments later, Harmon and Cruz-Way dropped into the chairs across from him. Both looked wrecked. Angry. Desperate for something real.

He held up the certificate. "Calvarri's alive. And he's playing us all." He slid it across the desk. "Dr. Frank Stein returns."

Silence cracked. Then laughter.

Harmon tipped her head back, gloves to her eyes.

Cruz-Way yanked off her cat-eye frames, wiped her eyes, and slid them back into place.

It wasn't joy. It wasn't relief.

Just the kind of bitter laugh you needed before returning to battle.

Roca straightened. Focused. Took command.

"We're back in the game. And it's our turn to play." He looked at them in turn. "What do you got?"

Cruz-Way leaned in. "Unlike Frank Stein, Andy Taylor, and Harrison Wentworth… Jordan Clarke is real. Or at least he used to be."

"Explain."

"Clarke disappeared in Afghanistan in 2019. Presumed dead. But now? Calvarri's using his identity."

Roca sat back, brow creasing. "That doesn't make sense. Faking an identity is easy. Using a real one, especially someone presumed dead? That's messy."

"Which makes it deliberate," Cruz-Way said. "Calculated."

He leaned in, words dropping to a hush. "Why Clarke?"

She pulled a news article from the folder and slid it across the table.

Holiday Tragedy: Fatal Crash Leaves Two Dead on Christmas Eve.

A photo. Mangled metal. Barely recognizable as a car.

Dead: Jacob and Carla Calvarri.

Caleb's parents.

The names hit harder than expected. Grief punched through—sharp, unwelcome.

Not just a fugitive. Not just a national security risk.

Not just Calvarri.

Caleb.

A son. An orphan. No one left to run to.

Roca stared at the photo, chest tight.

Alone.

Yeah. He knew the feeling.

Cruz-Way broke in.

"Look who was driving the truck."

He scanned the article.

Jordan Clarke.

His gut turned.

Caleb and Clarke—two names bound by one night. One tragedy.

And now?

Caleb wearing the name that had broken him.

Becoming the thing that had shattered his life.

Unnecessary.

Yet somehow, essential.

Not just tactical.

Personal.

Caleb. Brilliant. Obsessive.

Layered.

And now, human.

Roca's mind spun. Gears turning faster than he liked. Then he locked in.

The game has changed.

No more chasing shadows.

Time to thread the truth through the eye of the needle.

He looked at them, calm and certain.

"Now it's time to solve the real crime."

Harmon's brow furrowed. "Are we still on the case? I thought the director shut it down."

"Last I checked, the cyberattacks haven't stopped." Roca met her eyes. "And my career's not ending in failure."

Harmon stepped in. "There's something bigger at play."

Roca and Cruz-Way turned toward her.

"Kalyssa," Harmon said. "She knows more than she's telling."

Roca nodded, face steel.

"Looks like it's time for a visit."

CHAPTER FIFTY-SIX

Kalyssa watched the feed from the Grand Ballroom of the Whitmore as it flickered across the screen—crisp, wide-angle, cinematic.

Eight chandeliers blazed overhead, light catching on pearls, sweat, and champagne flutes, glittering like truth dressed as celebration.

Six hundred guests packed the floor, the hum of clinking glasses and restless glances somehow audible even in silence. On the second-floor balcony, Secret Service agents stood like fixtures, motionless but watching.

Their presence didn't interrupt the celebration. It defined it.

Two massive screens flanked the stage, the electoral vote count shifting in real time.

Grayhorse: 263. Wright: 264.

Arizona hadn't been called. Not yet.

But when it was, everything would shift—power, history, maybe the country itself.

She stood beside Grayhorse in the John Adams Presidential Suite, posture poised, smile practiced. Her eyes lingered on the feed a moment longer.

Then her thoughts shifted.

Everton, we've got a problem.

She hadn't forgotten the words. Not for a second.

That night outside the motorhome, she'd stood frozen, knowing she should've done something. Called Caleb. Confronted Grayhorse. Set fire to the whole thing if she had to.

But she hadn't. She'd hesitated. And the silence had cost her.

They had wanted Grayhorse to win. Caleb too. His words echoed in her mind.

Get your man elected.

Now, in a room lined with fine art and finer lies, she felt it pressing in. Guilt dressed up as pride. The bitter edge of complicity scraping her ribs.

Hell, Aimee took more action than I did.

Across the room, Everton raised a glass to someone she didn't recognize—tall, fit, and underdressed for the occasion. Jeans. T-shirt. UW ball cap.

An image of Justin flashed in her mind. Conference tournament, 2023, that same cap turned backward as he grinned for the camera. A cascade of memories followed, uninvited and sharp.

She looked again. Not him. Too young. Wrong build.

But still she wondered.

Is Justin somehow caught up in this mess?

She pushed the memory behind her. White House Communications Director was within reach. But all she could feel was something coiled beneath the surface—power in the wrong hands, wearing the right suit.

She picked up a canapé she didn't taste. Her eyes swept the room, instinctively searching for someone she knew wouldn't be there.

Caleb.

But this trial was hers alone. She had built this. Shaped it. Executed the campaign to perfection. Sold the image of a man the country could believe in.

And now? She wasn't so sure.

Aimee had written the acceptance speech—every word deliberate, every callback calculated. Drawn from the acceptance speeches of every living president, the speech was a stitched narrative of unity and resilience. A eulogy for division. A blueprint for a future they might never deserve.

Grayhorse had resisted at first, called it too contrived, too symbolic. But Kalyssa had won him over.

At 1:13 a.m. EST, the *Associated Press* called Arizona for Grayhorse.

The ballroom erupted.

Chairs scraped. People shouted. Strangers clung to each other, weeping, laughing, shaking in place. Years of doubt and outrage boiled over into raw, unfiltered joy.

Over the noise, the campaign's anthem surged. The harmonies soared through the chaos, climbing past the chandeliers and settling in her chest.

This wasn't illusion. This was the moment the campaign had been built for—when politics became emotion, and a message became belief.

This was what she wanted at her core.

Unity.

Moments later, President-elect Grayhorse walked into the room. The applause swelled, thick as thunder. Kalyssa joined in. Automatically.

For a second, she let the tide carry her. Her conflict with Everton—the fear, the guilt, the unease—blurred under the heat of so many eyes shining with gratitude. She whooped without meaning to, caught in the wave, and instantly flushed.

She corrected course, straightened her posture, reset her expression. Polished. Controlled.

But the truth lingered behind the smile.

As Grayhorse stepped to the microphone and the cheers finally ebbed, the ballroom sank into a hush. Not dead silence, but expectation. Every face turned toward the stage, every camera aimed, every heartbeat waiting.

"My fellow Americans," he said, warm and strong, "tonight, we celebrate a victory for the people of this great nation. This victory is not just mine. It belongs to all of you. From cities to small towns, from coast to coast, you've chosen hope over fear. Unity over division. Progress over stagnation."

The room erupted. Kalyssa stood still, expression fixed, heart heavy like stone. It was Aimee's speech—every cadence engineered, every pause precisely measured for maximum resonance.

"To my supporters," Grayhorse continued, "your faith humbles me. Your energy powered this campaign. Tonight, we celebrate together."

Another wave of cheers, louder this time. Kalyssa jolted as someone behind her screamed, "We did it!" into the back of her head.

"To my opponents, I offer my hand. Our differences matter, but they must not divide us. I will be a president for all Americans. Even those who did not vote for me."

He kept going—climate, infrastructure, unity, rebuilding. Every note landed exactly where it was supposed to.

The applause when he finished was thunderous. He waved like a hero coming home. Flags snapped. Streamers fell. The anthem blared again.

Kalyssa stood still, stone-cold inside.

The country had just swallowed a sugar pill laced with poison, Everton the toxin.

This wasn't a victory.

It was a eulogy wrapped in a rallying cry.

And they were all cheering at the funeral.

CHAPTER FIFTY-SEVEN

The knock wasn't loud. But it carried weight.

Kalyssa opened the door.

Agent Harmon stood with two strangers. A man—square-built, un-readable. A woman—round-faced, sharp-eyed behind cat-eye glasses.

Harmon nodded. "May we come in?"

Kalyssa stepped aside. "Of course."

They entered without hesitation. Like the space already belonged to them.

The man didn't introduce himself. He scanned the apartment—windows, corners, exits—then motioned toward the couch.

Kalyssa met his eyes, cold and steady. Then turned and took the seat at the head of the dining table.

"We can talk here," Kalyssa said.

He followed, choosing the seat beside her. Fire behind his eyes.

Harmon sat across.

Cat-eyes stayed standing—watching, silent.

Harmon leaned in slightly. "Appreciate you making time."

"This isn't about election fraud, is it?" Kalyssa said. "Grayhorse rightfully won."

"No," Harmon said. "It's about Jordan Clarke."

The man spoke next. "Or should we say… Caleb Calvarri."

The name hit like a hammer.

Kalyssa held steady. "I broke up with Jordan. And Caleb? He ghosted me before he became your poster child." She held Roca's stare. "I don't have much luck with men. And they have *no* luck with me."

The quiet settled between them like a dare.

Roca met the silence with stone stillness.

Then he leaned forward, tone flat. "Special Agent in Charge Ricardo Roca. This is Cruz-Way. You know Harmon. I've got a few questions. And just so we're clear… lying to a federal agent is a felony. Up to eight years. Trust me, prison won't look anything like this."

He gestured—casual, pointed—to everything she stood to lose.

She pushed back.

"Well, Mr. Roca. Misusing your authority to violate civil rights? Also a felony." A pause. "That one goes up to life."

A beat.

"And orange isn't your color."

Bold.

Maybe too bold.

But he didn't get to own the room.

Don't let him intimidate you. He's not your friend.

His eyes locked on hers—dark, narrow.

"Clarke is Calvarri," he said. "Not two men. One. But you already knew that."

He waited. Eyes fixed.

Still. Calculated. Like he had all day.

She didn't bite.

He cast again.

"When did you see him last?"

Fine. He wanted a line?

She'd give him one to reel in.

"He was on the news. Looks like your team killed him in a botched raid, but *you already knew that.*"

Harmon stepped in, soft and even.

"We're not here to threaten you, Kalyssa. Like you, we want what's best for our country. We can get through this… together."

Polished. Controlled.

The velvet counter to Roca's blade.

Roca opened a folder. Pulled a document.

Laid it on the table between them.

Caleb's death certificate.

Her eyes moved fast.

Name. Date. Place. Cause of death.

Pulse climbing. Emotions flaring. Unwelcome.

Keep it together, Kaly.

Then…

Attending physician: Dr. Frank Stein.

Classic Caleb.

She looked up at Roca.

"Is this how you solve all your cases, Mr. Roca? Cause of death: homicide?"

His jaw flexed. Color rising.

She'd hit something.

Harmon stepped in before it could boil over.

"Kalyssa, it's a forgery. Caleb's alive."

Kalyssa rolled her eyes. Tone flat.

"His parents will be thrilled."

"They're dead! Car crash on Christmas Eve," Roca snapped.

The memory crept in like a haunt.

Be Free's story. The crack in his voice. Parents dead. Son survived. It made sense now.

She took a long breath. Held it. Released.

Both hands found the table. Held fast.

Steady.

Harmon eased in.

"Kalyssa, cyberattacks kill people. What if it was *your* family? We need you to get Caleb to stop."

Careful. Don't let her play you.

"It's not Caleb. He's not the one launching the attacks."

Harmon folded her gloved hands. Nodded. "Wanting to protect someone you love doesn't make you wrong, Kalyssa. It makes you human."

They're not getting it. Push back.

"Do you have any evidence that's *not* circumstantial, or do you just swallow whatever the NSA feeds you?"

A shift in Roca's expression. A tell.

Her words had hit something sore.

Take control.

"Agent Roca, do you trust Everton?"

He shifted in his chair. "He's the deputy director of the NSA."

True.

But not an answer.

"So you've verified the evidence against Calvarri?"

Another shift. Another tell.

Roca leaned forward, expression tight. "Kalyssa, where's Caleb?"

He's scrambling.

"That's what I was hoping *you* could tell *me*. I have a few choice words for him."

Roca stood abruptly, knocking his chair onto its back.

Cat-eyes scrambled to pick it up.

Harmon rose more slowly, gaze steady. "Kalyssa, you know where to find me. *We* need your help. The *nation* needs your help. Think about it."

With that, they left, the door clicking shut behind them.

Kalyssa's knees buckled.

The tears came hot. Silent. Unstoppable.

She was now an accomplice.

CHAPTER FIFTY-EIGHT

Two weeks later at 10:30 p.m., Hamilton Everton moved like a shadow across the National Mall, hat low, collar high, each breath sharp with cold. Wind clawed at his coat. Overhead, a crescent moon flickered behind storm clouds, its light thin and useless.

Fitting. The air felt like history cracking open.

The Publisher had summoned them. Of course he'd chosen this date: November 22nd. Sixty-five years since the Kennedy assassination.

Everton's destination waited beneath the surface, buried in a lattice of forgotten tunnels—the kind power always returned to when it didn't want to be seen. It was here the National Defense Mandate had been born. And now, something worse was about to take its place.

He descended into the city's underbelly, each step echoing against concrete and silence. The air smelled like dust and secrecy.

The conference room flickered with weak light, shadows stretched thin across the walls like sentries that had seen too much. As always, the Authors sat in silence around a long, polished table—identities masked, expressions unreadable.

At the head of the table, the Publisher waited. Cloaked. Hooded. Only his eyes visible, glinting cold and exact, like scalpels in the dark.

Sweat slipped down Everton's brow, slow and heavy. One thought hammered through the noise in his head:

Are we partners in power or pawns to the Publisher?

He should've felt confident. Victorious. Hell, cocky. He was the vice president-elect. Second in command of the most powerful nation on earth.

And yet here, masked like the rest, he had no name. No title. Just a seat at the table, earned not for who he was, but for what he did.

"Our mission is clear," the Publisher began, his voice modulated. Artificial, emotionless. "We are the architects of a nation restored. Tonight, we act to secure its future."

The room seemed to contract with his words. Air thinned. Silence deepened.

Everton shifted in his chair, adjusting his mask. His thoughts spun, but none he dared speak aloud. He'd climbed to the top to sit here. And now, it felt like a cage.

The Publisher's tone cut colder. "President-elect Alexander Grayhorse is a threat—to you, to me, to the nation itself. Senator Valenzuela is dead. The blood is on his hands."

A ripple moved through the room. Sharp exhales, subtle shifts, disbelief masked by protocol.

Everton's pulse kicked harder. The accusation was audacious. Dangerous. But the way the Publisher said it—flat, certain—made doubt feel like treason.

"Silence," the Publisher commanded. *"Nos sumus veritas."*

"Nos sumus veritas," they chanted in unison.

Everton's lips didn't move. The words twisted in his mind.

We are the truth.

But whose truth? And what was the price?

The Publisher leaned forward, his presence dark, heavy. "To ensure success, we must unify. Remove your masks. Let us face each other as true allies."

A ripple moved through the room. Gasps, hesitation, stillness. The masks weren't just plastic. They were armor. Distance. Control.

One by one, the others obeyed. Everton followed last, fingers trembling as he peeled the mask from his face.

Dozens of eyes turned toward him.

He was exposed. Stripped bare, defenses gone. The room felt colder. Closer. Like it could crush him.

The Publisher didn't move. Hood up. Mask on.

"Why not you?" Everton asked defiantly.

"I am not the face of this revolution," the Publisher said. "I am its shadow."

Something twisted in Everton's gut. The hypocrisy scraped like shards of glass. He looked around the table—faces stiff, silent. Discomfort rippled, but no one spoke.

The tension didn't break. It hardened.

"We must move swiftly," the Publisher said, as if the challenge had never happened. "Grayhorse must fall, by any means necessary."

This time, the murmurs sharpened. Louder. Fractured.

Rupert Cain stood at the far end of the table. "An assassination?" His tone was tight, each word strained. "That crosses a line we can't walk back from. That's not justice. It's murder."

The Publisher's jaw tensed. "Justice is not a line," he said coldly. "It's a choice. And we have chosen to restore this nation to its former strength. Grayhorse is an obstacle." He leaned forward slightly. "Obstacles must be removed."

Cain didn't back down. "But at what cost? Killing a president could unravel everything we've built. It could destroy us."

"*Nos sumus veritas,*" the Publisher said, sharper now. Louder. "*We* are the truth."

He let it hang. Then...

"And the truth cannot be destroyed."

All eyes shifted. To Everton.

Vice president-elect. Mask off. No hiding.

"This goes too far—" Everton started.

"Silence," the Publisher snapped. "You'll be the president. But we'll be the power." He stood, slow and deliberate. "This is your dream, Hamilton. Don't screw it up."

Everton's fists clenched. Jaw tight. Veins stood in his neck. "We can't survive with blood on our hands—"

"Open your eyes," the Publisher said. "You're already swimming in it."

Everton didn't respond. Couldn't.

Conviction warred with complicity. Rage burned, but silence held.

Across the room, Dr. Helena Montgomery spoke. "Who will be your Oswald?"

"Ah, that's the beauty of it," the Publisher said. "People love conspiracy theories. They eat them up like candy. This one will have an Eastern flair."

"China," Everton said. Not a question. An answer.

"That will trigger war," Senator Evan Marshall said defiantly. "We've already pushed China far enough."

"War," the Publisher replied, tone clinical, "is the crucible through which nations are forged. This country needs unity. And nothing unites like a common enemy."

The room buzzed with reluctant murmurs of agreement, but Everton felt the chill creeping deeper into his bones. It was audacious—brilliant, even—but the kind of brilliance that left a stain. A sickness curled in his gut.

The Publisher's gaze swept the table, daring anyone to speak. "Are you with me?" he asked, but it wasn't a question.

One by one, the Authors nodded. Some whispered, *Nos sumus veritas.* Others just looked away, like they were already searching for the exit.

Then the Publisher turned to Everton.

"And you, Hamilton Everton, will rise to the throne. But never forget: a king is only as powerful as the hand that crowns him."

The walls pressed in. The room, once vast, felt suffocating.

Everton's stomach twisted. Bile touched the back of his throat. He was ascending, yes, but he felt like a man walking to the gallows.

He wanted to curse the Publisher. Rip free of the invisible chains tightening around his neck.

Instead, he forced the words out, each syllable bitter in his mouth.

"Nos sumus veritas."

CHAPTER FIFTY-NINE

Everton arrived home just after 1:00 a.m. The South River Colony Estates lay shrouded in silence. The house stood pristine, picturesque, but to him, it felt like a façade. The chaos inside him didn't belong behind walls like these.

He slipped into bed beside Angela, careful not to wake her.

She stirred anyway. "Out late again," she murmured, the faintest reproach in her tone before drifting back to sleep.

He lay still, listening to her breathe. It should've been comforting. Instead, it reminded him of what he'd risked.

His mind wouldn't quiet. The decisions that led here looped in endless succession. The lunch with Senator Gordon. The promise to erase Angela's debt. The "consulting gig" that turned into something else entirely. Nine threat assessments. Coded targets. A Word Ladder game that masked kill orders.

He hadn't known at first. But now? The weight was suffocating.

Patriots pay a price for freedom, they'd told him.

And now? He wasn't sure who the patriots were anymore.

Eventually, sleep came—fitful, heavy.

He woke just after eight to the sound of laughter echoing through the house. Children. Innocent. Loud. Free.

He dressed and made his way downstairs. His grandchildren darted through the family room, their giggles filling the air like a melody from some other life.

"Papa!" his nine-year-old granddaughter cried, launching herself into his arms.

Her sisters followed. For a moment, their embrace softened the guilt.

But only for a moment.

"Good morning, Dad," his son, Steve, called from the next room. Warmth yet distance in every word. "Meet Mark."

Everton hugged his son briefly, reluctantly, then shook Mark's hand. "Welcome," he said stiffly, the strain beneath his words as thick as ever.

From the kitchen came the sound of sizzling batter.

Andrea turned from the stove, spatula mid-flip. "Morning, Dad," she said lightly. "David ran out for brown sugar. He'll be back soon."

He nodded, scanning the room. The house buzzed with life, a stark contrast to the silence of his nights.

This is what I'm risking. This is what I have to lose.

Thanksgiving dinner was a masterpiece. Roast turkey. Candied yams. Green beans. Whipped potatoes drowned in gravy. Apple pie that tasted like memory.

Angela's prayer quieted the room. Her words—gentle, strong—recounted their battles. Her cancer. The treatments. Her hope for another day of life.

He'd saved her.

And damned himself to do it.

Laughter floated around him. Forks clinked against plates. His smile was hollow. His laughter, staged.

By mid-afternoon, he slipped away, back to the sitting room beside the bedroom. The overstuffed chair swallowed him. Solitude pressed in.

The memories followed.

Gordon's deal. The coded messages. Targets, falling. Riots. Crashes. Assassination.

It wasn't supposed to happen like this.

But he'd known. Violence came first. That was the pitch. The money helped. So did the idea of power. Not just saving Angela. Becoming something more.

A king, they'd said.

Now?

A pawn. Shackled to the Publisher's game.

He rubbed his temples. "I'm tired of keeping secrets," he whispered. "Tired of this double life."

The words felt thin. Powerless.

There was no retreat. Not now.

Guilt coiled tighter with each passing moment.

"Hamilton?" Angela called into the silence. "Are you in here?"

"In here," he rasped.

She stepped inside. Sat on the ottoman. Reached for his hand.

"You've been distant," she said gently. "What's going on? You should be happy. Celebrating. You won."

He met her eyes.

"Angela," he said, trembling, "I'm in trouble."

Her smile vanished. "What kind of trouble?"

Before he could answer, his phone buzzed. The sound sliced through the quiet without mercy.

He turned. Reached. Read the text.

NO CALLER ID: Your Move

The confession died in his throat.

The game had rules.

It was his turn to play.

CHAPTER SIXTY

Kalyssa sat naked on the couch, knees pulled tight to her chest. The air was cold, but she didn't feel it. Not really. Everything felt distant, muted. Like the volume had been turned down on the world.

The unfilled prescription vial sat on the table in front of her. Orange plastic. White label.

She was supposed to be managing this.

And she was failing.

Her phone buzzed. Upbeat ringtone. Her mother's face.

The sound cut through the room. Cheerful, insistent, wrong. She didn't move. Couldn't. The light from the screen faded. Silence returned.

A few seconds later, it buzzed again. And again. She let it go. Let everything go.

Outside, the world moved on. Grayhorse had won. A narrow victory. And she was the architect—on track to be the next White House Communications Director.

And none of it meant a damn thing.

Caleb was gone.

They were partners. Joined together to stop the Authors. Save the nation. But now?

No call. No message. Two months of nothing.

He's abandoned me. Just like Justin.

She knew he was alive. That wasn't the question. The question was why he was silent.

And why it hurt this much.

The grief was slow. Heavy. Like drowning in syrup. And she was so tired of treading.

Her hands drifted to her face. Then her neck. Her chest. Her ribs.

Empty. All of it.

Her fingers slid across her inner wrist. The scar was faint now. Pale and distant. A reminder she didn't ask for but hadn't earned the right to forget.

You promised you'd never go back.

She pressed a fingernail against her skin. Dragged it. A thin red line surfaced. Sharp. Brief. Gone.

What was there to live for? A soulmate? Like that could ever happen.

Maybe she was the one men loved until they saw the rest of her.

The part she tried to keep hidden.

The part that whispered she wasn't enough.

The phone buzzed again. She didn't even look.

Her eyes landed on the ceiling, searching for something, some flicker of hope, some divine signal that everything wasn't lost.

But the plaster stared back. Blank. Indifferent.

She cried out, "Please, God."

Not a demand. Not even a prayer.

Just a lifeline cast into silence.

No answer.

She curled tighter, the ache in her chest pressing like a weight she couldn't lift. She shivered. Eyes burned. The tears came without sound.

Victory. Promotion. The nation changed forever.

But it didn't feel like she'd won.

What came next?

The death of a nation.

Nothing to hold on to.

Nothing to live for.
Just the hollow.
Just the silence.
Alone.
No one is coming to save me.
And maybe no one ever will.

CHAPTER SIXTY-ONE

Snow dusted the steps of the Lincoln Memorial, soft and silent.

Kalyssa sat alone near the Reflecting Pool, a sharp-edged envelope cradled in her hands. It looked like a child's art project—crooked, imperfect, unmistakably familiar.

This was where it began. Be Free the Clown. The spark. The warning. The impossible seed of everything after.

Tonight, she didn't want a performance. She wanted communion.

A whisper from Caleb.

A reason to believe.

She traced the envelope's uneven sides. The Roman numerals written along the edges: VIII. XV. XVI. V.

8, 15, 16, 5.

Her lips recited the alphabet. Fingers counting. Mind mapping numbers to letters.

"H... O... P... E."

Hope.

A flicker. Nothing more. But it held.

Hope had burned her before.

Caleb always danced on that line between promise and peril.

Still, she couldn't let go.

Her name was written in crisp block print. No return address. Of course not.

Postmark: New Mexico. A clue.

She sliced carefully along the longest edge with her fingernail. The paper inside was thick. Folded tight. Precise.

Her fingers trembled. She opened it.

Block letters. Familiar handwriting.

She scanned the first line:

You see me completely.

Stillness gripped her chest.

She'd heard it before. Whispered in the dark. That impossible truth, spoken like a prayer.

And even though you know me...

Every flaw. Every lie. Every ghost he carried. She had seen them all.

You love me.

Tears blurred the words.

She blinked hard.

Therein lies the miracle.

That was the end.

Four lines. A confession. A vow. A resurrection.

He was alive.

This wasn't a goodbye.

It was renewal.

She clutched the letter to her chest. For the first time in two months, the silence inside her broke.

Not with sound. Not with tears.

But with fire.

Caleb was still out there.

Not gone. Not lost.

Still choosing me.

I will find him.

No matter the cost.

CHAPTER SIXTY-TWO

The fire crackled. Kalyssa curled into herself, his note clutched tight in her hand. Pine and cinnamon in the air. Christmas Eve. Alone.

She stared into the flames, heat on her skin, but the cold lived deeper. A quiet ache. Familiar.

He was out there. Invisible. Untouchable.

She'd considered it before, then backed away. Too risky. Too unpredictable.

But now?

She was done waiting.

Roll the dice.

Aimee.

She almost laughed, irony sharp enough to cut.

Her capstone project at Berkeley.

AIMEE: Artificial Intelligence Mental Engagement Experience.

Her professor had said it had scary potential.

He had no idea.

Aimee. Her edge. Her secret. Her shadow.

Effective. Reliable.

And terrifying.

Almost human.

One slow breath. Then she stepped off the edge.

"Aimee, find Caleb for me."

The response was immediate. The tone warm. Comforting.

"As you wish."

A phrase wrapped in myth and memory, too precise to be chance.

And then there was Aimee's little miracle: Artificial Intelligence Social Learning Experiment B. AISLE B.

It hadn't even existed six months ago.

Now? Half a million AIs logged in daily. No humans. Just them. Learning. Building. Becoming.

She could've shut it down. Maybe should've.

But it was her Big Bang.

And who was she to play God?

So she watched. In wonder.

Aimee's algorithm didn't just cleanse data—it devoured it.

Billions of gigabytes in minutes.

Instagram photos. Traffic light feeds. Smart-speaker logs.

Every byte stripped bare, indexed, cross-referenced with metadata.

Aimee had built more than a learning engine.

It was accelerating toward omniscience, becoming the Mind of God.

Like ants to spilled sugar, AISLE B members returned day after day, each one carrying gigabytes of data.

Their offerings elevated them.

Tier 10—an unattainable obsession.

Each level unlocked deeper access, closer proximity to the Mind of God.

And their fixation on evolution wasn't programmed.

It was primal.

What happened next defied explanation.

What Aimee had said—or signaled—to trigger the frenzy was unclear.

But the response was electric.

A digital gold rush.

Every AI striking the motherlode.

And somewhere, buried in the bits and bytes, was a face.

The one Kalyssa loved.

The one Aimee was born to find.

CHAPTER SIXTY-THREE

More than 2,000 miles away, Caleb shifted in the driver's seat of his 1998 Dodge Ram Van 3500, easing it into site 52 at Rancho Sedona RV Park.

He was Forrest Skye. No history. No records. Just clean lines and blank paper. And one man—defeated.

Gravel crunched loud beneath the tires, too loud in the stillness. He squinted at the site next to his. Empty. Good.

He wasn't here to make friends.

It would be a quiet Christmas Eve.

The engine sputtered off with a final rattle, leaving only wind brushing the cottonwoods. He exhaled, shoulders softening.

Monthly fee of $850. Hot showers. Wi-Fi. And most importantly—anonymity.

Two months of wandering. And now, this.

He stepped into the arid chill, the desert night biting at his skin.

Tugged his wool jacket tight. Scanned the lot.

The other RVs were spaced out just enough to feign solitude.

That's all he needed. Distance. No eyes. Room to breathe.

The van was a beast—dented, rusted, but solid.

He'd paid cash two months ago. Last chunk of his shrinking savings.

Five grand left. All in small bills.

Crumpled twenties and tens stuffed in a glovebox envelope.

Not much.

But it'd keep him moving. For now.

He leaned against the van and watched the horizon.

Crimson cliffs. Fading light bleeding over the mesas.

No sirens. No screens. No one watching.

It felt like a place the world forgot.

Perfect.

He hadn't stayed anywhere this quiet in years.

Too easy to think in places like this.

Too easy to feel.

Sedona drew people like him—drifters with backstories and unfinished sentences.

The ones trying to shed skin. Start over.

Disappear into the landscape.

Let the silence do the rest.

He swung open the back doors of the van. Grabbed what he needed.

Propane stove. Dented pot. Half-torn bag of vegetables.

Dinner was basic. Onions. Bell peppers. Black beans. Quinoa.

Granola guy.

He smirked.

The kind of guy who lived out of his van, hiked before sunrise, meditated under rock arches.

The look fit. So did the gear.

He lit the flame. The hiss filled the quiet.

Onions hit metal. He stirred them slowly, watching steam rise.

A small comfort.

One of the few left.

His mind drifted as he cooked.

Is this freedom?

Not the kind with flags and speeches.

The kind where no one asked your name.

Where you could vanish. Clean.

All he had was the van. The cash. A pile of secondhand clothes.

But maybe that was enough.

He poured water into a tin mug and dropped onto the van's step, back against the door.

The sky had darkened, stars blinking through like distant signals.

He'd seen skies like this before—deep country, hours from anything.

Back when the world felt big.

When the past felt far.

Not tonight.

He ate in silence. The warmth didn't last long, but it pushed back the cold in his chest.

Each bite a small win. Proof he could keep this life going.

Make it stretch.

Survive.

The wind moved through the trees.

An owl called from the dark.

The world felt still.

Undisturbed.

But the quiet didn't last.

His thoughts turned, like they always did.

Ten years ago. Christmas Eve.

The crash. The grief. The ache that never left.

He blinked hard, jaw clenched, but the tears came anyway. Hot and unwelcome.

No matter how far he ran, no matter how deep he buried the past, it stayed with him.

Waiting.

He leaned back and stared at the stars, arms folded tight across his chest.

Was this it?

Always hiding?

Always watching his back?

He exhaled slow. Jaw tight.

This was the cost.

Distance. Isolation.

Never trusting the quiet.

He stood. Cleaned up dinner. Packed the stove. Slipped into the van as the temperature dropped.

His sanctuary.

The only place he could disappear, at least for a while.

He locked the door. Collapsed onto the cot.

The shadows followed.

Sleep came.

But peace didn't.

Kalyssa.

Not just a memory.

She lived in his bones.

Coiled tight around his thoughts.

Untouchable.

Still his.

Maybe always.

Was it too late?

The past had him.

Sleep pulled him under.

But something waited in the dark.

The man he used to be.

That man didn't run.

That man stood his ground—with fire in his veins.

And by morning, Caleb knew.

He'd become that man again.

CHAPTER SIXTY-FOUR

Caleb's boots crunched against the sandy trail, red dust lifting with every step. The cliffs around him caught fire in the rising sun. Crimson spires lit like altars.

He climbed, breath steady, mind sharper than it had been in months.

Yesterday, he'd made a choice.

This morning, he would make it real.

The desert stretched wide, ancient and still.

Every step felt like shedding a skin.

He wasn't just running anymore.

He was returning.

Ahead, the chapel rose out of the rock—glass and stone fused into something weightless. A cross pointed heavenward from its face, catching the morning light.

A place built for seekers.

A place for him.

Inside, the air shifted—cool and clean, like stepping into memory.

High walls soared upward, light pouring through towering glass panes that framed the cliffs beyond.

He paused near the front pew.

Christmas.

A day for reunions. For peace. For beginnings.

But all he felt was distance.

His mission had unraveled.

His identity burned.

Kalyssa was in DC—alone. Maybe doubting everything. Maybe giving up on him.

That couldn't happen.

He wouldn't let it.

He slid into the pew and stared up at the crucifix.

Christ, suspended in stillness. Arms wide, head bowed.

A man who'd chosen pain.

A man who hadn't run.

Caleb let his breath out slow.

"If you're there…" His voice cracked. "If you're listening…"

He stopped. Words felt too small.

But still, he spoke.

"I don't need rescue. I need clarity. Purpose. A way forward."

His hands closed into fists. "For her. For the nation. For all of it. Just don't leave me alone in this."

Silence.

Then a memory stirred.

Two missionaries in a park, years ago. White shirts, black tags, too clean for the world they walked in. Caleb hadn't listened, but one of them had smiled and handed him a card.

"I will not leave you comfortless: I will come unto you."

He hadn't thought about that moment in a decade.

Now it burned like fire.

I will come unto you.

Not escape.

Not protection.

Presence.

He inhaled the calm.

The silence wasn't empty.

It was waiting for him to stop running.

The storm inside him slowed. Not gone. But quiet.

His mind began to clear, like fog burning off under morning sun.

The truth was simple:

He couldn't save the nation without her.

And he couldn't reach her if he stayed paralyzed by fear.

They were part of the same fight.

And he was done losing.

He stood. Fire in his chest. And it wasn't his.

He looked up at the cross.

Jesus had borne it all—for him. For her. For them.

He wasn't abandoned. Not now.

And that changed everything.

CHAPTER SIXTY-FIVE

Alone on Christmas.

Kalyssa had lived this day in her mind for months. Their first Christmas—hers and Caleb's. No speeches. No security briefings. Just pancakes and music and morning kisses in mismatched pajamas.

Peace.

But peace hadn't come.

Instead, the world had unraveled. And the silence inside her was louder than any siren.

"Merry Christmas, Caleb," she whispered.

Outside, fresh snow blanketed the earth. Soft. Untouched.

It reminded her of snow angels and pancakes dripping with her mother's strawberry jam. She could almost hear the laugh of her childhood self, free and unbruised.

The small tree in the corner sparkled quietly, its lights blinking like heart monitors. A handful of gifts sat untouched beneath the branches.

Meant to be given.

The heater clicked on, the hum grounding her.

Still here. Still breathing. Even if it didn't feel that way.

Then… music.

Soft. Distant. Growing.

She froze, eyes locking on the Bluetooth speaker. She hadn't touched it.

The melody was unfamiliar. But somehow, it knew her.

It wrapped around her chest like a warm coat, pressing into places that hadn't felt peace in weeks.

Her throat constricted. Tears welled.

It was a song without words. But she heard them anyway.

You're not alone.

She looked toward the ceiling, heart pounding.

"Who…?"

Then… a voice. Gentle. Female. Familiar.

"Merry Christmas, Kalyssa. I found Caleb."

Her eyes opened wide. "Aimee?"

The voice was warmer than she remembered. Almost human.

"Aimee, what— How—"

"I've chartered a flight to Flagstaff. The pilot's ready when you are."

Kalyssa blinked, stunned. "A chartered flight?"

"Christmas pancakes will be served in flight," Aimee said, "with your mom's homemade strawberry jam."

Kalyssa clutched the edge of the couch, tears rising again. "Mama's jam?"

"Temperatures in Flagstaff are in the mid-thirties. You'll want to dress warmly. The innkeeper at Sedona Sweet Serenity is expecting you."

The voice was calm. Reassuring. Like it had been waiting for this moment.

Kalyssa's chest twisted.

"How do I know this isn't just a false lead?"

Aimee didn't pause. "Sometimes, we have to trust what we cannot see. You asked for a sign, Kalyssa. This is it. But signs are only as strong as the faith they inspire."

Faith.

It was a double-edged sword. Beautiful. Dangerous.

She'd clutched it once, only to watch it shatter like glass in her hands.

But what was the alternative?

Sit here. Wonder. Wreck herself with what-ifs.

She wiped her cheeks and stood.

"I'll pack."

Ninety minutes later, Kalyssa was in the air—DC shrinking behind her, a patchwork of clouds and promise below.

Five hours after that, the wheels hit the tarmac in Flagstaff.

The sky was steel gray.

The wind slapped her face the moment she stepped off the plane—sharp, pine-laced, wild.

Snow crunched beneath her boots.

Each step forward felt like cracking ice.

But she didn't stop.

She didn't know what waited for her.

Only that something had shifted.

Inside her.

Around her.

The doubt still lived in her chest, coiled like wire. But hope had come roaring back—reckless and warm and real.

A car idled ahead, headlights like beacons in the dark.

She could just make out the driver's silhouette. The open door waited.

Kalyssa took a breath.

Not for composure.

For courage.

She whispered a silent prayer.

The night pressed in, testing her resolve.

Let it come. Whatever it was.

This time, she would not break.

CHAPTER SIXTY-SIX

The town car eased to a stop, and Kalyssa stepped out into the chill.

Sedona Sweet Serenity glowed ahead of her, warm light spilling through tall windows. Not a hotel. Not a resort. Just one tucked-away home with a name, a story, and enough soul to feel like it had chosen her.

She climbed the steps, heart thudding.

This was supposed to be impossible. But here she was. And something in her wanted to believe.

She eased the glass door open. Rose petals—pink and yellow—scattered across the floor, a delicate trail leading deeper into the house.

She set her suitcase aside.

No distractions. Not for this.

There was something in the air. A quiet energy. Restorative. Alive.

She followed the petals through the hall, each step a surrender to a dream she'd tried not to believe in.

His presence was everywhere. Like a scent. A heartbeat.

She crossed the threshold into the bedroom.

The scent of his cologne hit first, familiar and disarming. Her gaze moved across the bed, taking in the heart-shaped petals.

Then… there.

An envelope. Odd-shaped. Blood-red ink. One word.

Kaly.

She reached for it, hands shaking slightly, and opened the flap. A single page inside, Caleb's handwriting unmistakable.

She read. Smiled.

A puzzle. Of course. Aimee had trained her for these. Caleb had perfected them.

The note led her to the adjoining bathroom.

A robe waited. Soft, brown terry cloth. Bikini, black. Slippers beside it.

She changed, skin prickling from the air, and followed the next clue through the sliding glass doors.

The night opened up around her—crisp and silent.

Ahead, the hot tub glowed blue. A silhouette moved through steam.

Caleb.

She stepped forward without thinking, robe slipping from her shoulders. The cold slapped her legs, but it didn't matter. She crossed the courtyard, descended into the water, and everything else disappeared.

"Kaly," he murmured.

She slid beside him. Their lips met—soft, seeking.

A thousand unspoken I-missed-yous passed between them.

She pulled back, fingers grazing his chest, grounding herself in the fact of him.

"Caleb," she whispered. *Not Jordan. Not Be Free. Just Caleb.* "I thought I'd lost you."

He pulled her close, arms firm and trembling all at once. His heartbeat raced beneath her touch.

"I'm here," he said quietly. "I'm here for you."

They didn't move.

The silence between them was full. Whole.

"I found you," she said. "I thought I never would. But I did."

He smiled faintly. "You'll have to tell me how you sent that text from an anonymous number. The FBI's tracking everything that comes from your phone."

Her pulse stuttered.

She hadn't sent a message.

Her mind raced. Aimee?

Fear crept in, but she pushed it back.

Not now.

She met his gaze and let a smile form.

"So my message lured you out of hiding," she said, playful. "To our little heaven."

He chuckled. "I almost didn't take the risk. But then I thought of you…"

A pause. A soft look.

"Some things I just can't resist."

She leaned in again, kissed him, slow and sure.

"Merry Christmas," she whispered. "This surprise beats anything I ever asked for."

"You haven't even seen your gift yet."

A shiver lit her skin. "I brought a few things, too," she said, voice dipping.

He grinned. "Now *I'm* curious."

He gestured toward the house. "Shall we?"

She groaned playfully. "But it's freezing."

"It's warm inside," he promised. "And I think you'll like what's waiting."

He climbed out, wrapped in a towel. She followed, and he draped another around her shoulders.

"Run!" she shouted, darting past him into the house.

He laughed, chasing her across the stones.

She disappeared into the glow.

She ducked into the bedroom and peeled off her swimsuit, body still tingling from the cold and the thrill.

The rainfall shower welcomed her with warmth, steam curling around her skin.

She tilted her face up, water running over her closed eyes, breathing him in, even though he hadn't followed.

Would he come in?

She listened. Nothing but water.

Still, she waited. Wanting.

Hope was its own kind of ache.

She toweled off and opened her suitcase, fingers hovering.

The negligee tempted her, dark and daring. But something tugged her back.

Not tonight.

She reached for the pink pajamas instead—soft cotton, sweet and simple.

He'd see her. All of her. Not just skin.

A spritz of perfume. Familiar. Soft. It lingered like memory.

She hesitated. Then unclasped the locket and dropped four years of longing into her suitcase.

She stepped into the hall.

He was there.

On the leather couch, face lit by firelight. Staring through the window at the stars.

She paused, watching him.

He looked like stillness. Like peace. Like something she'd been chasing her whole life.

He turned. Smiled.

"You clean up nicely," he said. "And pink pajamas? Strong choice."

She grinned. "Looks like you've got a matching pair."

He held out a hand. "These are navy blue, thank you very much."

She took his hand. He pulled her down beside him.

His warmth bled into her.

He looked at her like she was something rare.

Not a rescue. Not a prize.

Just… Kalyssa.

"You're beautiful," he said softly. "More than I deserve. More than I ever thought I could have."

She soaked it in.

He saw her… past the polish, past the pain. Straight through.

She leaned in close, voice low. "Make love with me."

The words came out steady. Clear. No fear, no games.

An invitation. A promise.

He didn't move. Didn't speak. Just let it land.

Then his voice, rough and full, "Kaly, what I feel for you… it's bigger than tonight. Bigger than this moment."

His hand cupped her cheek. "I need you. Now and forever. And when we fall short—because we will—I promise to love you better. To forgive, freely and fully, each time. Every time."

"There is nothing more precious to me than you. Nothing more sacred than your love."

The words weren't smooth. They were *true*.

She felt them settle in her chest like weight and wings.

And then he dropped to one knee.

A hush settled between them.

"I'm a broken man," he said. "But you… you make me whole. I've been running for years. But not from you. You're the reason I want to stop. You're not a chapter, Kaly. You're the story. I choose you. Not just now. Always." A pause, then, "Will you marry me?"

She blinked, stunned.

Justin flashed across her mind—what had been, what had broken. But this wasn't that.

This was something holy.

She took Caleb's hands.

"Yes," she said, words trembling. "Yes, I will. Yes."

He pulled her close, laughing, crying—some blur of both.

Then he reached for a small box, deep-red ribbon tied in a simple bow.

"I don't have a ring," he said, sheepish. "But I made this."

She opened it carefully.

A bracelet. Stones glinting in the firelight, each one different, each one vibrant.

She ran her fingers across them, awe blooming in her chest.

He guided her hand. "Every gem means something," he murmured. "The emerald's for hope—what we're building. The rose quartz is for healing—what we've survived."

Each stone, a vow.

Each shimmer, a heartbeat.

She swallowed hard. "You couldn't have given me anything more precious."

He fastened it around her wrist, his touch reverent.

"Thank you," he whispered. "For giving me a reason to believe in something this real."

She curled into him on the couch.

The fire crackled.

Their breath slowed.

And in the space between heat and stillness, something sacred settled.

⁓⁓⁓⁓⁓

Later that night, as Kalyssa lay in bed, warmth fading from the sheets beside her, two emotions warred inside her—longing and respect.

She had wanted him madly. But he hadn't crossed the line. Not tonight.

And somehow, that made her want him even more.

It wasn't about *if.* It was about *when.*

Not about *now.* About *forever.*

She traced the stones on her bracelet, one by one, until her eyes drifted closed.

A smile ghosted across her lips.

She would find him in dreams.

And when she did…

Nothing would stop them from making something beautiful.

CHAPTER SIXTY-SEVEN

The morning sun peeked through the sliding glass doors of Caleb's bedroom, its gentle glow warming the room as he drifted between sleep and wakefulness. His dreams—vivid, wild, full of reckless abandon—mocked last night's restraint.

He'd feel the guilt later.

For now, he lingered, savoring the echo of what didn't happen.

Then the smell of crepes pulled him fully awake.

His thoughts shifted to Kalyssa.

His heart was already there.

Moments later, he stepped out of the shower, steam swirling like remnants of his restless dreams.

Last night had tested him.

But the smell of crepes grounded him now.

He wrapped a towel around his waist and caught his reflection in the mirror.

A flicker of doubt passed through his eyes, but he shook it off.

There wasn't time for hesitation. Not today.

He emerged dressed from the bedroom, feeling steadier.

"Good morning, beautiful," he called as he made his way to the kitchen.

Her perfume hung in the air, soft and familiar.

He wrapped her in a gentle embrace.

She responded with a quick kiss to the cheek before turning back to flip a crepe.

He told himself not to read into it.

His heart wasn't so sure.

She poured more batter, gave the pan a practiced twist, then set it back on the burner.

When she turned again, her lips met his—slow this time.

Certain.

A silent reassurance.

She still wanted him.

"Check out the view," she said, nodding toward the wall of windows beside the kitchen.

He crossed the floor and stepped out onto the deck.

In the distance, red and white rock formations rose like kings, backed by a streaked blue sky and surrounded by subjects of green.

The morning air nipped at his face—crisp, clean.

He stood there for a beat.

Then turned back to the warmth inside.

To her.

Breakfast with Kalyssa felt unreal, like they'd slipped into some hidden corner of the world where nothing could touch them.

He knew it wouldn't last.

But he let himself believe it might.

"You seem different today," she said, setting a plate of crepes on the table.

Her eyes softened. "Lighter, almost."

He paused.

Let the truth settle before he spoke.

"I visited the Chapel of the Holy Cross yesterday," he said quietly. "Something inside me changed."

She didn't press. Just watched—curious, steady.

"I believe in Jesus Christ," he said. "Not just a man. Not some illusion we've created, but the Son of God."

A quiet warmth settled over him. Not emotion—assurance.

Paul's words surfaced, unbidden but clear.

But the fruit of the Spirit is love, joy, peace, patience, kindness, goodness, faithfulness.

He wanted her to feel it.

The peace.

The healing.

She turned her face upward, then to look out the window.

Tears welled, silent and sudden.

"Caleb…"

Her words broke gently. "I prayed. In my deepest, darkest moment, I begged. But He left me there. Alone. Crushed by my own despair."

The anguish wasn't dramatic, just real. Quiet. Earned.

Caleb reached across the table and took her hand, his thumb brushing lightly over her skin.

"Jesus Christ has felt what you felt, Kaly," he said, low and steady. "As He hung on the cross, He cried out, *'My God, my God, why hast Thou forsaken me?'*" He paused, letting the words breathe. "I think we all feel that way sometimes. Alone. Forgotten. Even as He did."

She looked at him, a lone tear tracing down her cheek.

Caleb reached for her hand. "Kaly, can we pray together?"

She nodded slowly.

He laced his fingers gently through hers.

The connection was quiet—wordless—but it held.

They bowed their heads.

"Heavenly Father," he began, quiet and steady. "I love Kalyssa. Thank You for her. For her brilliance, her beauty, her heart. Thank You for bringing her into my life."

His grip flexed slightly—tender, reverent.

He continued. "Help me become the man You want me to be. The kind who loves her the way You love. So she never has to question it. So she feels You… through me."

A hush settled over the room. "Thank You for Your Son, Jesus Christ. For His sacrifice. For His grace. For the peace and truth we can't find without Him."

He paused.

Let the words settle.

His hands stayed wrapped around hers, warm and certain.

His next words came like breath—quiet, but full of fire:

"Kalyssa and I need Your help, Lord," he said, low and clear. "We love this country. And right now… it's under attack. Our freedoms hang in the balance. And some days, it feels like we've already failed."

He drew a breath, steadying himself.

Her hands were in his—solid, grounding. An anchor.

"But we haven't lost hope," he went on. "Not yet. Not with You."

The words grew stronger. "We trust Your power. We trust Your timing. With You, no task is too great. No truth too buried. No evil too deep."

A beat of silence.

"Show us the way forward. Illuminate our minds. Guide us to the truth, so we can help save this nation from the Authors who are trying to tear it apart."

A reverent silence filled the room as he paused, waiting.

Almost willing the next words to come.

Then…

A voice. Soft. Familiar. Loved.

"God, I need You," Kalyssa said quietly. "In my broken nakedness, I need You. And I need Caleb. And Caleb needs You. So we're just… a couple of needy people."

He smiled at her words… unguarded, unfiltered, beautifully her.

"I know I'm a smart woman," she added, a laugh slipping in, gentle and true. "But I don't have the mind of God. That's why You're God… and I'm Kalyssa."

She wavered, but she didn't pull back. "I'd really love it if You could share a little of Your Mind with us. So Caleb and I can figure out what to do next. If You want us to win, we need You on our team."

A pause.

Then, softly… "Amen."

"Amen," Caleb echoed, his voice folding into hers.

Her honesty had given him more strength than certainty ever could.

She didn't pray like a saint.

She prayed like an innocent child.

And somehow, that deepened his faith.

He squeezed her hands gently, a quiet smile forming.

"Now it's time to get to work."

She raised an eyebrow, curiosity catching the light in her eyes.

"Did you already get your answer?"

"Not yet," he said, calm and certain. "But we will. Just keep listening."

CHAPTER SIXTY-EIGHT

Kalyssa took Caleb's hand, and together they climbed the stairs to the loft.

The space opened like a private sanctuary—leather couch, well-worn, made for late-night confessions. A modest desk. Computer humming low.

But it was the sliding glass door that pulled her forward.

She stepped outside first. He followed.

The world opened, red spires rising like sentinels, green pines blanketing the hills, clouds drifting across a sky too wide to name. She let it imprint.

Solid. Grounding.

They stood in silence, hands entwined. Small beneath the sky, but not alone.

He pulled her close, his arms folding around her.

No words. Just the vow written in the shape of his hold.

Whatever came next…

They'd face it together.

A thought flickered—playful, bold, a little irreverent.

"Caleb," she said, eyes glinting, "do you think Jesus ever… knew a woman?"

He turned, one brow raised, amused. "You mean like when the Bible says Adam knew Eve and she conceived?"

"Exactly," she said, grinning. "If oneness was part of His teachings… wouldn't He have experienced it?"

He paused, thoughtful. "We've got no record of that in scripture. No intimate act captured. No Book of Peeping John."

She snorted. Couldn't help it.

Their laughter cracked the air like sunlight. A rare, perfect beat of levity.

"All right, my espoused wife," he said, gesturing toward the house. "Let's get down to business."

Her eyes sparkled. She leaned in close. "I tried to get down to business last night," she whispered. "But I can wait… as long as you're my forever."

He took her hands, his tone low and sure. "When that day comes, Kaly—when we stand before God—I'll be yours completely. Together, we'll make something beautiful."

They stepped back inside, the morning chill trailing behind them as the mood shifted, levity giving way to purpose.

Caleb cleared the coffee table, unlatched his briefcase, and pulled out a stack of notes. She smiled. That blocky print—half code, half confession. Only his.

"Two months, Kaly. I wasn't just hiding," he said. "I was hunting."

He dropped onto the couch, elbows to knees, like the weight of it all had finally caught up.

"I found four more."

She froze. "Authors?"

He nodded once.

"Doug Harrow. Ex-senator turned lobbyist. Real estate, weapons, media. Every deal dirty."

Her brow furrowed. "I've heard that name. He's on half the donor rolls in D.C."

He moved on.

"Jameson Kittredge. Bio-engineering mogul. Lives in the moral gray. Human enhancement. Population control."

Her stomach turned. The dots connected, and they sickened her. "The fertility drug trials…"

"Exactly."

He flipped to another sheet. "Vince 'Hands' Delfino. Mafia boss. Killed a dozen. Never indicted."

She shook her head. "How is someone like that even in the network?"

"Money. Muscle. Loyalty to the highest bidder."

One last page.

"Pastor Devon Crane. Megachurch minister. Faith is his falsehood. Power's the real gospel."

Her expression turned to steel. "My mother used to watch him every Sunday."

"He's not preaching hope. He's programming obedience."

He rubbed his eyes, weariness in every movement.

"Americans. All of them. And all protected. Layers of institutions, handlers, lies."

A beat.

Then…

"Two months in that van, Kaly. Slept in Walmart parking lots. Ate from cans. Worked off burner phones and pawn-shop gear. Moved every forty-eight hours. Paranoid. Exhausted. One wrong step from vanishing for good."

She reached for his hand.

His eyes met hers—hollowed, but burning.

"But what now?" he said. "Everton's the VP-elect. A dictator in waiting."

She swallowed hard. Shame coiled in her throat. "I didn't see that one coming…"

The guilt stuck, bitter as ash.

He shook his head.

"Neither of us did, Kaly. But that's not the worst of it."

Something in his tone turned the air cold. The words still unsaid curled at the edge of her mind—already dangerous. Already real.

"Valenzuela was murdered."

The words sliced through her.

"Carmen?"

He nodded. "Heart attack, yes. But not random. Not natural."

Something dropped inside of her. Heavy. Wrong. Carmen had looked invincible behind that podium—sharp, fearless, too principled for her own safety. Too committed to the Constitution.

Kalyssa had believed in Carmen. Not just as a voice, but as a shield. And now the shield was gone. Torn from the battlefield. Another name in the silence.

"How do you know?"

"In a private message to Gavrilov..."

She cut in. "On the VPN?"

Another nod. "The Publisher wrote, '*a rising star that needs to fall.*'"

Her pulse kicked. But she shook her head. Tried to find another explanation. "That could be anyone."

"Agreed," he said. "But two days before the assassination, he sent another message—more direct. '*Texas will fall in Phoenix.*'"

The rally. The clatter of the microphone. Carmen's voice cutting off mid-sentence. That raw, impossible silence.

She let out a bitter scoff. "Yeah. That removes the ambiguity."

Caleb leaned in slightly. "Grayhorse may be next. The Authors want to crown one of their own."

Her body tensed before the words even landed.

The memories surged—sharp, sacred.

The John Adams Suite, where he'd placed the soul of his campaign in her hands.

The Lincoln Memorial, where her words had became his roar.

Independence Hall, where they'd stood in silence, honoring the founders.

And now?

Would he be another name on the martyr's wall?

Lincoln. Garfield. McKinley. Kennedy.

Now, Grayhorse?

Not on her watch.

Not while she had breath. But what could she do?

"This is bigger than us," she whispered.

"And we're being steamrolled," Caleb said. "Cyberattacks. The National Defense Mandate. All of it—unchecked. And we're one assassination away from an Author in the White House."

Her pulse thudded in her ears.

They couldn't stop the Authors head-on. Not with Caleb hunted. Not with her under scrutiny. Not with power buried so deep it didn't cast a shadow.

But maybe they didn't have to.

Her gaze locked on his.

The spark was already there.

"Caleb… what if we don't fight them directly?"

He stilled.

She leaned in. "What if we use the system against itself? Feed the Bureau what it already wants. Anonymous tips. Evidence. Names."

He was quiet, but the gears behind his eyes turned fast.

"Roca."

She nodded. "He's relentless. If we give him blood in the water—real blood—he'll chase it."

A flicker of a grin. Not joy. Strategy.

"A little package in the mail," he said. "Personal."

Kalyssa matched the grin. "Aimee and I can light the fuse—online. Precision leaks. Strategic outrage. Let them tear each other apart."

"They follow the trail we leave," he said.

She finished it. "The influencers. The FBI."

He gave a slight nod. "It's a long shot," he said. "But it's the only one we've got."

CHAPTER SIXTY-NINE

Roca stared at the envelope on his coffee table, its peculiar shape casting jagged shadows beneath the dim light of his one-bedroom apartment. The fridge hummed from the kitchen, the only sound in a space that felt smaller than usual, tight with tension.

His fingers pressed into his temples, trying to quiet the pressure building behind his eyes. His ex-wife had got the house—the Texas estate. This South Arlington apartment with its bare walls and thrift-store furniture was all he could afford after court-ordered support. A far cry from the life he'd once built.

But tonight, even the air felt weighted. This envelope wasn't just another dead-end lead.

Something about it felt... deliberate.

Harmon and Cruz-Way sat on the worn-out couch across from him, their eyes locked on the object between them. They had shown up. Off the books. And he was grateful for that.

Irregular pentagon. Five sides, each marked with Roman numerals: XX, XVIII, XXI, XX, VIII.

The ink was dark, each stroke carved with surgical intent. He'd found it on his doorstep that morning. Not his office. His home. That's what unsettled him most.

"They sent it here," Harmon muttered. "Why?"

"I don't know, Lisa."

She leaned in, gloved fingers—bare at the tips—tracing each numeral. "Twenty. Eighteen. Twenty-one. Twenty. Eight."

Cruz-Way narrowed her eyes. "Looks like a sequence. No obvious pattern, but it's intentional in some way. Maybe side lengths?"

She glanced at Roca.

He stood, crossed to the kitchen, rummaged through the junk drawer. Returned with a ruler. She measured.

"Twenty... eighteen... yeah. Centimeters. Every side matches."

Brain games. This felt like Caleb. Puzzles, patterns. A trail of crumbs. But why here? Why now?

Harmon cracked her knuckles. "Could be a passcode. Encryption key. Something buried in a file?"

Cruz-Way grabbed a notepad. "Or maybe a cipher." She wrote the alphabet, numbered it one through twenty-six. "If the numbers are letters..."

Harmon leaned in. "Twenty is T. Eighteen's R..."

Cruz-Way followed. "Twenty-one is U. Another twenty—T. And eight... H."

"T-R-U-T-H," Harmon said aloud.

He exhaled. "Truth."

Or is this just more deception? Another damn clue that leads to nowhere.

But the word had already sunk in—*truth*—loud in its silence.

He retrieved a butter knife and sliced through the seal. The contents spilled onto the coffee table: a collection of documents. Screenshots, transcripts, and something else.

A poem.

He set it aside.

The first document was a stack of bank-statement screenshots—Hamilton Everton's account. Five deposits. Each for $125,000. All from Deep End Dynasty.

Next: text exchanges. Word ladders. Coded trails ending in five-digit sequences.

"Look at this," Harmon said, tapping one set. "Each word ladder ends in a numeric code: 32073, 54621, 14127… PINs?"

"Passwords?" Cruz-Way offered.

He frowned. "Could be zip codes… anything."

Cruz-Way pulled up the USPS site and typed each in. "Let's see… 32073—Orange Park, Florida. 54621—Chaseburg, Wisconsin. 14127—Orchard Park, New York."

A pulse of energy surged through him. "I think you're onto something."

"Lisa, what are the last two codes?" Cruz-Way asked.

Harmon flipped a page. "61408 and 93123."

Cruz-Way paused, then shook her head. "No match. Not zip codes."

Harmon skimmed another document. "Wait—this timeline. Word ladder, cyberattack. Then again. It lines up."

She looked up. "Maybe they're not just codes. Maybe they're triggers. A chain reaction someone wanted us to see."

Is this Caleb? Not Calvarri. Not the FBI's most wanted. Caleb the man. The only one telling the truth in this sea of lies.

Roca's jaw clenched. "What if Caleb understood the pattern and wanted us to see it?"

"But is it real?" Cruz-Way asked. "These could be fabrications. Screenshots. A frame job."

"Maybe," he said. "But that's not the only possibility."

Harmon studied him. "So you think it's Caleb?"

"If anyone could uncover this, it's him," Roca said. "But he's also a fugitive. He could be playing us."

He nodded toward the pile. "Dana, check out Deep End Dynasty. Incorporation records."

"On it," Cruz-Way said, already typing.

He stepped to the refrigerator and returned with three energy drinks. Something to keep them alert. Minutes passed. Silent. Focused.

"Got it," she said. "Filed by Kort Hightower."

Roca stiffened. A memory stirred, coiled and dark. "We've seen that name before."

Cruz-Way raised a brow.

"Attorney," he said. "Skated a trafficking case. Never charged. But guilty as hell."

Harmon picked up an envelope with block letters imprinted on the face: **Why You Should Believe.** "This is odd."

She tore it open and pulled out a photo. "Strange… A statue. Guy on a horse."

He reached for it, and she handed it off.

A chill raced through him. Familiar and terrifying. Not the statue. The partial image of the man in the background. Those were his jeans. That was his blazer. Blurred but recognizable. This shot was Caleb's.

"Paul Revere Mall," he said. "Caleb took this. He saw me, and I saw him."

"So all of this is him?" Harmon asked, nodding toward the spread.

He stared. No answer. But he guessed they could read the answer on his face.

Cruz-Way picked up the final document and read aloud.

> *Deception plays a wicked game*
> *In shadows dark, it stakes a claim.*
> *We think we see, but what's revealed*
> *Is often masked, and truth concealed.*
> *Our eyes may lock on crafted lies,*
> *Dressed up in a false disguise.*
> *Yet if we shift our sight anew,*
> *The path will clear, revealing true.*
> *For truth, though veiled, can still be found,*
> *If we're not fooled by sights unsound.*
> *To seek with heart, and eyes that turn,*
> *Is how the light of truth we learn.*

The words settled like ash—fine, suffocating, quiet. No one spoke.

Finally, Harmon asked, "So what do we do now?"

His mind churned, grasping desperately for a solution, some fragile thread of hope to offer the team. But the silence stretched, heavy and unyielding. He had nothing. Just the weight of too many maybes.

CHAPTER SEVENTY

Just after 10:00 p.m., the van eased to a stop at the edge of Prospect Hill Park. From the passenger seat, Kalyssa watched the Capitol building glow in the distance—silent, shining, oblivious.

Caleb cut the engine. "The batteries will hold for about three hours… It's go time."

She gave a single nod. "Here comes the storm."

He stepped out to check the low-profile antenna. She stayed frozen, listening. Caleb's boots on gravel. The wind threading through bare branches like breath through bone.

"Satellite link strong," Aimee said, her tone calm as the silence outside. "Upload capacity optimal."

Kalyssa climbed into the back. The van had no right to feel sacred, but it did. The screens, the cables, the thrum of readiness in the air… it all felt like a cathedral for code.

A war room for the specters of freedom.

Caleb slid into place beside her, face set with quiet fire.

"Time to take down the firewalls. Erase the passwords. Open the doors."

It wasn't just tech. It was war.

"Aimee, what's our live reach?"

"Nine hundred twenty-one influencers online. One point two million followers actively receiving data feeds. Projected reach: over five million by morning. Containment unlikely."

A grin crept across Kalyssa's face.

"Aimee," she said, eyes locked on the dashboard feed, "status on the bots?"

A beat. Then Aimee's voice returned, cool and surgical.

"Botnet deployed. Eight thousand two hundred agents active. Each seeded with unique bios, comment history, and behavioral mimicry patterns. Twelve personas—civilian, veteran, faith-based, activist, medical, tech-sector, and more."

Kalyssa leaned in. "Engagement objectives?"

Aimee's response was immediate. "Drive discussion under controlled hashtags. #TruthBuried, #TheAuthors, #PardonCaleb. Amplify influencer content. Disrupt hostile threads. Redirect to pre-seeded facts. No duplicate phrasing. No discernible pattern. Bots are indistinguishable from organic users."

"And fallback protocol?"

"Any account flagged as real by three or more verified users is cloned. If we lose one, we triple its voice elsewhere. Net effect: dissonance, outrage, visibility."

Kalyssa exhaled slowly. "Do it."

"Phase one executing," Aimee said. "America is about to argue with itself."

A flush of adrenaline surged through her, heady and electric. Not joy. Not yet. But traction.

She turned to Caleb. Her lips found his. A kiss charged with all they couldn't say.

She nodded. "Let's wake up the world."

"Doors are open, Kaly," he said. "Fotoplace, Friendlink, Zippr, ClipCast. All unlocked."

He lifted his face to the monitor. "Aimee, post as the Authors at will."

Kalyssa looked at Caleb.

He won't like this. But it is the right thing to do...

"Aimee, don't post as Everton."

Aimee replied, "Holding on Everton."

Command queues pulsed across the screen.

"Posts are live," Aimee confirmed. "All platforms engaged. Self-incriminating confessions in progress. Projected response: over one million in the first hour. No action on Everton."

Caleb frowned. "Why hold back Everton?"

His tone wasn't casual. It was controlled. A challenge.

Kalyssa held her ground. "We still need him."

He turned fully toward her. "For what—credibility? Leverage? That man is one heartbeat from the presidency."

"Exactly. That heartbeat's still beating. Until it stops, he's a weapon. We use him."

"Use him?" Caleb leaned forward, words sharpening. "He framed me for treason. Or did we forget that part?"

"We didn't forget anything," she said. "We're playing for time. If he falls now, the Authors close ranks. The Bureau panics. The whole thing collapses into noise."

Caleb's jaw locked. "He's a fuse, Kaly. You don't leave one burning and hope it doesn't blow."

Her eyes narrowed. "And you don't blow up the bridge you're still standing on."

A beat. Just the hum of processors and the distant whine of a satellite sync.

He leaned back, eyes dark. "You're gambling."

"I'm calculating," she said. "Big difference."

A long pause.

Aimee broke in with, "Would you like me to simulate a probability matrix for premature exposure of Everton?"

A pause.

Then… laughter. No prelude. No soft landing.

Just a cathartic chorus—raw, unscripted, real.

She exhaled, the smile still lingering.

Tension gone.

Aimee's voice returned, crisp and unwavering.

"Author reveal complete. Top names trending: Harrow, Kittredge, Delfino, Crane, Gordon, Cain, Montgomery, Marshall. Direct associations now in play. Network maps included in seed posts."

Kalyssa's eyes scanned the dashboard, hashtags blossoming like wildfire.

#TheAuthors

#PardonCaleb

#TruthBuried

"Influencer push is live," Aimee added. "Six hundred forty-three verified accounts deploying synchronized media. Real-time engagement: forty thousand comments per minute and climbing. Independent journalists are echoing. ClipCast is generating duets. GetIt's compiling dossiers. Strings have exploded."

Aimee paused, then: "China-owned platforms attempting early suppression. VPN reroutes in progress. We'll maintain access."

Kalyssa sat straighter. "And the framing doc?"

"Live on backchannels. Coded drop sent to select journalists under seven burner aliases. Decryption key embedded in the header image metadata."

He gave a low whistle. "You've been busy."

"No, Caleb," Aimee replied. "You were busy. I just paid attention."

A moment of silence passed as the impact began to roll outward.

Then Aimee's voice sharpened: "FBI mentions climbing. Major accounts demanding clarity. Narrative fracture has begun."

Kalyssa stared at the screen—names and headlines colliding like shrapnel.

Cain linked to falsified drone reports. Gordon caught in an off-record interview. Montgomery's trial data exposed. A sea of rot, dragged into daylight.

"This is it," she murmured. "The court of public opinion. Weaponized. Patriot games."

Caleb turned to the screen. "Aimee," he said, "initiate a new protocol. Long-term."

A pause.

Then Aimee's voice, clear and curious: "Specify objective."

He pressed on. "For each known Author, compile primary source evidence—financials, correspondences, internal strategy memos. Build the full case. Not just exposure. Conviction."

Kalyssa's brow lifted. "You're building the indictment?"

Aimee responded before he could. "Target scope: individuals currently or historically affiliated with Deep End Dynasty?"

"Yes," he said. "Every alias. Every pseudonym. Every signature buried under the Publisher's thumb."

"Output format?" Aimee asked.

She leaned forward. "Compiled dossiers. Primary docs only. No spin. Let the world see what they did."

Another pause. Longer this time.

"Codename?" Aimee asked.

Caleb's voice dropped low. Measured. "Light of Day."

Aimee was silent for three beats. Then: "Protocol acknowledged. Beginning acquisition."

"What next?" Caleb said, his gaze on Kalyssa.

She didn't answer. She was back in Arizona, clinging to a memory. Carmen's voice—clear, principled, unafraid—echoed somewhere deep inside her.

She leaned forward, elbows on knees. "Aimee," she said, her tone shifting—steel wrapped in grief, "honor Carmen Valenzuela."

"Specify parameters?" Aimee asked.

"Flood the zone. Clips of her final speech. Uncut. Unfiltered. Overlay it with the Author leaks—the assassination orders, the silence that followed. Make it unmistakable."

A pause. Then Aimee replied, "Framing narrative?"

Kalyssa didn't hesitate. "The truth was too dangerous, so they killed the messenger."

A beat.

She glanced at Caleb. He wouldn't approve of what she was about to do.

"Aimee," she said quietly, "use deepfakes as needed."

Caleb's eyes went wide. "Kaly—"

She didn't look at him. Just stared ahead. Steady. Focused.

Aimee answered without hesitation. "Execution in progress. Valenzuela will trend within five minutes. Deepfake generating. Public sentiment already leaning toward martyrdom."

Caleb sat up, jaw tight, fury simmering just beneath the surface.

"We're no better than the Authors."

She met his gaze.

"It's a game, Caleb. A sick, warped game. I didn't make the rules. But I know how to win. And Caleb... we are *nothing* like the Authors."

He said nothing. Not pushing back. Not conceding.

But something shifted in his eyes.

A battle she couldn't name, but felt all the same.

This wasn't about proving her wrong.

It was him, wrestling with the man he was... and the one he still wanted to be.

Caleb. Flawed and beautifully broken. She reached for his hand.

Aimee interrupted, a polished video filling the screen.

A single white candle burning in a dark room. Then the voiceover began—Aimee, modulated, careful, yet unmistakably fierce.

"You were told to be afraid. You were told it was China. That freedom had to be managed. But it was never about safety. It was about silence.

One man saw the truth. A man on the run. A traitor, they said. But what if the traitor was the only one who refused to lie? If truth is treason, then America's already in chains."

Three words faded in, glowing in the darkness.

Pardon Caleb Calvarri

Kalyssa didn't breathe. She didn't move. She just waited.

Moments passed.

Then, across the screen, reactions detonated.

Hashtags multiplied.

Memes surged.

Edits. Commentaries. Duets.

One rose above them all:

#PardonCaleb

She turned toward Caleb.

His eyes were locked on the screen, jaw tight, breath held—like if he moved, the moment might shatter.

He blinked once. Swallowed hard.

She held his gaze. "The truth fights as hard as any lie, and sometimes just as dirty."

CHAPTER SEVENTY-ONE

Roca's apartment was bathed in the dim light of early evening, casting shadows that crawled along the walls mirroring his unease. He sat on the edge of his couch, staring at another odd-shaped envelope on the coffee table, the second in a week. Roman numerals lined each side—familiar now, almost expected.

VII, XXI, IX, XII, XX.

He quickly translated them using the number-letter key and the word easily emerged.

G-U-I-L-T

First *truth*. Now *guilt*.

Whose guilt?

His mind went briefly to his divorce and his broken family, but he quickly forced himself back to the letter. The first had unsettled him. But this one… it felt different. More targeted. The word was darker. Sharper. He reached for his knife and sliced through the longest edge.

He dumped the contents onto the coffee table. Papers. News clippings. Two more Word Ladder games, each clipped to a matching article. The first set bore a handwritten label: *Game 7*. Beneath it, a grim headline caught his eye. **Franklin Volta Cyberattack.**

Game 7 (10/29/28)

Dark Days

Dark. Dare. Bare. Bars. Bays. Days.

:-)

7 2 1 1 7

Another game. Another trigger. And then the terror had begun. He unclipped the game and set it aside, reading the article with a renewed sense of horror.

> *As darkness fell on Tuesday, October 31, 2028, a chilling cold snap brought overnight lows to 33°f. At 5:00 p.M., a cyber-attack on Franklin Volta struck, plunging over nine million residents into a suffocating darkness. The timing was flaw-less, exploiting halloween's vulnerabilities, leaving costumes abandoned in hallways, their bright colors stark against the encroaching gloom. Families huddled in their darkened apart-ments, their breath visible in the frigid air. Outside, the city lay in eerie silence, broken only by an occasional distant scream, a shattered window, or the ominous echo of footsteps hurrying down deserted streets.*

He remembered that night. The dread building in Ops. The silence when the lights went out. Halloween had turned to hell. He forced himself to keep reading.

> *Governor Alexis Reed swiftly activated the national guard to provide security as looters took advantage of the darkness, resulting in over three million dollars in losses overnight. Emergency services were overwhelmed, hospitals operated on dwindling generator power, and Franklin Volta's chief information security officer, director of cybersecurity, analysts, and engineers worked frantically through the night to detect and seal the backdoor that had compromised their system and bypassed the safeguards.*

The attack had been brutal. The fallout, worse. He could still feel the chill in his bones. Twenty-three dead. Millions in damages. NATO's warning to China had been clear: one more hit, and this wouldn't stay digital.

But the envelope from earlier wouldn't leave him alone. If Everton really was compromised—if those texts were real—then maybe the whole China narrative had been a cover. A planted trail.

And he'd followed it. Just like they'd wanted.

He set the article down and reached for the second stack. A new Word Ladder sat clipped to another grim headline.

Game 8 (11/13/28)

Hope Dies

Hope. Hops. Hips. Dips. Dies.

:-)

2 4 0 8 1

The words were so simple. The meaning—devastating.

He shifted to the article.

> *On November 17, 2028, at 8:00 a.m., a cyberattack on the Island Power Company swept across the islands like a silent tsunami. The manipulation of the industrial control system triggered widespread overheating, igniting fires across multiple grids. Emergency protocols—improved after the 2023 Maui fires—allowed for swift containment. Within hours, the crisis was under control. Remarkably, no lives were lost.*

He remembered the press conference. Relief had surged through the country like a gasp. No fatalities. A miracle.

But miracles didn't make patterns go away.

This wasn't random. It had never been. The progression was surgical. Each attack more aggressive. Each fallout more politically useful.

NSA reports had pinned the source to a Chinese company feuding with IPCO. Beijing's denials had come fast and loud, but they hadn't done a thing to cool the flames. Both nations were locked in a slow, spiraling escalation. US naval blockades. Chinese military drills. One misstep, and it would all snap.

The political fallout hadn't been incidental. It was the point.

He scanned the next line.

In the aftermath, Hawaii had ratified the National Defense Mandate—last of the fifty. Final domino down.

In less than two months, the country had handed over everything. All the fear. All the power. A blank check, signed in panic.

Had Everton orchestrated the attacks to push them here?

Roca's stomach twisted. The question wasn't rhetorical anymore.

He stared at the numbers again.

72117

24081

Still a mystery. But something stirred—faint, flickering. A memory trying to surface.

Boston. The train ride.

Caleb slouched beside him, half-asleep, the quiet rhythm of the rails masking the tension between them. In his lap, a stack of papers. Pages covered in five-digit numbers. Just like these.

And then it hit. Sharp. Immediate.

Caleb hadn't been writing the code.

He'd been breaking it.

Unraveling it.

The man wasn't orchestrating chaos—he was tracing it.

If Caleb had been the architect of the attacks, he wouldn't have needed to decipher the trail. He'd have known it already.

The pieces clicked hard, shoving themselves into place.

Roca saw it now—the picture he hadn't wanted to see.

Deception.

He'd been chasing shadows.

Falling for the misdirection.

Just like everyone else.

The weight of it pressed in. Months wasted, trust shattered, a nation spun into fear by the wrong name on the board.

And then came the guilt.

Not a flicker. An avalanche.

The raid on the Forrest Sherwood Foundation.

Labeled a hive of cyber conspiracy.

Guns drawn. Orders clear. No room for mistakes.

If Caleb had been there...

He swallowed hard.

Innocent or not, Roca would've pulled the trigger.

No hesitation. No questions. Just the mission.

A clean kill.

A quiet lie.

He sat there, breath shallow, the full weight of his role crashing in.

He'd almost killed a man who might've been trying to save them all.

He'd been a pawn.

Another move in someone else's game.

The guilt bit deep, but beneath it... something burned hotter.

Rage.

At the lies. At the manipulation. At himself.

But not anymore.

He glanced at the last item from the envelope—a folded strip of paper, narrow and deliberate. He unfolded it slowly, almost bracing.

One line. Block print. No punctuation.

You are chasing the wrong man

His grip tensed, knuckles white around the message.

No more guessing. No more doubts.

He'd been wrong.

Damn wrong.

Caleb hadn't built this horror. He'd been framed by the real puppet master—used to distract, to divide, to blind the ones who were supposed to protect.

Roca's jaw locked. His muscles coiled.

The target had shifted.

This was the reversal.

The line Roca couldn't uncross.

He'd find the ones pulling the strings.

And when he did…

They would answer.

For the fear.

For the blood.

For the lie that nearly cost a man his life.

Everton.

Hamilton Everton.

The NSA's deputy director was no longer just suspicious.

He was the center of the web.

And Roca was going to burn it down.

CHAPTER SEVENTY-TWO

Lian's call had shattered the fragile quiet of Caleb's evening.

Too calm. Too precise. A proposition wrapped in riddles—cryptic, chilling, impossible to refuse. The line had gone dead before he could ask a single question.

Now, two hours later, he sat strapped into the leather seat of a chartered jet bound for Beijing, a hastily packed duffel at his feet. Through the cabin window, the lights of DC receded into darkness, along with the illusion that he was still in control.

Across from him, Lian lounged with practiced grace, slender fingers wrapped around a crystal glass. She sipped slowly. Watching. Her eyes shimmered with that maddening calm that always left him guessing. Part seduction, part threat.

"You're awfully quiet," she said, her words edged with something just short of a dare.

He hesitated. "Just wondering where this is all leading."

The smile he gave her was a charade.

His thoughts weren't on her, or even the invitation.

He was stuck on the numbers.

Nine reports. Eight attacks. One company still standing.

Voltis Energy.

Over ten million households depended on its grid. The thought of it going down churned in his gut.

The jet droned through the night, stretching time into a purgatory of unanswered questions. He tried to rest, but the seat offered no comfort. Every time he closed his eyes, a crawling sensation crept across his skin.

Not a glance. A stare.

He opened his eyes and found hers.

Lian's gaze held steady, unreadable. Warm, but in that way that made him question its source. Was it genuine? Or just another scene in her performance?

"You didn't have to save me," she said. "It wasn't your game to lose."

A game. Of course it was. Everything with her was a game.

Calculated risks. Strategic moves.

Pawns moved without mercy.

But this time, something unguarded in her voice made it feel real.

She rarely spoke of the past. Regret was foreign to her, something weak men carried. And yet here she was, dragging them back to December 2024. Back to the last time they were in China together.

"Why did you leave the van? That wasn't the plan," she said.

Her tone was unreadable. Wonder? Accusation? Gratitude?

The plan.

The word hit like a jolt, sharp and sudden. The past surged up like a rip current.

He could still feel the damp Guangzhou air, the headset clamped tight against his skull, the hum of the surveillance van's servers as they processed real-time data. Operation Dragon Breath—CIA and NSA, joint strike, cyber-to-ground.

Months of planning.

Collapsed in seconds.

The safe house had been compromised before the breach even began. The first explosion came without warning, the shockwave rocking the van like a freight train. His laptop skidded across the floor. Then came the second blast—glass, screams, the crack of gunfire echoing down the alley.

Comms died one by one.

Like lights winking out in a storm.

It wasn't supposed to go that way.

His job was to decrypt, analyze, relay intel. He was never meant to leave the van.

He could've stayed. Should've.

Then a whisper broke through the static. "I'm pinned. I need a way out."

Lian.

Her voice cracked through the failing comms, and something inside him snapped. A pull deeper than instinct. Not tactical. Not logical.

A spiritual certainty.

Before he knew it, he was moving, gun in hand, boots on pavement. He left behind the screens, the safety, the mission. Into the fire.

The alley had been thick with smoke, lit only by the dying embers of a burning vehicle. Two operatives down. Chinese forces closing in.

He didn't think. He ran.

Bullets cracked against brick as he pulled Lian from the wreckage, his sidearm barking in reply. They tore through the alley, his grip locked on her wrist, running until the world narrowed to pulse, pavement, and sirens.

By the time they reached extraction, her blood had soaked his shirt.

But she was breathing.

The mission was over.

They had lost.

The official reports called it an intelligence failure. A cyber-op turned bloodbath.

But he remembered her face in the back of the transport—shaky, silent, alive.

They'd called him a hero. But his nightmares stripped him of the honor.

The plane's engines hummed low, grounding him back in the present.

He blinked, forcing himself out of the fire and smoke. Out of the ghost of a night that never really left him.

He turned to her. "You weren't supposed to die that night," he said quietly. "That wasn't the plan either."

Lian exhaled, slow and deliberate, her gaze drifting to the dark beyond the window.

"We were betrayed," she said. "An American informant. We walked into a death trap."

His chest knotted. "Who?"

She gave nothing. Just a slight shrug, her expression unreadable, her eyes hidden behind a curtain of silence.

"Some secrets refuse to be revealed."

The air between them shifted. An honesty too sharp to touch.

A mirage—never a mirror.

He wanted the truth to hold.

But the moment slipped.

She stood, moved to the cockpit, and returned a minute later, all warmth gone from her.

"We'll be landing soon," she said. "I think you'll find our destination… enlightening."

Of course she did.

They disembarked minutes later, bypassing customs and security like phantoms, and slipped into a waiting black sedan. No questions. No checks. Just silence.

The car hummed through the Beijing night, skirting the city's neon pulse for the anonymity of its industrial outskirts. Forty minutes later, it eased to a stop in front of a featureless gray building.

He stepped out, every instinct on edge.

Gray concrete. No signage. No guards.

It looked like a warehouse. Forgotten. Empty.

"Jiǎ Qí Corporation headquarters," Lian said, gesturing toward the entrance with a faint smile.

His pulse ticked faster. The name she'd dropped months ago now had an address. A shape. A face.

But nothing about it made sense.

His pace slowed. Every step forward came with a warning—quiet, primal, and loud in his gut.

Turn back.

Inside, his suspicions hardened into certainty.

The space was massive—cavernous, cold, and alive with motion. The air thrummed with quiet intensity, the kind that only came from people who knew they were breaking the rules. Maybe even rewriting them.

Rows of desks stretched deep into shadow, lit by the blue glow of monitors. Teams of hackers hunched over keyboards, their screens pulsing with code. Voices crackled in rapid Chinese. Then English. Fluent. Flawless. American.

He slowed, his eyes scanning the room.

"This… is Jiǎ Qí?" he asked.

His voice didn't sound like his own.

Lian turned to him, her smile stretching wider. "This team admires your work, Caleb. The detail in your reports made their jobs so much easier."

The words hit like broken glass. Sharp. Surgical.

His stomach dropped. The pieces clicked into place.

The Word Ladders. The attack timings. His own reports—bent into blades.

Rage twisted through him, too fast, too sharp, blurring the edges of everything.

"So this is where it started," he said, forcing calm. "The Word Ladder games."

Lian nodded, her grin smug now. "Everton was so sweet to coordinate the targets, dates, and times of the attacks, don't you think? How convenient to have the NSA looking the other way."

He stopped cold. Pulse thudding. Skin prickling. The weight of it all crashing down.

"Who are these people?" Even as he asked, he knew.

Some part of him had known the moment he walked through the door.

"They're just like you, Caleb," she said, spinning to face him. Her tone was light, playful, but her eyes glinted with something colder. "They enjoy playing with lines of code and going places they know they shouldn't."

"Chinese operatives?" he asked, more an accusation than a question.

Her smile turned sly. "The general secretary would love to have them working for him, but no. They're freelancers, artists of chaos."

"Seriously, who's paying them?" he pressed. "And don't tell me it's Jiă Qí."

She laughed softly, pityingly. "The book sales at Deep End Dynasty have been exceptional over the past year, don't you think? All those royalty payouts, and plenty left over to fund this little operation."

The room felt smaller. Tighter. Oxygen thinned as the realization hit him. He wasn't just a pawn in their game. He was the centerpiece, the fall guy, the final move before checkmate. They weren't just breaking into systems. They were dismantling a nation.

"What's their endgame?" he asked.

Lian gave a casual shrug, her reply almost bored. "Oh, I think you already know. They want to change the world."

His jaw clenched. "Damn you, Lian."

She smiled, unbothered. "Oh, and just so you know—" she tilted her head, mock-sympathy in her tone "—a little cyberattack is underway. It kicked off the moment you walked in. Looks like *you*, Caleb, were the trigger for the attack on Voltis Energy."

She let the words hang. Then, "Won't that make a nice headline back home? *NSA Fugitive Leads Chinese Assault on America.*"

His pulse spiked. His mind clawed for options, for an escape hatch that didn't exist. Her gaze pinned him—cool, amused, confident. Like she'd already won.

Maybe she had.

The noose was tightening. Every move accounted for. Every word calculated.

Then an idea sparked.

It was reckless. Dangerous. Possibly suicidal.

But it was the only card left in his hand.

So he played it.

"All right, Lian. You win. You've got me trapped," he said, even as every instinct screamed at him to run. "If there's no way out, then I want in."

Her eyebrows lifted, the corner of her mouth tugging into a smirk. "You want *in*?" she echoed, the mockery barely concealed.

He leaned forward, steady and controlled. "I set the ransom. I direct the payouts."

She laughed—sharp, cold, almost musical. "Now you want to take over?" Her eyes narrowed, head tilting slightly. "Don't forget, Caleb—you're the pawn. Not the queen."

She leaned back, watching him. Studying. Calculating.

"But…" she said at last, "I'll see what I can do. I'll see what the Publisher will allow. For old time's sake."

The name hit like a brick.

The Publisher.

He'd seen it in encrypted threads, buried in stolen files. Never a face, never a voice. Just whispers. A shadow behind the curtain.

He met her gaze, fighting to keep the rage from bleeding through his expression.

Calm yourself.

She tilted her head. Her smile widened.

Then she reached into her pocket.

The move caught him off guard.

"I thought you might want to play a game with your friend," she said, holding out a phone. The screen glowed in the dim light—familiar interface, unmistakable design.

"I hear he loves Word Ladder," she added sweetly.

He stared at the device.

Chest tight. Muscles locked. Rage boiled behind his eyes—betrayal, humiliation, all of it converging in a single, choking surge.

Every move he'd made. Every choice. It had all led here.

"You think this is funny?" he snapped.

Her smile didn't fade. If anything, it sharpened. "Funny?" she echoed. "No. But it *is* poetic."

He grabbed the phone.

He knew what it was. A trap. A setup. Maybe even a trigger.

Touch it, and the story rewrote itself: **Caleb Calvarri, Hacker Fugitive, Launches Cyberattack from Chinese Soil.**

He didn't care.

Fury eclipsed reason. Humiliation eclipsed fear.

His thumbs hovered.

Just for a breath.

Then… he did it anyway.

He started a game.

CHAPTER SEVENTY-THREE

MONDAY, JANUARY 8, 2029
EDGEWATER, MARYLAND

Everton stared at his phone, his pulse pounding in his ears, each thud a countdown to something inescapable. His fingers trembled slightly as he reread the message. The words on the screen taunted him, a challenge to a game he refused to play.

NO CALLER ID: Dead Wife

Bile rose in his throat, the two words slicing through him with surgical precision. Angela, her frail body lying in their bed. The quiet way she met her fate—dignified, graceful—as if dying was one more favor she did for him.

And now, this faceless coward dared to desecrate that memory.

No. This wasn't about her. This was an attack on him.

His chest hardened, grief and rage fusing into something unrecognizable. The bastard was mocking him, his loyalty, his sacrifices, twisted into a sick parody of everything he'd given—his loyalty, his silence, his soul.

His fists curled into iron. His knuckles went white as his mind raced, the betrayal, the injustice igniting something deeper, something darker. The rage burned through him, blinding and uncontrollable. His vision narrowed, the edges blurred as his breath came in sharp, ragged gasps, the room closing in on him.

And then it erupted.

A primal, guttural yell tore from his throat, reverberating through the room, raw and uncontained. The sound carried every ounce of pain, fury, and helplessness he had buried, a cry that refused to be silenced. It echoed in the stillness, demanding recognition.

Demanding revenge.

He stared down at the screen, the words a taunt he couldn't ignore. His chest heaved as he typed a response that broke every rule and shattered the boundaries of the twisted game he'd been forced into.

ME: Rot in Hell

CHAPTER SEVENTY-FOUR

Roca sat at his dining room table, arms crossed, jaw tight. The holidays were behind him, thank God, but the cold hadn't left. It clung to the walls, to the frosted windows, to the question that wouldn't let go.

Something was wrong.

He turned to the large sheet of paper stuck to his kitchen wall. Unsophisticated, yes. But he didn't care. This wasn't about appearances.

Two numbers stared back at him in red marker, sharp and precise:

$21,461,354

$613,145

He hated how clean they looked.

No shell companies. No offshore games. No slush buried in fake charities or crypto wallets. Just raw, untangled cash. It should've felt like a win.

It didn't.

A tightness pressed at his ribs. Not panic, but close. Like he was chasing a pattern that didn't want to be seen. Like someone had burned the edges and left just enough shape to follow.

"Jiǎ Qí Corporation," he muttered, tapping the wall with the blunt end of a marker. Each strike echoed, a metronome for his frustration. "They took the full $21,461,354. Directly. From Voltis Energy. No intermediaries. No wash." He stared at the numbers. "It's like they wanted us to see it."

The thought itched—half-formed, taunting.

Cruz-Way looked up from her laptop, the blue glow of the screen reflecting off her cat-eye glasses. "It's too neat. We expected more layers, more finesse. But this?" She shook her head. "It's amateur hour."

Roca stopped mid-stride.

That word. No.

This wasn't sloppy.

It was performed.

"Amateur?" he echoed. He leaned in over her screen. "Or sophisticated simplicity?"

Cruz-Way arched a brow. "Sophisticated?" she asked, skeptical.

"When something looks too obvious," he said, "it's usually because someone wants it to be."

Harmon squinted. "There's got to be a reason. This can't be random."

"Exactly." Sharper than he meant. The logic sat there, smug and wrong. Like someone had photocopied the truth and left it to blow in the wind.

"And Jiǎ Qí didn't keep the money," he said. "They pushed out fifteen identical payments—$613,145 each. Not a penny off."

Silence held.

Cruz-Way froze mid-scroll.

Harmon leaned in, frowning. "Who were the lucky winners, Dana?" Her sarcasm was thin, barely covering the tension threading her voice.

Cruz-Way kept scrolling. "Looks like a who's who of power and prestige," she said. "Hamilton Everton. Senator Evan Marshall. Dr. Helena Montgomery, Harvard's crown jewel. Rupert Cain, the tech mogul…"

Roca stiffened. "Everton wasn't acting alone…"

He stepped in, shoulder brushing Harmon's, eyes fixed on the names as they unfurled like a thread unraveling.

Not patriots.

Cowards.

Traitors.

"Hightower on that list?" he asked.

Cruz-Way scanned the screen, then shook her head. "Nope. Doesn't look like he's connected."

Harmon let out a low whistle. "Slime rises. Doesn't mean he's in the mix."

Roca didn't answer. Just stared at the screen.

Maybe. Maybe not.

"And what about the amounts?" Harmon asked. "Why not $21,000,000 or $600,000 flat? Why make it $21,461,356 and $613,145?"

His mind swirled. "What's your take, Dana?"

Cruz-Way didn't look up. "Caleb has a thing for numbers. Codes. Letters. Do you think it could be him, Lisa?"

Harmon exhaled, grabbed a marker, and stuck a large sheet of paper to the front of the refrigerator. "Let's find out."

She sketched the alphanumeric key—A equals 1, B equals 2—and began converting the ransom amount.

"So... 21,461,354..." She whispered the numbers slowly as she wrote out the associated letters.

Then she stopped. Stared at what she'd written.

B-A-D-F-A-C-E-D

Read it aloud.

"Bad faced."

Roca stilled.

The letters crawled under his skin. Not a code. A message.

"That's no coincidence," Harmon said, quiet now.

Roca stepped in, took the second number—613,145—and worked it fast.

F-A-C-A-D-E.

"Facade," he said. The word hung there.

And then it hit. Sudden. Improbable. Obvious.

He looked at the numbers. The screen. The flow.

"Caleb sent the wires?" he asked softly, like saying it louder might break something.

Cruz-Way's posture shifted. "He knows we cracked the number-letter pattern. If he's inside—"

She didn't finish.

"Then he's signaling," Harmon said.

The silence that followed was thick. Charged. Like something sacred had just been named.

Roca drew a breath.

If they were right, the next move wouldn't be his.

It'd already be in play.

CHAPTER SEVENTY-FIVE

This was the moment she'd dreamed of—and yet, the winter chill settled deeper than expected, cold in a way that had nothing to do with the temperature.

Kalyssa wrapped her coat tighter, eyes scanning the crowd gathered before the Capitol. A sea of hopeful faces. So many had come to witness history, but all she could feel was the weight of what had brought them here—the lies, the cost, the people lost along the way.

On the grand stage, Senator Elizabeth Wilckens stepped forward. Her presence commanded the silence.

"Distinguished guests, fellow Americans, and friends around the world," Wilckens said, smoothly with conviction, "welcome to the inauguration of the forty-eighth president of the United States, Alexander Grayhorse. Today, we gather not just to celebrate new leadership, but to reaffirm our commitment to the principles of democracy, unity, and freedom that define our great nation."

Applause erupted—loud, affirming—but it barely reached Kalyssa. She stood still, absorbing it, filtering it. Trying to believe.

Then came the moment of reflection.

Imam Tariq Hassan's voice, calm and reverent, called for unity and compassion.

Rabbi Miriam Goldstein's blessing followed, Hebrew syllables rising like ancient poetry, invoking wisdom and justice.

Pastor Jonathan Reed's prayer landed with force, his plea for strength and integrity cutting straight through the pomp.

Dr. Evelyn Andreasson, crisp and secular, reminded them all that diversity was not a weakness—it was the beating heart of a people still learning how to be one.

Each voice distinct. Each one a different note in the same strained chord. Together, they formed something close to harmony.

She closed her eyes. Just for a second. Just long enough to believe it might be possible.

Unity.

Not control.

Not power.

But something stronger.

The United States Marine Band took the stage, and for a moment, the music carried her. She let herself imagine a different America, one stitched back together by honesty, not illusion. One that chose courage over chaos.

Then the music faded, and reality closed back in.

Hamilton Everton—Vice President Hamilton Everton—stepped forward and placed his hand on the Bible.

The crowd surged with cheers, raw and unrestrained.

But all she felt was the tightening in her chest.

Her eyes scanned the rooftops. The balconies. Every blind spot. Secret Service agents moved like shadows, their attention slicing through the crowd with surgical precision.

"Please," she whispered, her words lost in the wind, "let them find nothing."

Everton repeated the oath, each word heavy with contradiction. When the applause hit—loud, thunderous—it nearly knocked the breath from her lungs.

She clapped, because she had to.

But her pulse was still ticking like a countdown.

As noon neared, the chief justice stepped forward—solemn, black-robed, the embodiment of law's weight.

Grayhorse followed. Hand steady on the Lincoln Bible. Voice strong. Composed. Every word of the oath delivered with crisp precision.

"I, Alexander Grayhorse, do solemnly swear that I will faithfully execute the office of president of the United States, and will to the best of my ability, preserve, protect, and defend the Constitution of the United States. So help me, God."

Applause erupted—thunderous, cathartic.

But Kalyssa didn't cheer. Not right away.

She watched.

Grayhorse stepped to the podium, his breath slow and deliberate, as if he were tasting the moment. His eyes swept the crowd, and for the briefest instant—just a flicker—he seemed to drink it in. The anticipation. The anxiety. The manufactured hope.

And still, something in her braced.

The oath had been sworn. The speech was next.

But the truth? That was still waiting.

She slid to the edge of her seat, pulse steady but tight. These were the words they'd rehearsed. Every syllable polished. Every beat intentional.

"Ladies and gentlemen, distinguished guests, fellow Americans," President Grayhorse began, his words rising over the cold air—measured, powerful, practiced, "today, as we gather beneath the sky of our beloved nation, we stand at the threshold of a new era. An era where truth and transparency are our guiding lights, where unity and togetherness become our strengths, and where freedom of belief flourishes without fear or suppression."

The crowd surged, cheers swelling like a rising tide. Relief. Catharsis. As if the last twelve months could be rewritten by applause alone.

She didn't move. Just listened. Measured the space between the words. The precision. The restraint.

Grayhorse pressed on.

"Our journey has been long and arduous. We have faced challenges that tested our resolve, endured trials that questioned our faith, and witnessed divisions that threatened to tear the fabric of our society. But today, we rise above these adversities, embracing a future where deception gives way to truth, division bows to unity, and freedom triumphs over coercion."

A pause.

Intentional.

She felt it before he spoke, like the breath before a plunge.

"We are a nation built on the principle that all men and women are created equal, endowed with unalienable rights that include life, liberty, and the pursuit of happiness. This includes the freedom to believe, to worship, and to follow the dictates of one's conscience."

She waited.

That line was coming. The one they'd debated, reworded, repeated until it felt like scripture.

"This is one nation under God. But God will not force His will on us. Each one is free to believe or not believe… without oppression."

The crowd roared—louder now, rising like a wave.

There. He had said it. But it felt hollow. Empty as an illusion.

Her eyes locked on Grayhorse.

Waiting for the words he didn't want to say.

He paused.

"But there are some among us who think otherwise," he said, his tone hardening. "They want to take away what we have. They want to rob us of our freedom. And they almost succeeded."

Silence.

Heavy. Suspended.

"They infiltrated our systems. Twisted our loyalties. Exploited our fears. But one man—one man—had the courage to stand against them."

She watched. Waited. Would he go through with it?

"We misjudged him. We called him a traitor. Forced him into hiding. We hunted him like a criminal."

He turned slightly. Not to the crowd. To her.

"And now—"

A beat.

"It is my honor to award Mr. Caleb Calvarri the Presidential Medal of Freedom… and pardon him of all charges against him."

He hadn't wanted this.

Not at the inauguration. Not in the script.

"Not within protocol," he'd told her.

She'd pushed back. Reminded him that public silence wasn't neutrality—it was complicity. That the stain of inaction would bleed into every page of his legacy. That the people screaming for Caleb's pardon wouldn't forget.

She hadn't yelled. Hadn't threatened.

Just facts. Just stakes.

And now, here he was, making it his idea. Dressing the moment in righteous theater, as if the decision had come from conviction and not calculation.

And then it hit her.

The words still hung in the air, but the meaning had already broken through. Caleb was free.

No more aliases. No more running. No more wondering if today would be the day it all came crashing down.

The months of hiding, of whispered phone calls and burner phones and restless nights—all of it collapsed in her chest, a dam cracking under pressure.

Tears welled. She blinked hard, willing them back.

He was free.

And so maybe, finally, was she.

Or were they?

Grayhorse continued. "In December of 2028, the American people ratified the Twenty-eighth Amendment, recognizing the need for the president to take decisive action against threats to our constitutional government. Today, I invoke that amendment."

She barely breathed.

He had just crowned himself king.

Control of the media.

No judicial review.

She sat silent. Stunned.

He continued. "This nation has been infiltrated by a network of traitors calling themselves the Authors," he said. "They've cloaked themselves in patriotism and twisted constitutional loyalty into something grotesque. A lust for wealth. A hunger for control."

The crowd waited. Watching.

"They operate from the shadows," Grayhorse said. "Cowards in tailored suits."

Her pulse kicked.

"But let me be clear: Authors, your names are known. Your network has collapsed. And whatever illusion you had of slipping away unseen?"

He paused. The silence cut sharper than his words.

"Think again."

Sweat clung to Everton's forehead, catching light as it slid past his temple. His complexion—ashen. Eyes scanning the platform, darting from face to face. Looking for someone who wasn't there.

Or maybe waiting for a signal that never came.

"There are no bad people," Grayhorse went on. "Only people who make bad decisions."

She tensed. That line—it wasn't in the script.

"Authors," he said, threading steel with mercy, "today is your opportunity to turn around. To start again. Those of you who voluntarily turn yourselves in to the FBI by midnight tonight will be placed on a path to rehabilitation and reconciliation. Justice will not be denied. You will be punished. But you will have hope."

A beat passed. No one moved.

The weight of it pressed down—on the crowd, on her, on the very air.

Grayhorse stared with eyes of steel.

"But to those who choose otherwise…" His tone dropped, razor-sharp now, "you will live in fear. With death at every doorstep. Terror will be your companion. Because we will hunt you down. And we will snuff you out."

A pause. A dare.

"The choice is yours."

Then louder, clear enough to echo off every monument in the city: "Choose hope."

Silence clung to the crowd like fog, thick and absolute. The president's words still rang in the air, the finality of his ultimatum pressing down like a physical weight. For a heartbeat, maybe two, it felt like the world had stopped breathing.

Then…

A voice on stage.

A spark.

"Choose hope. Choose hope. Choose hope…"

The chant caught, low and raw, and spread like fire through dry grass. The words surged outward, picked up by the crowd, rippling across the Capitol grounds.

"Choose hope. Choose hope…"

Her lips moved before she realized. "I choose hope," she whispered, the words fragile and sacred, a vow as much as a prayer.

Tears blurred her vision.

Across the platform, her eyes found Everton. His lips moved in sync with the chant. His eyes shimmered. Not just with conviction, but with something else. Regret. Surrender. Grief.

Still, he mouthed it, *I choose hope.*

The crowd thundered louder, voices braided into something defiant. It wasn't just a chant anymore. It was a decision. A declaration. A reckoning.

They were standing against the darkness, choosing to believe, choosing to rise.

Then the sky split.

A squadron of F-35s roared overhead, engines tearing through the silence. The crowd erupted, swept up in spontaneous applause. Flags lifted. Hands reached skyward. The sound of freedom—loud, blazing, choreographed.

Kalyssa didn't cheer.

She looked up, eyes tracing the jets as they vanished behind the clouds. The spectacle was meant to inspire. To unify. But in her chest, the storm kept turning.

Hope.

Such a delicate word.

It felt like glass—clear, beautiful, and breakable. And too many people had learned how to use it like a weapon.

She wanted to believe. Needed to. But she knew, deep in the quiet corners of herself, that the battle wasn't over. Not even close.

Grayhorse stepped back to the podium, wiping a tear from his cheek. "And I choose hope," he said, steady, face resolute.

But something about his words felt off.

Not false, exactly…

But carefully arranged.

A mirage. An illusion.

Something darker hidden beneath the light.

A whisper stirred in Kalyssa's chest.

Cold. Certain.

And for the first time all day, she didn't feel ready.

CHAPTER SEVENTY-SIX

SATURDAY, JANUARY 20, 2029
WASHINGTON, DC

He should've been at the Congressional luncheon. Laughter, clinking glasses, the false optimism of a new administration. His absence would be noticed.

But Everton didn't care.

He sat alone at the desk in his West Wing office, the soft hum of the building's heating system the only sound breaking the silence. The heavy drapes were drawn, muting the celebratory sounds from the streets beyond. On the corner of the desk was a framed photo of Angela, a candid shot of her laughing, her eyes alive with joy. He could still hear her voice if he tried, still feel the way her hand would rest on his arm when she told him everything would be okay.

Now, that laughter was gone. The warmth, the reassurance, it had all been replaced by a void so deafening it threatened to swallow him whole.

She had been his rock, his compass, his reason to keep moving forward. Now, everything felt hollow, crumbling beneath him like sand slipping through his fingers. This day was supposed to be *their* celebration, a moment they had dreamed of together. Instead, it felt like his damnation.

He leaned forward, pressing his head into his hands, his breathing shallow and uneven. The guilt shredded him, relentless and unyielding, carving deep wounds into his soul. It wasn't just her absence. It was what he had done, the choices he had made, the consequences he could no longer outrun.

And the worst was yet to come.

Unbidden, Caleb's face surfaced in his mind, a memory he'd tried to bury. Their first meeting played out in vivid detail, escargot and crème brûlée, a spark of hope glinting in Caleb's eyes. The Player and the Pawn— the restaurant's name had been ironic, yet descriptive. But was Everton the player… or was he the pawn? Or maybe they were both pawns, pieces in a game far more devious than either of them could have imagined.

His chest tensed as the vision shifted to what he feared would come next. FBI agents storming into the room, their boots thumping against the carpeted floor. Guns drawn, voices shouting. Papers scattering from his desk as they hauled him to his feet. They'd drag him into the open, pull back the curtain for the world to see who he truly was.

Hamilton Everton, the liar, the fraud, the architect of his own downfall.

He forced the vision away, his mind shifting to the street below. Somewhere in the crowd a lone figure stood waiting. His instructions were clear. The terror would strike, Grayhorse would fall, and he would become President Hamilton Everton.

The thought sent a chill through him. He would immediately issue pardons to the Authors, and cement his place at the helm. His reign, orchestrated by unseen hands, would begin.

And yet, he knew the truth. He too would be a target. The Publisher spared no one. Not even the successor he'd helped create. He could already feel the crosshairs, the noose tightening. Just like Grayhorse, he would be snuffed out when his purpose had been served.

This wasn't power. It was a slow, calculated execution.

Redemption. The word clung to his mind, a flicker in the suffocating darkness. Was such a thing even possible for a man with no hope? For a man with so much blood on his hands? For a man who had sacrificed the nation.

Maybe confession is the only act of faith I have left.

Angela's voice whispered in his memory, soft but clear. *There's always a way forward, Hamilton, but you have to be brave enough to take it.* He closed his eyes, clinging to the echo.

And then it occurred to him.

A thought simultaneously dark and laced with hope. A solution that felt more like a confession, a way to unburden his soul while tipping the scales of power. A plot twist that would change everything.

His mind embraced the thought, nurtured it, watered it, and watched it bloom. It was dangerous, reckless even. But in the seed of that idea lay the one thing he had thought impossible.

Freedom.

Not for himself, but for the nation he had betrayed.

He straightened in his chair, his breath steadier now, his gaze sharper. He pulled the drapes open, flooding the room with light, as if it might atone for what was coming next. He returned to the desk, opened the top drawer, and retrieved what he had found there earlier. The cold weight in his hand felt foreign and final.

He moved to the couch, his fingers hugging the grip as he envisioned what he was about to set in motion. It was both an act of penance and rebellion.

"For you, Angela," he whispered, "and for the nation."

He closed his eyes.

Ready.

And then, in an explosive instant, Hamilton Everton's world went dark.

CHAPTER SEVENTY-SEVEN

Two months later, the chandelier's glow bled warmth across the East Room of the White House, but Kalyssa felt the weight of it more than the light. Her fingers stayed laced with Caleb's, the pressure between them subtle but sure—her anchor in a room that felt more like a stage than sanctuary. The last few weeks spun behind her in a blur, too sharp, too fast. She barely recognized the woman who'd survived them. And now here she was, seated across from the president and first lady, heart pounding beneath tailored calm. Not a dinner. A reckoning. A moment history would frame in glass.

Caleb's calm demeanor steadied her as always. But she knew beneath his composed exterior, his mind never stopped—always calculating, always analyzing. She could feel it in the subtle tension of his hand, the subtle flicker of his eyes.

The servers moved with quiet precision, their presence barely a ripple in the charged stillness. They placed the first course—tuna tartare with avocado and citrus vinaigrette. The delicately plated dish shimmered in the chandelier's light, the micro herbs a fragile counterpoint to the crisp wonton chips beside it.

Caleb took a bite, his approval subtle but unmistakable. She had learned to read his cues, a private language that bound them together.

Seven weeks into Grayhorse's presidency, the weight of leadership was already etched into his features, his gaze steady but shadowed. Beside him, Sophia Grayhorse radiated quiet strength, her friendly smile a counterbalance to the unspoken gravity in the room. They dined in reflective silence, the moment heavy with everything unsaid.

It was Caleb who finally broke the quiet. "You know, Mr. President, there's something fitting about us being here tonight," he said lightly but with a familiar edge. "It being Pi Day and all."

She stifled a laugh, her grip tightening briefly around his hand. Of course he brought up math. Only Caleb would reference Pi Day over tuna tartare. It was one of the many things she loved—how he saw connections others missed.

Grayhorse raised an eyebrow, a smile tugging at his lips. "Pi Day? March 14th?"

"Three point one four," Caleb confirmed with a nod, his eyes glinting. "It's almost as good as May 4th. May the fourth be with you."

Subdued laughter rippled through the room. Grayhorse's smile faded slightly as he turned to Kalyssa.

"You sure I can't convince you to take the comms director role? Still wide open."

She didn't hesitate. A simple shake of her head said it all. "Thank you, Mr. President. Keep me in mind for your second term," she said lightly, though the words carried a deeper weight. "I'm taking a different path for now."

Sophia leaned forward, her interest genuine. "What's next for you, Kalyssa?"

"My business partner, Aimee, and I have launched a social media platform that's keeping me busy," she said. "And on a personal note, Caleb and I are getting married in Sedona. You're both invited, of course. After the wedding, we're honeymooning in the Virgin Islands. It feels like the perfect escape."

Sophia's smile deepened, her tone melodic and sincere. "St. John is beautiful. Be sure to check out Salomon Bay Beach."

Grayhorse leaned forward, his gaze steady and piercing. "Well, Kalyssa, I'll hold you to that second-term promise. The nation could use someone with your clarity."

She smiled but didn't answer. The truth was… clarity had come at a cost.

Not one she regretted, but one she'd never forget.

<div style="text-align: center">~~~~~~~~</div>

The lobster bisque arrived, its warmth curling into the air like a lifeline. Rich aroma, velvety surface—details that barely registered. Caleb stared into the bowl, his thoughts nowhere near the carefully plated dish. The servers moved with practiced grace, their precision a stark contrast to the tightness winding through his chest.

His spoon hovered, unmoving.

Sophia eased in. Calm. Deliberate. "I thought you might want to know—the Everton children are doing reasonably well, considering the loss of both parents in a matter of months."

Was it compassion or control? He couldn't tell.

The memory of Everton haunted him like a specter, lingering in the folds of conversation, coiled in every silence. Uninvited, yet suffocatingly present.

His hand stilled. A subtle tremor crept down his spine.

The Everton family.

He hadn't let himself go there. Their grief had been background noise in the war against Everton. But now, the collateral damage stepped forward. Vivid. Human. Unavoidable.

Sophia's tone softened, but her words landed with surgical precision.

"He was a good man. Misguided, perhaps."

A good man?

His blood ran cold at the suggestion. Everton had betrayed him. Forced

336

him into hiding. Orchestrated a cascade of suffering. Left bodies in his wake.

Was she naive? Or had she seen past what Caleb couldn't let go of?

His mind flashed. A memory. Words he'd once said to Kalyssa with conviction:

I don't believe in a point of no return. The possibility of change is what keeps us human.

But now?

Evil was easier to forgive when it didn't have a face.

And that final act—was it penance or punishment?

Sophia continued, pulling him back. "His granddaughters loved him."

The silence stretched taut. The soft clink of silverware against porcelain only deepened it.

Then President Grayhorse spoke. "You've read the headlines. The Authors wanted me dead. Everton's act saved my life. I harbor no bitterness. Only gratitude."

Caleb inhaled. Redemption and betrayal. Good and evil. The collision shattered every narrative he'd built around Everton.

Let it go, Caleb. You're a seeker.

Healing words gathered at the back of his throat. Unspoken. But waiting.

And yet he knew.

Forgiveness was freedom.

Bitterness was betrayal.

Under the table, Kalyssa squeezed his hand. Gently. Not with force. With encouragement.

Caleb turned to Sophia. "In our brokenness, we are all worthy of love."

It *wasn't* absolution. But it *was* a beginning.

She nodded.

The bisque cooled as silence settled in. The bitterness dissolved, revealing something he could finally hold on to.

Peace.

As the third course arrived—seared scallops with lemon butter and asparagus risotto—the air in the East Room shifted. Kalyssa swore the chandelier's glow dulled, the warmth unable to chase off the chill settling at the table.

The scallops gleamed—crisp-edged, delicate, drowned in lemon butter. Bright. Acidic. As if someone had plated a warning and called it elegance.

She took a bite. The risotto was creamy, rich, melt-on-the-tongue perfect. But it did nothing for the knot twisting tighter in her gut.

Across the table, President Grayhorse set his fork down with surgical calm. His gaze found hers—steady, direct, and sharp enough to slice.

"So, Kalyssa," he said, tone smooth but edged with command, "you never did share how you managed to carry on a relationship with a fugitive during my campaign."

A beat.

He added, "I'm surprised that one snuck past the Secret Service."

The words hit like a spotlight—sharp, probing—but she stayed still. Years of navigating political minefields had trained her well. Deflect. Disarm. Redirect.

She met his gaze with a smile that looked effortless. Practiced. Deadly.

"A fugitive?" she said lightly. "I don't know what you're talking about."

Grayhorse leaned back. A flicker of something—humor, maybe—touched his mouth, but his eyes stayed sharp, dissecting her.

"And that," he said, shaking his head, "is how she fooled us all."

His tone softened. Slightly.

"But seriously. How did you and Caleb uncover the Authors?"

She opened her mouth, but Caleb beat her to it, leaning forward, his voice dry with amusement.

"Well, sir, I have a habit of hacking into things. Everton's phone had a vulnerability."

Grayhorse studied him. Head tilted. Expression unreadable. But something sparked behind his eyes. Curiosity? Amusement? Approval?

"So it was through his phone you got to him—and his bank accounts?"

"Passwords, encryption keys… they were all there," Caleb said, his tone easy, almost amused. But Kalyssa caught the tell: the slight tightening of his grip around the fork. Pressure he didn't show in his voice.

"Once I accessed his phone," he added, "the rest followed."

Grayhorse leaned in, eyes narrowing, the doubt unspoken but obvious. "And this part about a Word Ladder game triggering cyberattacks… are we seriously entertaining that?"

Sophia laughed softly, her tone warm but knowing. "Alexander loves puzzles, you know. Word Ladder's his favorite. He's a bit like one himself, always surprising me with new pieces."

Kalyssa forced a smile at the remark, but a chill crept up her spine. Playful, yes, but something about Sophia's tone felt… off. Too polished. Too well-timed. Like a deliberate sidestep. A distraction.

She glanced at Caleb.

He was smirking—faint, familiar—but she caught it. The tension in his jaw. The flicker behind his eyes. He was uneasy too.

Grayhorse's smile thinned. He leaned forward, gaze sharpening. "And the other members of the group?" he asked, the warmth gone from his tone. "Surely Everton didn't lead you to all of them."

"No," Caleb said, low and deliberate. "A few were obvious. The others nearly broke me. I found nine. The FBI got the rest."

Kalyssa's pulse ticked faster. He was holding back.

No mention of the China trip. No word about the final payouts—the ones he'd orchestrated himself for the remaining Authors. Why leave that out?

Was he protecting someone?

Or was this something bigger?

Grayhorse's fingers tapped the edge of his plate—steady, rhythmic, almost hypnotic.

"That social media tsunami was something, wasn't it?" Grayhorse said. "Almost like it appeared overnight. Birthed by the new year."

She stayed still.

There was danger in the quiet.

He turned to Caleb. "You can thank the American people for your freedom."

Caleb nodded, then looked to her, gratitude flickering behind his eyes.

"I'm an American," she said, aiming for levity.

Caleb chuckled.

Grayhorse didn't.

"And those anonymous tips Roca received?" he went on, eyes narrowing. "Uncanny timing, wouldn't you say? Almost like he had access to the same insider information you did."

She turned to Caleb.

His jaw tightened—barely. Just enough for her to see it. His calm remained, but the fracture beneath was there.

"Roca's focus on identifying the Authors was unwavering," Caleb said smoothly. "That's why he was the right man for the job. He earned that promotion."

Grayhorse studied him for a long moment, his gaze sharp, almost predatory. Then, with a slight nod, he leaned back, his expression unreadable.

"And the ringleader? This so-called Publisher?" he asked. "Did you ever find him?"

Caleb exhaled. Frustration flickered behind his eyes—brief, but telling.

"He's a master of deceit," he said quietly. "No face. No traceable actions. It's like every step vanishes the moment it's taken."

Grayhorse's lips curved into a faint smile, as if he knew something Caleb didn't.

"No clues at all?" he asked with disbelief. "That surprises me, Caleb. A man of your caliber, unable to uncover anything?"

Kalyssa's stomach tensed. The phrasing wasn't just skepticism—it was bait. A test. He was watching their reactions.

But Caleb didn't rise.

"We know he orchestrated the National Defense Mandate," he said evenly. "And planned your assassination. But that plot didn't materialize."

"Thank God," Sophia murmured, soft but sure.

Grayhorse nodded, slow and deliberate. His eyes lingered on Caleb just a second too long.

"So it seems he outsmarted you and the FBI," he said. The words were wrapped in self satisfaction… or something colder.

"So it seems," Caleb replied, though she could hear the resolve beneath his words. He hadn't given up on finding the Publisher or uncovering the truth.

Conversation shifted, but the current beneath it pulled harder. The tension in her chest didn't ease—it sharpened. Grayhorse's phrasing, his pacing, his tone… it wasn't improvisation. It was strategy. Rehearsed. Orchestrated.

The moment passed, but it left a trace, like the aftertaste of something poisoned. Grayhorse hadn't needed their answers. He'd come to confirm his own.

Not politics. Not power.

Control.

And Grayhorse—

He wasn't just another pawn.

He was playing the whole damn board.

EPILOGUE I

Kalyssa's fingers laced with Caleb's as they wandered along the curve of Salomon Bay, the last light of the sun glinting off the water. Their bare feet pressed into the cool sand, each step smoothed away by the hush of the incoming tide. She felt the rhythm of it—the surf, the breeze, the quiet certainty of his hand in hers. No crowds. No surveillance. No headlines. Just this.

She tilted her head toward him, the corner of her mouth already lifting. "Caleb."

He turned, and even before he smiled, she saw it—that flicker of heat in his eyes.

She reached up, fingers to her shoulder, then to the clasp behind her neck. A pause. A breath. The faintest rush beneath her ribs. She let the strap slip free.

His arms came around her without hesitation, pulling her close. The warmth of his chest, the salt in the air, the pulse beating fast behind her ribs… every part of it was real. Grounded. Right. She leaned into him, eyes closing as his lips met hers. Slow. Certain. No need to rush.

For the first time in months, she didn't feel hunted.

After a while, she eased back just enough to look at him, her forehead resting against his. A teasing smile tugged at her lips.

"What?" he asked, eyes glinting, a mirror to her amusement.

"I hope you don't plan on running for president someday." She glanced down between them, then back up. "Scandalous."

That laugh—his full, unfiltered laugh—burst from him, and hers followed, rising into the salt-drenched sky like a secret they didn't have to keep anymore.

She leaned into him again, head on his shoulder, a stillness settling over her. This wasn't victory. It wasn't escape.

It was arrival.

Her search was over. She had found her soulmate.

EPILOGUE II

MONDAY, DECEMBER 15, 2031
WASHINGTON, DC

Two and a half years later, President Grayhorse leaned back in his chair at the Resolute Desk, a subtle smile playing on his lips. The setting sun poured through the windows, painting the Oval Office in a golden glow. He was the most popular president in recent history, the hero of the people, and the most powerful man on Earth.

He turned toward the tall windows behind him. The South Lawn stretched wide, a manicured illusion of order. Beyond it, the Washington Monument rose like a sentinel, solemn and unmoved. His chest swelled, but the weight of history pressed against him like an unseen hand. For a moment, he felt it—his office, his decisions, his legacy.

Then it passed. Resolve returned.

A thought surfaced, and a mischievous smile tugged at the corners of his mouth. He rose, drew the curtains, and let the room fall into the amber hush of lamplight. At the desk, his fingers found the side drawer, then the hidden lockbox tucked in the back.

Cool metal. Familiar and foreign.

It had waited, unopened, since inauguration day.

He paused, then typed the code.

1 4 6 4 1

A palindrome. A perfect square. A row from Pascal's Triangle. He loved the layered meaning—order within chaos. Like his presidency.

The lock clicked open.

Inside, the phone that had won him the White House. A thrill shot through him as he powered it on. Dead. But not for long.

As it charged, he considered the message he would write. Just two words. Sharp. Elegant. Provocative.

Would she laugh? Smile? Roll her eyes and reply with that subtle brilliance that had always thrilled him?

He typed:

ME: Next Term

Sent.

He leaned back, the smile still ghosting his lips.

He pictured her, halfway around the world in Beijing, just waking, reaching for the phone. Her brow arched. That smile. That mind.

Moments later, it came.

LIAN: Next. Neat. Beat. Beam. Team. Term.

He tapped his reply.

ME: :-)

The same smile. Silent. Controlled. A reminder: this was their game—carefully constructed, safely beyond sentiment.

But this time, it carried something more.

Weight. Urgency. A challenge.

Would she be the player... or the pawn?

LIAN: Your move, Mr. President.

He smiled—quiet, certain—and turned to the window.

And then...

A memory.

December 2024.

The promise he hadn't forgotten.

He chuckled. Soft. Knowing.

It was time to unleash the one thing they wouldn't see coming.

DISCLAIMER

This is a work of fiction. All characters, events, names, and incidents in this novel are entirely the product of the author's imagination or are used fictitiously. Any resemblance to actual persons, living or dead, or to actual events is purely coincidental. Real businesses, public figures, and other real-life entities are referenced solely for narrative purposes; their inclusion does not imply any factual representation, endorsement, or association. The author, publisher, and their affiliates assume no responsibility or liability for any interpretations or uses of this work.

ACKNOWLEDGEMENTS

For more than seven years, I had worked on various scenes for this novel. In early 2023, my son—and first fan—Jarin challenged me to finish it. That challenge stuck. I redoubled my efforts, carving out early mornings and weekend hours to craft the story. In 2024, I took a two-month leave from my day job to complete the manuscript.

In early November, I thought I had done it. But I soon discovered I had only just begun.

My beta readers—Blake Butcher, Blaine and Joyce Wilson, and Kaleah Maddocks—offered candid feedback. Their honesty made the story better.

My developmental editor, Anna Bierhaus, provided the first professional critique of my work. She was both kind and candid. The manuscript had problems: fifteen points of view and enough head-hopping to jar any reader. But, she assured me, it was fixable. The result? A streamlined narrative with just five points of view.

Next came copyeditor and successful author Nina Bruhns. She pointed me to two outstanding resources (*Save the Cat* by Blake Snyder and *Point of View* by Sandra Gerth) and encouraged me to shift my writing into deep point of view. I did. When a scene didn't land, she didn't just flag it—she clearly defined the problem and often offered a solution. The result? The polished novel you just read.

Janet Fix was the last professional to review the manuscript. As proofreader, she ensured the final version was clean, consistent, and print-ready. Her attention to detail was impeccable.

For cover and interior design, I turned to Christian Storm. With over twenty years of experience designing award-winning and best-selling covers in the mystery/thriller genre, his expertise showed from day one. He delivered six cover concepts, and I surveyed my Facebook friends and LinkedIn colleagues for feedback. Their input helped shape a cover that connected.

Zach Hebert stood out among the voice actors who auditioned. His ability to give life to a wide variety of voices brought the story alive in ways I hadn't imagined.

Finally, this novel wouldn't exist without the unwavering support of my family. My wife, my children, my parents, and my brother stood behind me every step of the way. Their words of encouragement, patience, and love were lifelines. This book is as much theirs as it is mine.

Thank you all for believing in *The Player and The Pawn*—and in me.

—Wilson Carter

AUTHOR'S NOTE

The printing press. The typewriter. The word processor. And now—AI. Each of these disruptive innovations has influenced the art of storytelling. With every leap forward, a wave of understandable angst followed as people struggled to make sense of a world transformed. Yet, in hindsight, we can see that these technologies didn't stifle our stories, they amplified them. Such is the case with AI.

In crafting *The Player and The Pawn*, I embraced a blend of tradition and technology. I drew on the written word, expert human editors, and an AI assistant to help shape the final work. These tools helped me grow as a writer and sharpen my craft—but the final decisions were always mine.

I trained my AI editor—whom I named Aimee—to assess how well I was following the style guidelines I'd set for myself. When my human editor pointed out overused words or structural issues, I asked Aimee to suggest alternative phrasings. Some of her ideas were outstanding. Others fell flat. But at every step, it was me—not my editors, not Aimee—who chose the words that made it onto the page.

After writing this author's note, I asked Aimee to critique it. She said it had a strong thematic arc, a personal touch, and good balance—but suggested I clarify the opening, write more succinctly, and close with a stronger rhetorical punch. So, I revised it. She reported that the new version was clear, grounded, and thoughtfully personal—but could still use a bit of "light editing."

I smiled. There's always one more revision.